At the End of the Line

At the End of the Line

by

Kathryn Longino

MW
MEDIA WEB
PUBLISHING

CLEVELAND OHIO

Published by Media Web Publishing, Inc.

ISBN: 09895463-4-9
ISBN: 978-0-9895463-4-8

irst Printing September 2012
Printed in the United States of America

10 9 8 7 6 5 4 3 2 1

Lyrics to Hello, Little Girl, by Duke Ellington, Willow Weep for Me by Ann Ronell, and Pony Time by Don Covay and John Bell were used by permission.

Library of Congress Control Number: 2014940136

To Our Mothers,

Helen Dionne
Leslie Vandiver

Chapter One

Hildale, Utah
November 2, 1958

"Mama, please don't make me marry that man. I don't love him." Beanie swiped at the tears dribbling down her cheek with the back of her hand then ran it underneath her runny nose. She started to wipe it on the skirt of her floor-length cream chiffon dress when her mother grabbed her by the wrist and held it.

"Beatrice Mae Eddleston, don't you dare soil your grandmother's wedding dress." Mrs. Eddleston snatched a flowered hanky from the corner of the dressing table and dabbed at her daughter's red and swollen eyes. "And stop your crying right now." She held the handkerchief under Beanie's nose and said, "Here, blow." Tossing the soiled hanky back on the dressing table, she said, "You are about to become a married woman. And married women don't act like babies." She grabbed the hairbrush from the same dressing table and began brushing her daughter's long hair. "It's time for you to grow up and start acting like a lady." She yanked on the long strands as if to emphasize her words. "Brother Peterson is a very nice man. And he will take good care of you."

Beanie winced as the brush grazed her scalp. She reached behind her head and pushed a finger through her hair to see if her mother had drawn blood, but her mother slapped it away before Beanie could find out. Her mother's harsh demeanor proved that Beanie had pushed the subject too far. So she softened her voice and said, "But Mama, he's so much older than me. He's Daddy's age." She fiddled with the yellowed lace that belled out around her wrists. "Besides, he already has two wives. What does he need with a third one?"

Mrs. Eddleston yanked on the brush again, entangling Beanie's hair in a strong hold, forcing her daughter to look at her in the mirror. "Now you listen here, Beanie," she shook her finger at her daughter's reflection, "Orson Peterson is a fine man. He's a well-respected elder in the church. And according to the teachings of our founder, plural marriages are required for exaltation. Even your father is considering taking on a second wife." She paused and smiled at her young daughter, forcing a look of joy. "Haven't you seen the way he looks at you in church?" Beanie shook her head. "Well, I have. And it's very clear that he's smitten by you."

"But I barely even know him." Beanie glanced at the wind-up clock next to the row of assorted cosmetics. Two hours had passed since arriving at the temple. "Where's Daddy?"

"Your father had something he needed to tend to," she said without elaborating.

"Why didn't he and the boys ride with us to the temple?"

Mrs. Eddleston raised her eyebrows and looked at her daughter in the mirror. "You would have rather had your brothers running up and down the hallways disrupting us while we're trying to get ready?"

Beanie shrugged and looked back at the door to the sitting room hoping that the rest of her family would come bursting through it.

Mrs. Eddleston steered her daughter's head back toward the mirror. "Don't worry, they'll be here." Changing the subject she said, "Are you excited about meeting your new sister wives? I hear they are very nice." She loosened her grip on the hairbrush and continued to brush Beanie's hair until it shined, and then she added, "You always wanted a sister. Now you'll have two."

Beanie's bottom lip began to quiver. "But I'm too young to get married."

Mrs. Eddleston separated the amber locks into three equal parts and then began to braid Beanie's hair. "Fifteen is not too young to get married, especially when you are marrying a good man and one of the most prominent real estate developers in Hildale." She tied a thin cream silk ribbon around the end of the braid and then whipped the braid around in a circle atop Beanie's head. "Just think of how well he will be able to provide for you and the wonderful life you'll have with him. Won't that be nice, Beanie?"

Beanie remained quiet.

"And if you're a good wife and do what Brother Peterson asks of you, I'll bet he'll even buy you a piano so that you can practice your lessons at home. You're getting so good that I'm sure he'll want you to keep taking your lessons with Miss Cora. And he'll be able to afford them." Mrs. Eddleston picked up an antique pewter hairpin decorated with pearls and marcasite and stuck it in the back of the bun to hold it into place. She pulled the ends of the silk ribbon from beneath the bun so that they hung down the back of her head. Then she grabbed an aerosol can of Spray Net and sprayed the hairdo until it hardened into place. She placed both of her hands on Beanie's shoulders and leaned down so that their cheeks touched. She looked in the mirror and said, "Oh Beanie, look how beautiful you look. So grown up. I think Brother Peterson will be very pleased." She sighed and added, "My baby is getting married in less than an hour."

Beanie stared at the stranger in the mirror. The bun on top of her head made her look five years older and confident. And the dab of rouge on her cheeks, the pink on her lips, along with the bit of mascara on her eyelashes made her look radiant, happy even.

But she was none of those things.

And she didn't belong there in that temple sitting room. She was still a child both inside and out. Her primary thoughts focused on her new hula-hoop and hopscotch, not a husband and homemaking. But she didn't have a choice. Her parents had made this arrangement with Brother Peterson without her consent, even without her knowledge. Last week she was a young girl who dressed in saddle shoes and poodle skirts, oblivious to this man named Orson Peterson. Oh, she'd seen him in church congregating with the other elders, but there was no reason to pay him any mind.

But today that would all change.

Beanie looked down at the borrowed off-white patent leather pumps her mother gave her to wear. Even with tissue shoved into the toes, they didn't fit well because they were two sizes too big and much too wide for her narrow feet. But they matched the antique wedding dress well enough. And they added two extra inches to her height, making her, once again, look that much older.

Beanie stood up and faced her mother. No amount of makeup could camouflage the distressed look on her face. She pleaded softly, "Mama, please. Please don't make me -"

Her mother cut her off. "Not another word about it, Beatrice. You are marrying Brother Peterson, and that's final." She began to grab the items off of the dressing table and shove them into a cloth tote bag. Her lips tightened into a thin straight crease across her face. Without looking at her daughter, she muttered harshly, "This is the right decision, a good thing for all of us. You'll see. You'll be fine."

Beanie waited for her mother to finish the sentence in the way she always did when she wanted to make Beanie feel better. "You'll be fine, *I promise*." But she said no more.

A knock on the door broke the silence. When the door opened a crack, her father stuck his head through the opening. He seemed to be slightly out of breath and a little out of sorts. "Are you ready?" That's all he said. No smile, no "You look beautiful, Beanie." No indication at all that this was to be a joyous occasion.

Mrs. Eddleston looked at her husband and said, "Where are the boys?"

"They're already seated in the temple."

Mrs. Eddleston grabbed a small hand-tied bouquet of antique white gardenias from the dressing table and handed it to her daughter. She looked back at her husband and answered for Beanie. "Yes dear, she's ready."

"Then let's go. Everyone's waiting," he said while holding the door open for them.

When Beanie shuffled awkwardly past her father in her big shoes, she looked up at him. She wanted to try one final time to beg him to call off the wedding. But he looked straight ahead, not giving her that opportunity.

The few minutes it took to walk the length of the hallway from the sitting room to the temple's sanctuary felt like a death march to Beanie. So many emotions tumbled around in the pit of her stomach causing it to ache - confusion, anger, fear, but not one ounce of joy could be found in the mix. No matter how much her mother tried to make the situation sound wonderful, Beanie knew that for whatever reason, her parents desperately wanted her to marry Brother Peterson. Beanie realized that at this point, the reason why didn't matter. Her life was about to be pushed into a direction she did not want it to go. But what could she do? She was a mere child, a fifteen-year old schoolgirl with no way to change this outcome. Her only choice was to try to make the best of it and pray that God, not her parents, had sanctioned this union.

When they reached the doors to the sanctuary, Beanie peered through the long rectangular windows. A few people were scattered throughout the pews. At a closer glance, she realized that she didn't know many of them. Strangers. They all seemed like strangers, including the man standing near the pulpit wearing a black suit and looking down the aisle at her.

"Come, Beanie. It's time." Her father spoke softly as he opened one of the doors for her. He still refused to look at her. But as she took the first step down the aisle by herself, she could have sworn she heard him say, "I'm sorry, Beanie."

Expressionless faces stared at her as she walked down the aisle. They could have worn smiles or frowns, but she couldn't make the distinction. All she saw were willing witnesses to her execution. *Shame on all of you*, she thought. And then her eyes caught sight of a girl mirroring her own age seated in one of the pews next to what could have been the girl's father. But on closer inspection, the man's hand laid draped way too high up over the girl's thigh. When their eyes met, the girl pulled hers away and started fiddling with the hem on her skirt. *I guess fifteen isn't that young after all*, Beanie thought.

When she reached the front of the church, she stood next to Brother Peterson as the temple sealer of the ward began the ceremony with, "Brother Orson Peterson and Sister Beatrice Eddleston, please join hands in the Patriarchal grip or Sure Sign of the Nail." Brother Peterson held his hand out to her, urging her to take it. With reluctance she placed her young hand in his.

Though the ceremony lasted barely five minutes, Beanie felt like she had been standing there for hours. Phrases like: *do you take Brother Peterson by the hand and give yourself to him* . . . and, *to be your lawful and wedded husband for all time* . . . raced through her mind causing her to feel faint. This was not how she thought her life would be. She thought that when the time came, several years from now, she would find a boy. They would court, fall in love, and then eventually get married. But standing there now with none of those options, she knew that this was to be her life from this point forward. Nothing she could say or do would change it. So when the temple sealer looked at her and said, ". . . of your own free will and choice," Beanie faced the stranger that was to become her husband. And for better or for worse, she offered him a slight smile and said, "Yes."

No rings were exchanged or kisses given, simply a one-word agreement sealed her to this man forever.

As they walked down the aisle amid claps and chatter, Orson continued to hold Beanie's hand up for all to see as though she were his prize. But once he ushered her out the doors of the temple, he let go, pointed to the blue Rambler parked along side the curb, and said, "Beatrice, go wait in the car. I need to talk to your father."

Beanie looked back at the people gathering by the front doors presumably to shake the bride's hand and said, "But what about -"

"I said, go wait in the car."

Not wanting to make her new husband angry, Beanie walked to the car and slid in the front passenger's seat. She watched as Orson walked over to where her father stood and shook his hand. They seemed to be exchanging pleasantries, but, clearly, there was no warmth coming from either of them. Orson reached into his inside breast pocket, retrieved an envelope and handed it to her father. Her father took the envelope, and peeked inside, shook Orson's hand again, and glanced at Beanie.

Though the look was brief, the effect was lasting for Beanie. Her father's eyes conveyed a deep sadness and a sense of something else, guilt maybe? His normal congenial smile lay hidden beneath the sullen features of a sad man.

Beanie wondered what was in the envelope that had made her father so melancholy. Since Orson was now her husband, surely he would tell her if she asked him.

Wouldn't he?

Chapter Two

"What are you doing there?"

Beanie's eyes fluttered open when she heard the car door creak. She hadn't realized she had fallen asleep in the front seat of Orson's car. It couldn't have been for more than a few minutes. But when she turned her head and saw Orson leaning on the passenger's door with two women standing behind him, she realized that her nap had lasted longer than she thought. Her father no longer stood by the entrance to the temple. In fact, most of the wedding attendees were gone, leaving only a few stragglers loitering near the main entrance.

"I asked you a question. What are you doing in the front seat of the car?" He pulled her out of the car forcing her to stumble over her big shoes. "The front seat always belongs to Margaret." He pointed to the older of the two women standing behind him. "Your place is in the back seat next to Dorothy."

"I-I'm sorry. I didn't know." Beanie reached her hand out to Margaret and said, "Hello, Miss Margaret, I'm Beanie."

Before Margaret could reciprocate, Orson said, "No, your name is not Beanie. It's Beatrice." He narrowed his eyes. "You are never to use that nickname again. I will not have my wife running around calling herself *Beanie*. Understood?" Beanie nodded her head. "Good. Now let's go home."

Beanie didn't even know where "home" was. She knew Orson lived on the outskirts of Hildale, but she had no idea where. She thought back to the simple dwellings of her neighborhood and wondered if Brother Peterson's house was anything like those.

Twenty minutes and two lectures later about the rules and regulations of the Peterson household, Beanie saw her new home. When Brother Peterson pulled the Rambler into the circular driveway, the new bride sucked in her breath. "Oh my goodness, it's so beautiful!"

Massive cement steps, at least ten feet wide, led up to two large white marble pillars flanking a set of deeply varnished double doors with large, oval beveled windows. Clipped back roses lining the grand walkway causing Beanie to imagine the fragrant rainbow of colors that would greet her in the coming spring. The three-story red brick structure looked more like the Peery Hotel in Salt Lake City than it did a private residence. It was boxy but elegant.

Getting out of the car and standing in the driveway, Dorothy smiled sweetly at her, making Beanie think that she might be a nice person to get to know, maybe even become best friends with. She looked to be no more than five or six years her senior, an acceptable age difference for a budding new friendship. "Yes, Beatrice, we are so blessed that Orson is such a good provider for us and the children. Wait until you see your room. Margaret and I put new curtains up for you and painted the walls a lovely shade of light green. I hope you like it."

Beanie stared up at the row of windows on the second floor and wondered which one was to be hers. But then realizing what Dorothy had said she asked, "Children?"

Orson opened his door and stepped out onto the driveway. He walked around the front of the car and started for the steps. He said over his shoulder, "Yes, Beatrice, I have six children; two girls and four boys. You will help tend to their needs."

Beanie thought about her own three younger brothers, remembering how uncomfortable they looked seated in the front pew. She wondered if they understood that the sealing ceremony meant that she would not be coming back home to help take care of them anymore. The thought of not seeing her brothers every day saddened her. She hoped that Orson, or one of the sister wives, would drive her back home every so often so that she could visit them. But what if they wouldn't? That thought made her blurt out, "Can I bring my brothers out here to play sometime?"

"We'll see," was all that Brother Peterson said.

Orson opened the front door and stood in the foyer watching his children play quietly in the living room. They hadn't noticed him yet.

"Well, where is everybody?" he said.

"Daddy!" they all screamed. An avalanche of children poured out of the living room and latched onto Orson's legs, arms and waist. "Daddy! Daddy! You're home!"

Orson bent down and scooped up the littlest child, a girl, and cuddled her while swaying back and forth. He smiled at the matronly woman waddling up behind his brood and said, "How were they, Mrs. Weller? Did they give you any trouble?"

Mrs. Weller offered him a broad smile presenting a jovial moon face. She clasped her hands together at her bosom and said, "They were angels, Mr. Peterson, absolute angels."

He eyed the child in his arms and said, "Angels, huh. I doubt that." And then he tickled the toddler making her squeal with delight.

That made Orson laugh. He carefully unpeeled his daughter's fingers and handed her to Margaret. After a few more communal hugs, Orson straightened up and said, "Children, I want you to meet your new mother." He gestured to Beanie and said, "This is Beatrice. Beatrice, these are my children."

Beanie stared at Orson. He seemed to be completely different around his children; loving, caring and happy, not the stern man she married a short time ago. She hoped to see more of that side of him. Maybe being married to *that* Orson wouldn't be so bad.

She moved her attention over to the children. All were dressed in clean and nice clothing with every hair combed neatly in place. The oldest was not much younger than her and nearly as tall. She figured six months from now he would be looking down on her. She wondered how she could be their new mother when she, herself, was still so much of a child. Just because the temple had sealed Orson and her as husband and wife didn't mean that she was qualified to instantly become a mother to six children. *What if I can't do it?* The thought frightened her. But then she remembered how easy it was for her to help tend to her little brothers. Maybe if she pretended to be an oldest sister instead of a mother to these children, the task wouldn't seem so overwhelming. Besides, they already had two mothers. They didn't need a third. She smiled at the revelation and said, "Hello, children. I'm very happy to meet all of you."

Margaret handed the baby to Dorothy and said, "All right children, go to your rooms until dinner is ready." She looked at Mrs. Weller. "Will you please make sure the older ones have finished their homework before you leave?" She pulled some money from her purse and handed it to the woman. "And thank you for babysitting while we were at the ceremony."

Mrs. Weller took the bills and smiled. "My pleasure, Mrs. Peterson." She looked at Dorothy and said, "Mrs. Peterson." Then she looked at Beanie and said, "Welcome, Mrs. Peterson."

Mrs. Peterson. Beanie thought. *I'm a missus.* That sounded so absurd to her. She wasn't even sure what it meant to be a *missus.* What were Orson and the others going to expect of her? If it was to babysit the children then that made her a babysitter. If it was to clean up the house then that made her a maid. What was the actual job of a missus? She thought about everything her mother did around the house, trying to put herself in her mother's shoes. Then she looked down at her feet and thought, *oh wait, I already am in her shoes.* The irony made her chuckle.

"What is so humorous?" Orson wanted to know. His laughter and carefree manner instantly subsided.

The grin fell from Beanie's face. "I . . . Uh . . . Nothing." She cleared her throat. "May I go change before dinner?" Although she wasn't sure what she might change in to. She had no other clothes with her, other than the ill-fitting wedding dress that she wore. She glanced at Dorothy, sizing her up to see if maybe she might be able to wear something of hers until she could get her own clothes from her parents.

"I'll take her to her room and get her settled in," Dorothy offered looking at Orson as if to make sure that her request had been met with approval.

Margaret was the one who replied. "That would be fine, Dorothy. But do it quickly. You have potatoes to peel." She nodded toward the kitchen.

The household rankings had become evident to Beanie: Orson, followed by Margaret, followed by Dorothy, followed by the children, and finally, her. Or was it Orson first and the children second? She might not be completely sure of her role as the third missus, but she was confident the details would be spelled out for her in no time, clearly and succinctly.

When Beanie entered her room, she wanted to cry. Not because it was so beautiful and filled with elegant furniture, but because all of her things, including a small box of piano sheet music, already filled the room. She opened her closet door and found what few clothes she owned already hanging on wooden hangers. She opened the dresser drawers and found all of her undergarments, socks, and trousers separated and folded neatly. How did all of her belongings get here? She looked at the familiar lime green suitcase tucked near the back of the closet and choked back the tears. Evidently, packing up her things was the 'something' that her father needed to tend to. It was as if they couldn't get rid of her fast enough. At that moment she felt totally unloved and unwanted.

"I hope you don't mind, but Mrs. Weller took the liberty of putting your things away while we were at the ceremony. Orson had one of the elders of the church pick them up from your father and deliver them here. He thought it might make your transition a little smoother."

Dorothy walked over and closed the new curtains in order to give Beanie some privacy. "After you've changed, come down to the kitchen, and I'll get you started on dinner preparations." She smiled at Beanie, a genuine smile. But she must have sensed Beanie's sadness and added, "You'll be fine, Beatrice, *I promise*." And then she exited the room.

That evening, Beanie could barely keep her eyes open during dinner. She fought to stay focused on the conversation. The day's events had taken an emotional toll on her, and she couldn't wait to go to sleep in that luxurious oversized bed in her room. It looked to be twice the size of her bed at home with two fluffy pillows instead of one, flattened from overuse. Being the wife of a wealthy husband was starting to appeal to her.

As she readied for bed, Beanie heard a quiet *tap, tap, tap* on her bedroom door. "Come in," she said as she buttoned the top button of her pink flannel nightgown.

Dorothy opened the door slightly and stuck her head through the crack. "May I come in?"

Beanie smiled. "Of course." She sat down on a small tufted seat facing an oval mirror, pulled out the marcasite hairpin, and laid it next to her brush. She unwound the plaits, pulled the silk ribbon off of the end, and unbraided her hair. Then she picked up her brush off of the dressing table and began to brush it.

Dorothy, standing in the bedroom said, "Margaret sent me up here to see if you needed any help." She walked over to the vanity, stood behind Beanie and said, "Here, let me do that for you."

Beanie handed her the brush and said, "Thank you. It's getting too long to do it myself." She enjoyed it when someone else brushed her hair for her. It made her feel like a princess. And tonight, more than anything, she couldn't wait to jump into bed, snuggle under the silk comforters, and fall asleep.

Dorothy took the brush and gently glided it down the cascade of crimped hair made wavy by the braid. "You're so lucky to have such beautiful hair." She inadvertently looked in the mirror and ran her fingers through her own. "Mine has never been as thick and beautiful as yours." She sighed again and then reiterated, "You're so lucky."

Another, but more robust, *tap, tap, tap* on the door stopped their conversation. Before Beanie could answer, the door opened wide. When Beanie saw Orson standing there, she instinctively put her arms over her budding chest. Even though her nightgown covered her, no man, other than her father, had ever seen her in her nightclothes.

Orson entered into Beanie's room and stood by the door. He didn't say a word. He simply gave a slow nod to Dorothy. She set the brush down, got up from the bed and quietly exited the room. Orson's eyes fell onto Beanie's nightgown, his lips parted slightly, he rubbed his hands down his pants along his inner thigh, and then he closed the door.

Chapter Three

Boston, Massachusetts
November 4, 1958

It should have been her, Adeline thought. All this fanfare. She was supposed to have been more than an onlooker. She had thought she was going to be somebody. Or at least married to *a somebody*.

She stood by the window in an empty room at 10 Kilby Street in Post Office Square. She could hear the horns honking, people cheering and shouting out in the streets and the muffled noises from the big room down the hall. The lights in the streets were bright, glaring and constant.

Adeline Stewart Garrison, "Liddie" to her husband and friends, dug down into her evening bag and pulled out her pack of Pall Malls. God she hated when people shortened names to make nicknames. But that was her life. The abbreviated version of what she had thought it would be. Her life wasn't bad. Just not what it could have been. Not what she had hoped it would be, especially after everything she had done to make it better. She lit up her cigarette and blew the smoke onto the window pane, clouding it up.

Well, she mused, as she wiped to clear the small, square glass, *all the cheering was appropriate. He will one day be president.* Staring out blankly she knew. No doubt about it. It'll be Jack. Holding the Pall Mall between her fingers she placed them on the cold pane of glass and remembered Jack's brother, Joe.

It was supposed to have been Joe rising to the top.

She brought the cigarette back up to her lips and smiled as the smoothness from the tobacco tickled her tongue.

Joe and me. Together.

She wet her lips, gazing out at the blur of lights coming through the window, it took her back. Back to the day when she first laid eyes on Joe. He looked dapper with that big wide smile. She hadn't thought that someone like him would ever notice her.

It was the 1940 Democratic Convention in Chicago. She had snuck into the stadium where it was being held and had ended up sitting next to him purely by accident. But he kept stealing glances, until finally he spoke. Even now she still blushed at the thought.

She wasn't even supposed to be there. And she had only ducked in the Massachusetts section to get away from the guards she thought had spotted her. After she had peered back to make sure she had lost them, she turned to see exactly where she had landed. Everyone around her was standing and cheering. Instinctively, she started clapping and smiling and that's when she turned and saw him.

He leaned over to her ear and shouted over the noise, "That's someone's seat."

"Oh," she said, and stopped clapping. "I'm sorry." She looked around to see where she could hide next, and started to step away.

"Don't go. It'll be a while before he gets back." He stuck out his hand and said, "I'm Joe."

That was the beginning of her fairy tale story.

Or so I thought.

Joe had finished Harvard College two years before. He was headed to law school, and according to his maternal grandfather, was going to be the first Catholic president of the United States. He had that quirky accent, drawing out the "a" in his words, and a tuft of hair on the top of his head that he had to constantly run his fingers through to keep in place. His smile was the biggest she had ever seen.

There was only one day left for the convention and he spent that evening with her.

She had let him do all the talking. She wasn't shy, but what would she say? This was certainly something that happened only in fairytales. And when he did ask her something she couldn't even find the words to answer him, just his presence flustered her.

"You're from Boston?" she had asked him. And then told him she was starting college there in the fall. How those words came out she never knew, they tumbled from her lips just as if it were really true.

"I bet you're going to Wellesley," he had said She shook her head. He smiled with that mouth full of teeth, and said, "I know, Simmons. Simmons College. Am I right?" She bowed her head blushing and nodded. "Good," he said, bending at the knee so he could look into her face. "So then, I'll know where to find you."

She knew at that moment she wanted to be with him. At whatever the cost. She didn't know how but she was going to Boston, and she was going to enroll in Simmons College wherever that was. It couldn't be that hard, she had thought.

And by golly, she had done it. She had enrolled in Simmons that fall, and became Joe's girl. Spending time with him at Hyannis Port sailing, playing football , she had been accepted into his large, almost identical looking family . She had been happy.

That is until he was killed by that bomb.

He had done twenty-five missions and was able to come home. She had begged him to come back. She missed him hopelessly, and she had told him so. "Just one more mission, then I'll come home," was his response and then he said, "I love you."

That had been the last thing he said to her.

The bombs attached to a plane had to be piloted close to the target. It was set to go off after the pilots cleared the plane. But it went off two minutes early before he and the other soldier could parachute out. That was all it took to take her dreams away.

Two little minutes.

And even though her husband Walter was a descendant of Boston's *Brahmin elite*, he was no Joe. His family had somehow managed to end up on the wrong side of that proverbial track. Adeline knew when he approached her to be that shoulder to lean on after Joe's death, it was only to get in with the Kennedy family. They had embraced her and he wanted those connections as well. Then, unexpectedly he had fallen in love with her. Over the years she had grown to love him too. But it was far from being in love. She reserved those feelings for someone else.

The door to the room swung open, and her husband, holding onto the doorknob, leaned into the room. "When are you coming, honey? He's going to win this by a landslide. You're missing all the fun."

"I'm on my way." Adeline ground her cigarette out in the ashtray on a desk next to where she stood at the window and turned to look at her husband.

"Well, you better hurry, Liddie." He let go of the doorknob and stood up straight. "Why are you in here?"

"I just needed to collect my thoughts, and have a cigarette." She turned around to him and gave him a smile, not sure if he could see it in the dim room.

"There's buzz going around that Frank'll be here. Old blue-eyes. I know how you love him."

"I wouldn't want to miss him." She took in a deep breath. "I'll be out in a minute."

"All right," he said with a nod of his head. "Get a move on then. Even Jack asked about you."

"I'm coming. I just need to fix my face," she said.

"You look beautiful tonight."

"Thanks."

"Hey, what's the last count . . ." Walter yelled at someone as he pulled the door closed.

Wiping away the single tear that persistently crawled down her cheek. She pulled her compact out of the silver evening bag that she had laid on the windowsill. Eyeing her reflection, she turned her head from side to side, pushed up on her hair, and then pulled her tube of lipstick out and applied a heavy coat, which she blotted with a tissue. Throwing her mink stole over her shoulder she walked out of the room. Standing in the hallway, her eyes still trying to adjust to the bright light, she heard someone shout, "They've predicted he'll win by a landslide. Massachusetts will once again be represented by Senator John F. Kennedy!"

Chapter Four

Hildale, Utah
January, 1959

The first three months of matrimony, though challenging, had its benefit - new and fashionable frocks. Every third Tuesday, Orson allowed the three sister wives to go to J.C. Penney's to shop for appropriate clothing for them and the children. As long as Margaret gave her consent, and the outfits followed Orson's strict guidelines, Beanie could buy them.

This morning Beanie stood in her closet scrutinizing her ever-expanding wardrobe. Even though the temperature outside was barely forty, she felt overheated and uncomfortable. So thumbing past the long-sleeved shirts, she paused at a short sleeve, pale blue blouse with bright yellow daisies lining the breast pocket. She stripped it off its hanger and put it on. When she tried to button it she found it fit more snugly than it did only a few weeks ago, leaving unsightly button gaps at her chest. She discovered the same problem with her new tan trousers, most likely a result of better quality of food in the Peterson house, along with larger portions.

She looked at her reflection in her bedroom mirror as she separated her hair into three equal parts and began braiding it. Her cheeks looked more round, as of late, which made her blue eyes appear smaller and closer together. She touched the hint of a layer of fat gathering underneath her chin and frowned. *When had that happened?* With all of the running around, chasing children, picking up toys, and cleaning this large home, she assumed that she would have lost a few pounds, not gained them. *Guess I better stick to just grapefruit for a while instead of the bacon and eggs,* she thought.

When she opened the bedroom door to go downstairs, the familiar smell of hot homemade waffles with maple syrup hit her nose causing her stomach to lurch. Normally she loved the smell, but today the smell seemed overly sweet and made her feel like vomiting. She threw her hand over her mouth and ran to the bathroom just down the hall, slammed the door, and retched.

Fifteen minutes later, Beanie gingerly walked into the kitchen. Saturday breakfast was already in full swing. All of the children were dressed and seated around the massive, rectangular, oak table gobbling down scrambled eggs, bacon, and those awful smelling waffles as though it might be their last meal. "Do we have any soda crackers?" asked

Beanie as she rummaged through the large walk-in pantry. "My stomach is a little upset this morning."

When she walked out empty-handed, Margaret gasped. "Beatrice, you look terrible. Shall I call the doctor?"

Beanie went to the cupboard and pulled out a small juice glass. She poured some apple juice in it, leaned back against the counter and said, "No, Margaret, I'm okay. It must have been something I ate last night." But just in case she was coming down with something, she made sure to stay away from the children. She didn't want them to catch what she had.

Dorothy smiled at Beanie and said, "What time is your piano lesson?"

"I have to be at Miss Cora's at eleven." She looked at the clock hanging on the wall. That gave her only two hours to feel better. She didn't want to give Orson any reason to make her stay home, so she smiled and added, "I'm really looking forward to it. Miss Cora is going to teach me how to play *High on the Mountain Top* today."

Orson gave her a nod of approval. "Good. When you've learned it properly you can play it for the congregation." He took a bite of crispy bacon. "Have Miss Cora teach you, *Come Listen to a Prophet's Voice*. That's always been one of my favorites."

Beanie nodded, looking away from that repulsive piece of bacon hanging out of his mouth, smiled politely and said, mimicking his enthusiasm, "Oh yes, Orson, mine too. I've always loved that song." She took another sip of the apple juice hoping that he wouldn't ask her to sing the unfamiliar tune. Immediately, her stomach clenched. She grabbed the edge of the counter to steady herself and said with a forced smile, "I think I'll go upstairs and go through my sheet music and pick out some other pieces to take just in case we have some extra time."

Orson nodded. "Just make sure the music you choose is appropriate."

Beanie casually exited the kitchen and walked to the stairs. Once out of sight, she scampered up the steps, ran down the hall, and flew into the bathroom where she promptly threw up the few sips of apple juice.

Two hours later Margaret pulled up in front of Miss Cora's house, handed Beanie three dollars for the lesson and said, "I'll be back in an hour to pick you up."

"Thank you, Margaret. I'll wait by the curb." She grabbed her file folder of *appropriate* piano music and exited the car. As soon as Margaret drove away, Beanie took a deep breath and grinned. At that moment she felt like she could breathe again. She stood up taller and walked with anxious steps up the sidewalk to her piano teacher's house and rang the doorbell.

When Miss Cora answered the door, her smile vanished. "Beanie. You look awful. Have you come down with something?" She ushered her student in and said as she took her coat and hung it on the coat rack, "Go stand by the fire to warm up. I'll go make you a cup of tea before we begin."

"Thank you, Miss Cora." Though she wasn't cold, the fire felt nice and comforting on Beanie's back, as though she were wearing her new electric blanket as a cape. When the heat became too much for her, Beanie walked over to the piano and sat down. She scooted the bench in, positioned her feet on the damper pedals, spread her fingers over the keys and began to sight read the piece of music perched on the upright's fallboard. Instantly a jazzy and upbeat melody filled the house.

Miss Cora entered the living room carrying a porcelain tray with a Victorian style flowered teapot, matching china teacups, and a small plate of freshly baked blueberry muffins. She set the tray on the coffee table and said, "Beanie that sounds fantastic. I didn't know you knew how to play jazz."

Beanie stopped playing, turned to look at her teacher and said, "I don't. I've never heard this song before. But it's really nice. I like the rhythm."

"Yes, John Coltrane is one of the all time great jazz saxophone players. He's played with all the greats: Miles Davis, Dizzy Gillespie, Duke Ellington and Thelonious Monk. That song, *A Moment's Notice*, is from his latest album, Blue Train." She smiled at her student and said, "It's not an easy song to play, but you did it justice, Beanie. You're a natural at jazz. Now come here and have a bite to eat before we begin the lesson."

Beanie pushed the bench back and stood up. "It'd be fun to go see him play. Maybe if he ever comes here, you and I could go together."

Miss Cora laughed. "I think the only way we'll get to see him is if we go to Chicago or Philadelphia or somewhere

where jazz is popular. I don't think Mr. Coltrane would have a very big audience here in Hildale."

Beanie eyed the muffins as she sat on the couch. "Those look good. Did you make them?"

"Fresh out of the oven. Have one."

Beanie grabbed one, peeled back the paper cup, and took a big bite. As soon as she swallowed, her stomach lurched, again. She dropped the half eaten muffin on the plate and said, "I think I'm going to be sick." She didn't want to throw up on Miss Cora's beautiful peach colored, floral, area rug, so she jumped up, ran to the bathroom, and for the third time that morning, retched.

A few minutes later when Beanie returned from the bathroom, Miss Cora helped her to the couch, handed her a cool washcloth and said, "Here, put this on your forehead." She poured Beanie a cup of tea. "And drink a little of this. It's chamomile. It'll settle your tummy."

Beanie took a small tentative sip in case her stomach rebelled. When her gut didn't react negatively from the tea, she took another sip. "It tastes good. Thank you, Miss Cora. I don't know what could be wrong with me." She took a longer draw from the cup, savoring the warm liquid. "I'm just so tired. Maybe I'm coming down with the flu."

Miss Cora studied her young student's roundish face, and then she visually tracked the rest of her body. As the clues piled up, she asked, "Are your breasts tender?"

Beanie instinctively crossed her arms over her chest and said, "Yes. How did you know?"

Miss Cora placed an arm around Beanie's shoulders, pulled her close and said, "Sweetheart, you're not sick. I think you're pregnant."

"Pregnant? I just turned sixteen. It's not possible." Beanie's bottom lip began to quiver.

Miss Cora hugged her tighter and sighed. "I'm pretty sure, Beanie, which makes what I have to say even harder."

Beanie pulled away. "What is it, Miss Cora?"

"My husband and I are moving to New York."

"Moving? Why?" Beanie felt a wave of nausea. She wasn't sure if it was because of the pregnancy or the fear of losing her only friend.

"My husband got offered a job that pays twice what he's making here." She looked at Beanie with conflicted eyes. "I'm sorry, but we had to take it."

Beanie felt her world beginning to crumble under her feet. "When are you leaving?" She wasn't sure she even wanted to know the answer.

"The moving van will be here next week." She hugged Beanie. "I'm so sorry, but here -" she stood up, walked over to the piano and grabbed the Blue Train sheet music and a pen. She sat back down next to Beanie and said while writing on the top of the piece of paper, "This is my Aunt Lynnie's phone number. We will be staying with her until we can find a place of our own. I want you to call me any time you need to talk."

Beanie took the music and stared at the number through blurry eyes. "I'm going to miss you so much." She clutched the sheet music to her chest and cried while Miss Cora held her in a tight embrace and rocked her.

That evening during dinner Beanie didn't participate in the conversation. She was too distraught to open her mouth for fear of crying. So when Margaret told her to clear the table and start washing the dishes, Beanie gladly agreed. She just wanted to be by herself where no one would see her cry.

She was only half-way through the dishes when Orson stormed into the kitchen furious. "What is this?" he said, shaking the sheet of music in her face.

Beanie looked at it and said, "It's John Coltrane's new song, *Moment's Notice.*"

"I can see the name of it, Beatrice. Where did you get this?"

His tone made Beanie nervous. "From M-Miss Cora. She said I played it beautifully, better than she played it. So she gave it to me today."

Orson rattled it in her face again and said, "This is not the music I said you could play. Did you not remember our conversation over breakfast? *High on the Mountaintop* or *Come Listen to a Prophet's Voice.* Those were the songs you were supposed to learn, not this blasphemous garbage by one of those ignorant coloreds. Don't you know they are the devil?"

"Orson, it's not garbage, its jazz. Besides, Miss Cora said I'm a natural, and that if I practice hard enough I could become a professional jazz pianist. Maybe even play concerts somewhere."

Orson glared at her. "You best get that notion out of your head right now. Mormon women do not have professions. Your job is being my wife and the mother to my children, not playing *this* type of music in some seedy joint in the bad section of town."

Without thinking, Beanie rolled her eyes and said, "There's nothing wrong with playing jazz. My learning to play it on the piano doesn't interfere with the teachings of the church. In fact, this is a really interesting piece and quite intricate." She reached for the music. "Here, I'll play it for you on the piano so you can hear it for yourself."

Orson's face scrunched with anger as he yanked the music from her reach and slapped her hard across the face with the other hand. "Don't you ever roll your eyes at me again. I will not tolerate that kind of disrespect. And I don't care if President Eisenhower wrote that music, you will not play it again. Understood?" He ripped up the music, sending bits of jazzy confetti raining down on the kitchen floor. He tossed the bulk of them in the wastebasket nestled by the side of the refrigerator. "And I don't want to hear another word about it. Now clean this up." He turned around and exited the kitchen without saying another word.

Beanie gently touched the tender, stinging part of her cheek, fighting back the tears. She had never in her life been struck by anyone, not even her father. And now to know that her own husband was capable of such horrible things made her weep out loud. How could her parents have given her to this man in marriage?

As she swept up the mess she prayed, *please, please God, don't let me be pregnant.*

That evening when she went to bed, she just couldn't stop crying. Just turned sixteen, pregnant, and married to a mean man. How could her young life be ruined before it even had a chance to get started? What was she going to do?

For three weeks she did nothing but cry and watch her clothes grow tighter and tighter.

Then in the middle of one sleepless night, whether from the stress of keeping her secret, the sadness of not being able to share it with anyone, or just the biological need to pee, Beanie felt something churning in her lower abdomen causing it to cramp. She jumped out of bed, ran to the bathroom, and sat down on the toilet. The painful spasms caused her to grit her teeth and break out in a sweat. She yanked a few sheets of toilet paper from the roll and dabbed her forehead, then dropped them in the toilet. Then she grabbed more squares and wiped herself. When she stood up and turned to flush the toilet, she nearly fainted. Clots of mucus and blood turned the toilet bowl water a deep chunky red. There was so much blood.

She threw her hand over her mouth to stifle a cry, quickly flushed the toilet, and thought, *am I dying or did God just answer my prayer?*

Chapter Five

January 23, 1959

Beanie hadn't told any of them about the miscarriage, and yet, they found out. She thought that once she flushed the evidence down the toilet, no one would ever know that she had been pregnant. She didn't realize that the bleeding had started while she slept.

The following morning when she saw the blood, she stripped the sheets from the bed, shoved them in the back of her closet and went down to breakfast. When she returned to her room, Margaret stood by her bed holding the bloody sheet in her hands, her lips pulled into a tight scowl. She opened up the sheet, showing the dried clots to Beanie. "Why would you hide this? Is this from your period?"

Beanie lowered her head as if ashamed, but didn't answer.

"Well, what is it from then?"

When Beanie looked up at her with tears in her eyes, a realization came over Margaret. A mixture of anger and sadness filled her words. "You should have told us," she said. Margaret dropped the sheet to the floor and added, "How far along were you?"

Beanie shook her head. "I-I don't know."

Margaret tipped her head down as if in a silent prayer, slowly shook it, and said, "Well, Orson needs to know about this."

Beanie rushed to Margaret and grabbed her hand. "Please don't tell him, Margaret. I didn't mean for it to happen. It was an accident. Please, can't we just keep this between you and me?"

Margaret pulled her hand away and said, "I have no secrets from my husband, and neither will you."

That night while Beanie slept, Orson entered her room unannounced. He shut the door behind him and stood by her bed. She wasn't sure if it was his heavy breathing or his sheer presence that woke her, but her eyes shot open, and she sat up straight gathering the blanket around her chest.

Seeing the large shadow standing at the foot of her bed, Beanie whispered, "Orson, is that you?" She gathered the blanket tighter as if to protect herself.

"Take off your nightgown," Orson hissed.

Beanie didn't need to see his face to know that he was enraged. If having a piece of inappropriate music caused him to slap her, she could only imaging what hiding a pregnancy would make him do. She said quietly, "Orson please. I'm not feeling very well."

Orson came around the side of the bed, grabbed the comforter, yanking it out of her hands, and flung it to the end of the bed. "I said, take it off."

Beanie didn't move.

He reached down, grabbed her by the front of her nightgown and yanked her to her feet. "Take it off, or so help me, I'll rip it off of you." He reached for her buttoned neckline.

Beanie pushed back his hand. "Orson, no. Please don't do this to me."

Orson took a step closer to Beanie and grabbed her upper arm, wrapping his long fingers around it. "Why didn't you tell me you were pregnant? He seemed to go into a rage. "What did you do to my child?"

The smell of whisky on his breath caused Beanie to turn her head to the side. She cried out, "Please, Orson, I didn't do anything wrong. It just happened."

"Don't lie to me." Orson reared his open palm back and slapped it across her face knocking her to the bed. He grabbed her nightgown and ripped it down the front, exposing her breasts. He hissed, "I'm going to teach you a lesson, you filthy liar. You're going to pay for your sins". He continued to rip the nightgown until it opened up like a bathrobe. Then he unbuckled his pants and pulled them off. As he pushed her legs apart with his, he entered her hard and said, "You are going to give me another child to replace the one you stole from me. I'm going to make sure of that."

All Beanie could do was sob and submit.

•••••••••••

May 23, 1959

As she stood by the kitchen sink reliving that awful night four months ago when Orson found out she'd miscarried, she couldn't stop crying. The bloody clots in the toilet this morning meant that it had happened again. And once Orson found out that it had happened a second time, his punishment for this one would worsen ten-fold, she was sure. She couldn't even fathom what it might involve.

From the foyer, Beanie heard Margaret yell, "Beatrice! Dorothy and I are going to the grocery store. We'll be back shortly."

Beanie calmed her tears and yelled back, "All right. I'll finish cleaning the kitchen." When the front door closed Beanie sobbed loud and hard allowing all of those pent up tears to pour out.

Working through her sadness she scrubbed down the entire kitchen starting with the cupboards.

Cleaning seemed to help her think. And in this case, she really needed to figure out what she was going to do. After pulling all of the dishes out of the cabinets, wiping down the insides, and then putting the dishes back, she started on the floor. "Maybe he won't find out this time," she said to the broom as she swept along the baseboards. "I checked the sheets, and they were clean, no blood anywhere." She pulled the refrigerator away from the wall and stuck the broom back behind it, gathering all of the lint balls, cobwebs, dead bugs, and bits of paper. "So there's no way he could find out," she added as she grabbed the dustpan and swept up the dirt. "No possible way."

Just as she was just about to dump the dustpan, something caught her eye. A sense of familiarity made her heart pound harder. She shook the dirt and cobwebs off of a small shred of paper and uncrumpled it. Excitement caused her to suck in her breath when she recognized the handwritten numbers on it. "Miss Cora," she said. Her heart leaped with excitement as her mind quickly flashed on the night when Orson ripped up the music with the phone number on it. "It must have fallen behind the fridge." But as quickly as the excitement hit, it died away and she groaned, "Oh no. Where's the rest of the phone number?" Two numbers shy of Miss Cora's Aunt Lynnie's complete telephone number, Beanie yanked the refrigerator farther away from the wall and fell to her hands and knees looking for the rest of it. But when she found no other pieces of paper, she leaned against the wall, opened up her fingers and let the scrap of paper float to the floor.

But then a thought came to her as if it were a voice from God. *I remember there was a seven and a four.* She picked up the piece of paper and said out loud. "I'll just keep dialing numbers until I reach her."

Excited, she jumped to her feet, grabbed the phone from the wall and cradled it on her shoulder as she stuck her finger in the hole and spun the rotary dial. "Please, please, please pick up the phone, Miss Cora. I really need to talk to you right now."

But before the telephone could complete the connection, she heard the front door open and Orson's voice drift in from the foyer. "Beatrice, I'm home. Where are you?"

Reluctantly, Beanie hung up the phone, pushed the refrigerator back against the wall and moved over to the sink. "I'm in the kitchen," she yelled back. Then she tucked the partial phone number inside her bra, where it would stay safe and secret until she could try again later.

When Orson entered the kitchen, he stared at her and said, "What did you do?"

Beanie leaned against the sink and raised her eyebrows. *How could he possible know?*

"What do you mean?"

He glared at her and said, "You look guilty."

Beanie took the dishtowel, wiped her hands on it and said without looking at him as she folded it neatly and placed it back on the counter, "I haven't done anything wrong, Orson. I've just been here cleaning." She could feel his gaze boring a hole through her back.

"Good, because if you did do something wrong and I find out about it . . ." He let his words trail off as he turned and exited the kitchen.

Beanie instinctively placed her hand over her heart, covering and protecting the one bit of hope she had left. Fear crept in to strangle her spirit, choking out that tiny seed of optimism that had sprouted only moments earlier. She pressed the palm of her hand against the hidden telephone number and prayed, *please let me find her before he hurts me again.*

Chapter Six

Boston, Massachusetts
May 23, 1959

"Uuhh . . . o h . . . ba by. Ooh, you feel so goo d. Open your eyes. Look at me," he said, breathless. "Is it goo d to you? Is it goo d, ba by?"

Adeline opened her eyes and saw his dark brown eyes staring intently into hers. She felt his bo dy rhythmically, fluidly moving in her, the sensation causing her bo dy to tighten and flex. Letting out a slow moan, she smiled and no dded. She closed her eyes again and pushed har der into him.

And at that moment everything felt right to her. The lies she lived with daily somehow seemed inconsequential. The worries over being found out, even though she ha d led the masquera de for years, all seemed to dissipate. And with this momentary fulfillment of her desires, she felt all she ever wanted was within her grasp. She lifted her hand off of his back and reached straight up, arching her neck, her head rolled back and she grasped at the air above her. She balled up her fist as if she could capture this moment, take hold of it, and never let it go.

He rolled off of from atop her and wrapped his arm around her. Adeline lay in Melvin's arms, content. She rubbed the coarse, tightly curled black hair on his chest as it rose and fell with each hastened breath as he tried to slow it. She rolled over to the edge of the bed, and reached down into her purse that was on the floor for her pack of cigarettes, took one out and lit it. Rolling over to lay on her back, she blew out the smoke. Adeline let out deep sigh, and thought about how she could wallow in this moment and in these feelings forever. Finishing her cigarette, she willed herself to move. She pushed up on the bed, and swung her legs over the edge.

"I have to go," she said, grounding out the cigarette in the ashtray.

"Don't leave, baby. Stay a little longer." Melvin sat up and moved in close behind her. He whispered in her ear, "Stay with me, Adeline." Releasing a wisp of breath with each word, he stroked her soft, sandy blonde hair.

Adeline stood up and looked around the floor to find her bra and girdle. "You know I've got that thing tonight. And I've got to have time to do my hair. I've missed my appointment with the hair dresser." She glanced over at the mirror and pushed her hair up, wiped the mascara stain from under her hazel eyes, and then looked down at her watch. "I wish I could stay," she said.

Dressed in her underwear she sat on the side of the bed and pulled on one of her stockings. Pulling out the fastener made into the underside of her girdle, she hooked the stocking inside the rubber disc and clamped the metal clip. She ran her fingers up the nylon, smoothing it out.

"Here, let me do that." Melvin hopped out of bed and took the other stocking from the bed next to her. Kneeling down on one knee, he lifted her foot and ran the nylon up her leg. Stopping at her thigh, he caressed it, and leaned down and kissed it.

"Stop." She laughed. "I told you I had to go." Adeline pushed his hand away from her leg and reached for the hook.

"Okay. I'll do it." He looked up at her and smiled. "No hanky-panky." He brushed her hand aside and opened the hook, latching the stocking at the front, he then lifted her leg up onto his shoulder and fastened the hook in the back. He patted her thigh, lowered her leg and raised himself up and forward. Adeline could feel his breath on her face as he leaned in close to her, his arms pushing down onto the bed on either side of her. He asked, "Do you really wish you could stay?"

"Yes." She rubbed his dark face. The prickly stubble on his jaw rubbed against the palm of her hand and sent an electric rush through her. Letting her hand slide down his body she stroked his strong, firm chest. She wished she could have more of him. Not just here. Not just now. But always.

"I don't know about that," he said, as if reading her thoughts. "I think sometimes that you're just using me," he said, and got up. He walked over to the other side of the bed and picked up his striped undershorts.

"Using you?" she asked. "For what?"

"I don't know, Adeline."

"How could you not know?" Sliding on her slip and then dress, she said, "You just said it, you have to have some idea why you did. Just tell me what you mean, Melvin." She went over and stood with her back to him. "Here, zip me up."

He pulled the long zipper up slowly, but didn't say a word. As the silence lingered between them, Adeline slipped on her heels, put on her hat and leaned into the mirror over the dresser to fix her lipstick. She walked over to the door, and putting on her gloves she said, "Well, I'm leaving. Are you going to tell me what you meant Melvin Chambers, or will I have to spend the next few days fretting about it until I see you again?"

"You wouldn't fret about it." He looked over at her as she raised her eyebrows. "Sometimes I think you just use me to show that you haven't turned into a racist."

"A racist?"

"Yeah. Makes you feel better inside."

"If that was the purpose you were serving, I wouldn't keep your black behind holed up in this apartment. I'd flaunt you all over town."

"You'd never do that because you'd mess up your lily-white life. And I know that's more important to you than anything else."

Taking in a deep sigh, Adeline pulled open the door and left without saying anything else. Melvin's words had reached to grab a hold of her. Those words had ripped into her hart and her mind, and had cut down deep into her soul. She took in a deep breath and tried not to let the tear wedged in the corner of her eye fall.

Stopped at a traffic light on her drive home, the world around her became still. Sitting there everything went quiet except for the hum of the air-conditioning. Her eyes wandered out the side window. The noon sun was beaming and the cloudless blue sky blanketed her, its warmth resonating with reassurance and redemption. She lifted her head and closed her eyes. She was sure that the beauty of this day was a sign. A sign that exonerated her from all she had done. All she was doing. That somehow it could void those words that Melvin had spoken. After all, it was only freedom that she sought, or some reasonable semblance of it. That couldn't be asking for too much.

Lost in thought, Adeline ran her white-gloved hands around the steering wheel of her white convertible Thunderbird, and thought about her white life.

Surely I'm not racist, she mused. *I have a colored lover.* And colored help. Even her "in" to society, Jack Kennedy, was on the bandwagon for civil rights, even more so after he made that hiccup with the 1957 civil rights bill. She had always been one of his staunchest supporters.

So, why would Melvin say that?

Surely, he couldn't have meant it. He knew he was more to her than just her paramour.

A horn honked and pushed her out of her though ts, making her jump. She eyed the car behind her in the rearview mirror. Moving her foot from the brake to the gas pedal she thought, *I should have taken the top off the car*. Pulling off she headed home to Beacon Hill.

Chapter Seven

The house was abuzz with people and deliveries. It wasn't anywhere near ready to receive guests, and Adeline still had to get herself together. Her husband, Walter was no help. She was sure that once he got home he would probably do his usual - waltz in at the last minute, insist she help him get ready - tie his tie, help him find the right black socks. And then head downstairs without her.

Aren't all black socks the same?

This was going to be the biggest dinner party the Garrisons had ever hosted and she had spent the morning doing something that had put her seriously behind schedule. This dinner, one of the first campaign events, along with a tea the next Saturday that Adeline would host for Jack's yet unannounced bid for the White House, were important. And while Adeline was adept in organizing things, this day she was feeling a bit overwhelmed, and it showed in her temperament.

First her friend, Arlene Moore, was supposed to have arrived an hour early to help out, but she hadn't showed up or called. The rental company was setting up chairs. The bakery had arrived with the cakes. But there was no place to put them because the rental company found it more important to get the chairs set up for people that hadn't arrived yet, than to set up the small cake table Adeline had ordered. The colored help, mostly her own staff, but some she had hired out for the night, just couldn't seem to get anything right. The silver didn't sparkle like it should. They had brought out the wrong china from the cabinet. How could they have not known that the serving dish to that set had been slightly cracked at the last dinner party? She couldn't very well serve with that, and it appeared she couldn't very well trust them to get anything done without her standing over them. Just as she was about to yell at Jean, her maid for the past seven years, about the water stains on the wine glasses that she "could see all the way from over here," there came a knock on the back door and a chime from the front doorbell.

"Oh, my goodness." Adeline stood in the middle of the floor, curlers in her hair, wearing a black mohair turtleneck sweater and full red and black striped skirt. She was shoeless, a bad habit her husband always prodded her about, but it felt natural to Liddie. She spread her arms and raised her eyebrows, showing her exasperation.

"I'll get the back door, ma'am. You get the front." Jean, apparently seeing Adeline's frustration, placed the spotty crystal glass she was holding on the table and headed through the kitchen to the back door. "It's the man with the champagne," she called out.

Liddie barely heard her as she made it to the front door where the flower delivery man was being trailed by three others bringing flower arrangements up the walkway. She held the door open and let them squeeze past her. After she let the last one in, she pointed her finger toward the dining room. "In there," she said. Grabbing the last guy, she told him he could place the one he was holding on the coffee table.

"We have a couple more," she was told by the first deliveryman as he rounded out of the living room to go back to his truck. She started out toward the door to follow him when the phone rang.

"What now," she said. The caterers had called twice already, once to say they'd be late, and then another time, twenty minutes later to say they were lost. "If this is that darn caterer again..."

"Hello," she said.

"May I speak with Lynnie, please?" A distraught voice came through the receiver.

"Speaking. This is Liddie Garrison. May I help you?" It was a voice unfamiliar to Adeline.

"Oh. Good. I'm a friend of your niece's."

"My niece?"

"Yes. Miss Cora, um, I mean Cora Hampton."

"I think you must have the wrong number," Adeline said, and hung up. Placing her open palm over her forehead, she tried to think. "Now, what is it that I was getting ready to do

. . . Oh," she nodded her head. "I know. Jean," she called out, "who did you say was at the door?" Adeline headed toward the kitchen to check on who had knocked. Hopefully, it was the caterers. Before she could reach Jean the phone rang again. "Oh for Pete's sake." She just couldn't take one more distraction. "Will somebody please get that phone? Please!"

She found Jean standing at the kitchen sink. She looked around the kitchen. "I thought the caterers were here?"

"No'am. I told you, it was the champagne."

"Oh." She looked down and saw the case sitting by the back door. "Jean. Come now, let's get that case out of the doorway." She stood in the middle of the kitchen and looked at her. "Someone coming in the door will trip on it. Can't you pull it in? At the rate things are going, I'm going to have to pop a cork on one of those bottles before my guests start arriving."

Jean took her foot and started to push the wooden case filled with twelve bottles of 1945 Pommery Greno Brut across the floor with her foot.

"Can't you pick it up, Jean?" Adeline stood with her hands on her hips, tapping her foot.

"No ma'am. I can't pick it up."

"Well, go and find someone who can." Adeline walked back through the dining room and saw the petite dark-skinned woman staring at her from the living room. "Well what is it?" Jean's cousin, who had come in to help with the party, was standing there holding the receiver. "What?" Adeline asked again.

"The phone's for you, ma'am."

At the End of the Line   51

"Well, why didn't you say something?" Going over to her, Liddie snatched the phone, covering the mouthpiece she said, "Were you just going to stand there and hold it?"

"No ma'am, I was just waiting for you to stop talking."

Adeline, in a huff, pushed her aside and spoke into the phone. "Hello."

"Yes. Uhm . . . Isn't this Cora's Aunt Lynnie?"

"No dear, it isn't. This is 'Liddie,'" she said, emphasizing the "d." "Didn't I just tell you that you had the wrong number? I'm hanging up now. Don't call here again."

"Don't hang up. Wait. Please, don't hang up. This is the number that she gave me." The person on the other end sounded no more than a child. And this time Adeline noticed that she was crying.

"Are you crying? What's wrong with you? Where are your parents?"

"I'm just so afraid. I don't want to be here anymore and Miss Cora said she'd help . . . she said if I needed her, to call her."

"Well, this isn't her." Adeline paused. "What are you afraid of?"

"He's going to hurt me again." She broke out into a sob.

Adeline gasped and grabbed her chest. "What's your name?

"Beanie. I mean Beatrice."

"Tell me, Beatrice, who is going to hurt you?"

"My husband."

"Husband? How old are you? Where are you?"

Chapter Eight

Mississippi
1938

She tried to sneak into the house quietly. Taking her shoes off at the wire-screened back door, she held onto the door handle gently pulling it closed so it wouldn't slam. She tiptoed slowly across the kitchen toward her bedroom.

She had been crying so hard that it had taken a long time to quell the sobbing and catch her breath. Backed up against the house, she had slid down it to stoop by the back door, calming herself before she attempted to go in the house. Her momma was such a light sleeper. She had tried to fix her clothes, she tugged at the torn dress that hung over her body. It was nearly in shreds. No matter, she thought, she'd burn it just as soon as she could. And she was soaking wet. She had left that place screaming, near buck naked. Holding what was left of her clothes and her shoes in her arms, she had run straight to the creek. The water was cold but she didn't care, she just wanted to wash it off of her. To wash *him* off of her.

Now tiptoeing across the floor, she only had a few more steps. Hattie Jean Thomas knew she was late coming in, not to mention everything else that had happened that night. If her mother heard her she'd be in a heap of trouble. Hattie Jean could imagine her momma pointing her finger at her saying, *"No self-respecting sixteen year old girl stays out past dark. It just ain't right."* Now that statement made sense to Hattie Jean.

Surely, she had found that out tonight.

Just five more steps and she could hide away in the quiet of her room. She could curl up in her bed and be drawn up in the moonlight and pray for forgiveness and strength. Then she hoped to be able to rest quietly in the bosom of God and forget all that had transpired that night.

She knew that it had to have been something she did for something this terrible to happen to her. But she'd repent. She'd help out more around the house, not talk back to her momma. She'd even go up to the Stewarts house and help her momma with her work.

Her whole body trembled. She just wanted to get into her bed, pull the covers over her head and find some calm. She stopped and stood still, taking in a big swallow to fight back the tears.

Only a few more steps.

"Hattie Jean? Is that you back there?" A softly strained voice called across the darkness.

"Yes, Momma," Hattie said.

"Come here, chile. What you doing back there sneaking around? You thought I wouldn't hear you?"

Hattie Jean ran into her room and pulled out her two piece pajamas from under her pillow and hastily put them on. She threw the tattered dress under her bed and flung her shoes into the back of her closet. Sorry, once she did it because they made a thumping sound when they hit the back wall of the closet.

"Hattie Jean Thomas. Didn't you hear me, girl? I said come here."

"Yes ma'am. Here I come." Hattie Jean ran back out to the kitchen and splashed water on her face, drying it on the hand towel that hung over the sink. Then she went into her momma's room at the front of the house. She stood at the door and her mother turned on the light next to her bed. Her mother stared at her so long that Hattie Jean started to fidget. She wrapped her hand in the tail of her pajama shirt and chewed her lowered lip. Her eyes filled up with tears, and she didn't know how she was going to stop them from overflowing. She wiped her eyes with the back of her hand.

"What's wrong with you, chile? You sick or something?" Hattie Jean's mother threw back the covers and sat up on the side of the bed. "Why you standing there shaking?"

"I don't know, Momma."

"Come here closer to me, let me look at you." Hattie patted the bed for her to sit. Ophelia's skin was dark, but smooth with a natural sheen. She had high cheekbones, small slits for eyes, and large, ample breasts. At fifty, she still worked, cooking, cleaning and doing the laundry for the same white family she had worked for forty years. Hattie Jean lowered herself down and tried to keep as far away from her mother as she could. Not looking into her mother's face, Hattie Jean stared at her mother's fat feet and swollen ankles.

"Tell me." Her mother grabbed her and pulled her close. "I knows something is wrong. Tell me what it is."

"Charlie Ray raped me," Hattie blurted out. Wasn't no use trying to keep anything from her mother, she decided. She would either figure it out, or question her until she got too weary to stay quiet about it any longer. Plus, Hattie Jean knew that any moment the torrent of tears she was trying to hold in would come bursting out.

Ophelia hopped up out the bed and stood over her daughter. "What you mean he raped you?"

"We had a fight."

"A fight?" Ophelia took hold of her daughter's chin and turned her face side to side. "Did he hit you or did he rape you? There's a difference, you know."

"Yes ma'am, I know. We were . . . We . . ." Hattie Jean scrambled for words to tell her mother what had happened. She tried to overcome the fear of saying it out loud and of what her mother would think of her because of it.

"You were what? Don't lie to me, chile."

"We were kissing in old man Dooley's barn behind his store and . . ." The tears started coming down Hattie Jean's cheeks. "And I told him to stop, Momma. I got up and tried to leave. But he wouldn't let me." Hattie Jean's words came rushing out. "He kept grabbing on me and he wouldn't stop. He got ma dand started yelling at me, pushing me around.

"He asked me why I came in the barn with him if I didn't want to do it. Then. Then . . . well, then . . ". Hattie Jean lowered her eyes. "Then he pushed me down and got on top of me, and he started yanking at my clothes and pulling on my underwear. But I didn't want to do it, Momma. I didn't. I swear. I was just trying . . ."

"I'm going over his house." Ophelia took off her gown and directed Hattie Jean to "help me get my clothes on."

"No, Momma. Don't go over there."

"Hand me my brassiere."

"Please don't go." Hattie Jean pleaded. "It's my fault." Ophelia raised her eyebrow. Hattie Jean wrung her hands together. "I mean I just shouldn't have been trying to prove nothing and all this wouldn't have happened. Plus, Momma, he said if I told anyone he would hurt me and you, too. I don't want nothing to happen to you 'cause of me."

"Ha! That's a laugh. That boy ain't gonna do a darn thing. 'Specially after I tell his momma what he's done. I got a mind to call the sheriff."

"No. Momma. I don't want everyone to know. I just want to forget about it. Please."

"What you talking about? What kind of girl I done raised? You stand up to people that wrong you. Didn't I teach you that?" Ophelia put on her slip, and told Hattie Jean to, "Gimme my dress over there off that chair."

"But you don't understand, Momma," Hattie Jean picked up the dress but clutched it tightly, not wanting her mother to go to Charlie Ray's. "Everyone hates me anyway. They'll just say I deserved it. They won't think bad of him. They'll just think bad of me. I won't be able to show my face anywhere."

"Oh, but you can show your face after having that boy make a harlot out of you?" Ophelia snatched her dress from Hattie Jean. "Being a Jezebel will make people like you? Now that's some logic I surely don't understand."

"No, Momma, you're right. You don't understand. You just can't understand."

"What is that supposed to mean?"

"He said that I think I'm better than everybody else, always walking around actin' highfalutin. That 'cause I'm light-skinned with light eyes I think I'm better than anyone else. I think I'm as good as white folk."

"That's just some hogwash. What does that even have to do with anything?"

"Because everybody always teasing me, saying that you so dark that my daddy must've been white."

"Ain't that the most ridiculous thing I ever heard?" Ophelia sat down on the bed. "Here chile, come help me get these shoes on my feet." She looked at Hattie Jean. "Your daddy was colored, God rest his soul, and you is colored. He was right fair, but he had colored blood. One thing for sure, you can't change your color. You might be light, but you sho'll ain't white. Anyone can look at you see that you're colored."

Hattie Jean, with tears running down her face pleaded with her mother. "I know it, Momma, but that's all they see

– my light skin and then they keep goading me. They see me, they know I'm colored, still, it don't stop them from picking on me. You know it, Momma, they always been doing it. You can't do nothing to stop it. And if I hadn't been trying to prove something I wouldn't have got caught up in that barn with that boy."

"What you tryin' to prove?"

"That I'm just like everybody else. That I don't think I'm better than nobody."

"You are just like everybody else. Shoot. I was thinking you was gone do more than everybody else around here. That's what I was hoping. How you look ain't none of your fault. You shouldn't have to prove nothing to nobody at no time. Don't be no fool, Hattie Jean. People gone always try to get your goat 'cuz you colored. You gone always have to fight. And when bad things happen you can't think you deserve it 'cuz a yo' skin color."

"I get it twice as hard, Momma. You just don't know. White's don't like me because I'm colored, and the coloreds don't like me 'cause I'm light-skinned."

"And that's why you think it's okay to have that boy have his way with you? Lord, what kind of mind do you got?"

"I got a good mind, I'm guessing. I just wasn't using it tonight."

Ophelia put on her coat and picked up her pocketbook. "You take a bath and get that douche bag and clean yourself out. I'm going up to that boy's house. No matter what you say. Something's gone be done about this. If'n I have to do it myself."

Chapter Nine

Hildale, Utah

She said she'd call me back. Beanie stood by the phone wishing for it to ring. *Please call me back, please.* The lady, Liddie, who answered the phone yesterday said she would phone her back after her party. She was kind of glad she hadn't called back last night. How would she have explained the call to Orson? If he ever found out she was telling some stranger about their personal life, he would have a fit. And Lord only knows what he would do to her. But now that everyone was gone from the house, Orson at work, the children at school, Margaret and Dorothy in the park with the two youngest children, Beanie had the place to herself.

A loud *ring, ring* caused her to jump. She grabbed the phone off the wall and said in an anxious rush, "Hello?"

"Hello, may I speak with Beatrice?"

It was her, the woman from the wrong number. Beanie tried to calm her heart. "Yes, this is Beanie."

A very proper and crisp voice responded, "This is Adeline Garrison. You called me yesterday. I just wanted to call back to make sure you were okay."

The fact that this stranger called back to check up on her made Beanie's heart leap. "Thank you so much for calling me back, Miss Adeline. I'm sorry that I interrupted your party, but I was trying to call my friend."

A woman's voice said, "Did you reach her? Her name's Cora, right?"

"Yes, her name's Miss Cora, but I didn't get a hold of her. Actually she was my piano teacher. But she moved to New York about five months ago."

The woman on the phone grew quiet for a moment and then said, "I live in Boston. How did you end up calling my number?"

"Miss Cora wrote it on a piece of music. But my husband found it and tore it up. And then he hit me."

A gasp came over the line. "He hit you?"

"Yes, he slapped me across the face. But that's not the only time he's hurt me."

"What do you mean? How has he hurt you?"

Beanie hesitated. She wanted to open up to this woman, but a part of her was ashamed of her secret and afraid that if she revealed it, this stranger would think badly of her. But since she had no one else to talk to she said quietly, "When he found out that I had a miscarriage, he slapped me and forced me to have sex with him so that I would get pregnant again." She grew quiet and then added, "I've just miscarried again. I feel so ashamed. I didn't want to be pregnant, but I certainly didn't intend to kill another baby. Now I'm afraid of what my husband will do to me if he finds out."

"Did you call your parents? Maybe they can come and get you."

"No. I can't call them."

"Why not?"

"Because they don't care about me anymore." She wrapped the telephone cord around her finger and leaned against the wall. "They must not care about me otherwise they wouldn't have given me to this man."

"What do you mean by *given you* to him?"

Thinking back on her wedding day ten months earlier, she said, "They forced me to marry a man that I hardly knew." She remembered the trauma of her first night as Orson's third wife and said, "I've tried to be a good wife. I really have. But he just hates me. No matter what I do it's not good enough." She paused. "And the others, they hate me, too."

"What others?"

"The other sister wives. They treat me like I'm the hired help, not Orson's other wife. Especially Margaret. She's mean to me. Dorothy's nicer, but she always sides with Margaret."

Miss Adeline said, "Beanie, you know it's not right to have more than one wife. It's against the law."

"Not in Utah and not in our church. In our church, Orson is held in high regard and can pretty much do what he wants. As an elder he has the authority to do as he sees fit, especially when it comes to his wives."

"That still doesn't give him any right to hit you."

"Yes it does," Beanie insisted. "I'm his wife. And if he wants to beat me or force himself on me there's nothing that I can do about it. Nothing at all." She felt a sense of panic begin to fill her insides. "I just don't know how long I can live like this. I want to run away."

"Where would you go?"

Beanie shrugged her shoulders and picked at a sliver of wallpaper coming loose by the edge of the kitchen's doorframe. "I don't know, maybe Miss Cora's. But I don't even know where she lives."

"I think you should speak to your parents. I'm sure they love you and would want to help you."

"No they don't. They couldn't get rid of me fast enough. They had my things packed and shipped here before I even knew what was happening. And every time I try to talk to my mom about what's going on with Orson and me, she stops me and tells me to 'just make it work.'"

"I think you are overreact -"

Beanie interrupted her. "You don't understand." Her voice escalated. "He forced me to have sex with him. He hurt me. I mean, really hurt me. He's going to kill me next time. I just know it." Her voice grew softer, "It's just a matter of time."

Miss Adeline remained quiet for a moment and then said, "What is it you want me to do? I can try to help you, but I just don't know how. I don't know you, so I don't know if what you're telling me is the truth or something you've made up just to get attention. I'm not saying you're lying, but if it's really as bad as you say it is . . ." Her voice trailed off.

Beanie became solemn. "It's all true, Miss Adeline. Please believe me. I wouldn't make this up."

"Well, what do you want me to do?"

"Help me get out of here before it's too late."

"So where would you go? You said you didn't have anywhere to go."

Beanie thought for a moment and then said hopefully, "Maybe I could come to Boston to visit you."

"I don't know . . ." Miss Adeline's voice faltered, "I-"

"Please, Miss Adeline. I'm desperate."

"Do you know Cora's last name? Perhaps I could find her for you. I have friends who could look into it for me. Would that help?"

Beanie's heart sank. "No, I think it would take too much time. And I don't think I have that much time left."

Miss Adeline remained quiet for a moment. Finally Beanie said, "Are you still there?"

"Yes, I'm still here. I'm thinking."

"Thinking?" Beanie felt a slight flutter in her chest.

"Do you have any money?"

Beanie sighed, "No. Orson doesn't give me any. I've managed to save up a few dollars here and there, but nothing substantial. Why?"

"If I send you money for a bus ticket, do you promise to use it for that?"

"Oh yes, Miss Adeline. I promise." Beanie squelched the urge to jump up and down. "I'll get on the first bus that goes to Boston." She didn't know how she would do it or when she would get there, but at least she had a destination.

"All right, then. It's settled. You'll come here and we'll find your Miss Cora." Miss Adeline stopped for a moment and then said, "She will help you once we find her, right?"

"Oh yes, I know she will. She loves me just like a-" Beanie when quiet when she heard the front door open.

From the foyer she heard Orson yell, "I'm home. Where is everyone?"

Beanie whispered into the phone. "He's home. I've gotta go."

"Wait, I need your name. Tell me your whole name."

"Beatrice Peterson, and I live in Hildale, Utah."

"I'll wire you the money tomorrow through Western Union."

In a hushed voice, Beanie said, "Thank you so much for helping me." And then she hung up before Orson could catch her.

Chapter Ten

Boston, Massachusetts
June 30, 1959

Adeline sat across the dining room table from her husband, Walter. They always ate in silence. He'd grab a drink, bourbon neat, from the bar when he walked in the door from work, loosen his tie, throw his suit jacket across the back of a chair, kiss his wife and inquire as to what time dinner would be ready. Always in that order. Dinner was ready every night at the same time. That never seemed to break his routine. Tonight, however, Walter found his wife's actions required some dinnertime conversation.

"What do you even know about this girl, Liddie?" he asked, switching the fork into his other hand after cutting a hunk of the prime rib that was piled on his plate.

"I know that she needs my help. " She watched his cheeks bulge as he pushed the meat into his mouth and chewed. "And, I know that I plan on helping her."

"I'd think you need more information about her before you send my hard earned money all the way across the goddamn United States. How do you know she won't get it and buy cigarettes or spend it on some boy?" He picked up his water glass, trying to wash down his food. "What did you say her name was, again?"

"Her name is Beatrice. Beanie for short."

"And doesn't she have anyone that can help her out there in Wyoming?"

"Utah."

"What? Oh. Utah," he said, stuffing potatoes in his mouth and watching her as he chewed. He narrowed his eyes and pointed his steak knife at her. "You know we're not the goddamn American Red Cross."

Adeline closed her eyes and took in a deep breath. He always took to yelling to make his point.

"Are you listening to me?" Walter glared across the table at Adeline.

"Can't help but hear you, Walter," Adeline said, opening her eyes. "The whole block can hear you."

"I paid enough money for this huge house and yard to be able to speak as loud as I want. " He took a swig of the bourbon. "Doesn't matter how loud I talk though, does it? You do what you want. Taking in orphans, spending my money on clothes, and God knows what else."

Adeline smirked. "Yes. God knows."

"What is that supposed to mean, Liddie? You have that degree in biology from Simmons College. What did you think you would do with it? Women tried to pass that Equal Rights Amendment to make them equal to men. Didn't happen. Won't happen. Just like that civil rights bill won't happen to make the colored man an equal citizen to the white man. No place for women but running the household and having babies -" He looked at Liddie. "Sorry, honey, I didn't mean you. I know you can't have any children and that's no fault of yours. It was God. I never held that against you, you know that don't you?"

"Mmm hmm."

"I was just saying that that's a woman's place — in the home - and the Negra's place is to help them take care of it." Walter stuffed another hunk of meat in his mouth, before shoveling in one fork-full and then another of the roasted potatoes. "The blacks will always be beneath us." He tried to finish voicing his thought by pushing the food into his cheeks. "And you, Liddie, beautiful white woman that you are, will still be a step beneath me."

"If you keep talking with all that food in your mouth, you are going to choke to death," Adeline said. "And then once you're dead, I'll be able to do whatever I want with your 'hard earned money', including sending it 'all the way across the goddamn United States,'" she quoted him, a smile curling up at the edge of her lips. "Then the only person that'll be beneath anyone will be you. Six feet beneath us, to be exact."

"Is that all you have to say?" He took a sip of his water. "You're not defending equal rights for women? What about these civil rights for the Negroes?" Adeline lowered her head and played with her creamed peas. "I'm surprised you're not all over this civil rights thing with your college education and all these colored folks you hire. You want to see desegregation at work, just visit my house, that's what I always say."

"You want me to hire a white woman to do your laundry and cook your supper?"

"Hell no. Jean cooks better than my own mother did. God rest her soul." Walter laughed, and wiped his mouth with his linen napkin. "Jean," he shouted into the kitchen. "Is that apple pie I smell?" He didn't take his eyes off of his wife.

Jean came to the doorway of the dining room. "Yes, Mr. Garrison. I made it just like you asked me to this morning."

Walter looked over at Jean and smiled. "Well, thank you, Jean, looks like you're the only one in this house that listens to me." He glanced over at his wife and smiled. He pushed his plate back, downed the rest of the bourbon in his glass, and walked over to the bar to refill it. "Where's the ice bucket? We have any ice out here?"

"Are you insinuating that I don't listen to you?" Adeline picked the conversation back up.

Peeking behind the small liquor cart he spied the ice bucket. "I'm saying you don't do anything I ask you to do," he said filling up his glass with bourbon and ice. "And you do things without asking me. Like giving away my money."

"Are you asking me not to send money to this girl?"

"If I asked you not to, would you still send to her?"

"Of course I would. She needs my help. She needs *our* help."

"My point exactly. Why do you even ask me about doing things you want to do? You're going to do them whether I agree or not."

"To be honest, Walter, I didn't ask you if I could send the money, I just told you I was going to do it."

"It's a good thing we've got Jean, otherwise people would think I have no control over my own home." He nodded his head at his wife, sat back down at the table, leaned back in the chair straightening out his legs, and called out, "Jean, bring me some pie."

Adeline got up from the table, kissed her husband on his forehead and went upstairs to the bedroom she shared with Walter. She sat down on the bed with a sigh.

"That girl needs my help," she said out loud. "I just can't imagine her living there and suffering the way she says she is." Lifting up her dress she pulled it over her head and threw it on the bed. She sat down and unhooked her nylons and rolled each one down her leg.

I wonder if she is telling the truth.

If it is true, then shame on her parents. She's just too young to take the stress of a marriage, and evidently her body is too young to take the stress of a pregnancy. To have two miscarriages in the course of six months is a lot to put on anyone. How awful for her.

Adeline shook her head. She leaned over and picked up the pack of Pall Malls from her nightstand and pulled out a cigarette and lit it. She rolled her head back and let the smoke float out of her mouth. Getting up from the bed, Adeline's lips held onto the cigarette as she rolled the nylons together and tucked them away in a drawer. Resting the cigarette in the ashtray on the nightstand, Adeline walked over to the dresser and gazed at her reflection in the mirror, absentmindedly taking off her earrings and bracelet, and placing them in her jewelry box.

Certainly, I know how Beanie must feel, she thought, not releasing her gaze from the mirror. *Her life is not meant for anyone to have to endure.*

Poor child.

And to have a husband that would hit her because of it. Something in Beanie's story stirred an emotion inside of Adeline. A feeling she thought long buried. It's not that she *liked* the girl, she barely knew her. It's just that she *understood* the girl. And for that she wanted to help her. Help her get away. To start a new life. Somewhere that husband of hers couldn't find her.

"I don't know which is worse, the pregnancy or the cruel husband," she said in a hushed voice.

Adeline placed her hand over her stomach and stared blankly down at the dresser. *Walter would never think to do anything that cruel to her, even with his ranting and raving.* "I would never stand for anything like that," she said out loud. *And if he did,* she thought, *I wouldn't hesitate to kill him.*

"What are you doing, Liddie?" Walter asked as he came into the bedroom.

Adeline turned around and looked at Walter. "Thought I'd go out and tend to my rose bushes. Why don't you come along and have a drink on the patio? It's such a lovely evening." Adeline smiled at Walter as she found a pair of pedal pushers and a top in the dresser drawer.

"Sounds like a good idea." He pulled his tie over his head, unbuttoned his shirt cuffs and rolled up his sleeves. He walked into the bathroom and relieved himself, not bothering to close the door. Belching and talking at the same time, he said, "It'll be nice to spend a little time with my stubborn wife. I'll miss you after I leave for my business trip tomorrow."

"I'll miss you, too, dear. You'll be gone for three days?"

Adeline watched him as he walked back into the bedroom, picked up her cigarette from the ashtray and took a drag.

"More like five," he said. "We weren't able to get a plane back until Sunday night." Speaking through the smoke as it pushed it out through his nostrils, Walter asked, "What will you do with yourself while I'm gone? Find a group of wayward children to take in?"

She chuckled, picking up her sun hat off the hook on the closet door. "No. I promise I won't do that. Maybe I'll drive up to the Cape for the weekend." Adeline smiled at her husband. "It may be hard to find something satisfying to do with you away, but I'll try."

"Well, I'll call you on Friday night to see how you're doing."

"I'll look forward to it." Adeline kissed him on his cheek and pulled her hat over her head. "But if I do go up to the Cape, I'll probably leave on Friday, so don't be alarmed if you don't reach me," she said as she left the room. She stopped at the bar to make her husband a drink, which she placed on the patio table before heading out into the yard to see about her roses.

Chapter Eleven

Melvin opened the door before Adeline even had the chance to knock. He had a big grin on his face, his eyes beaming just at the sight of her.

"Well, looks like someone is happy to see me," Adeline said smiling. She had waited no longer than it took for Walter to leave for the airport for his business trip, before she snatched up a few things and left to go stay with Melvin.

He wrapped his arm around her waist and pulled her close to him. Adeline held her hat down with her hand, and yelped. "Melvin! At least let me get in the door."

"I missed you, sugar."

"I missed you too, baby." She kissed him on the lips, drew her head back so she could look at him and kissed him again. "Mmm hmm," she murmured. "How I've missed you, my love," she said, stroking his cheek with her gloved hand.

Melvin pulled her in the door with one hand, and grabbed her small overnight bag with the other. "Come on in, baby. I've cooked you a scrumptious brunch."

Melvin's apartment was a place she had become familiar with, even felt at home in, after her almost twice a week visits over the past seven years, and many overnight visits when Walter was away. And today she was almost giddy about spending the next three or four days with him.

Walking past her, Melvin dropped her luggage off by the bedroom door and went into the kitchen. Adeline stood in the middle of the living room, and smiled. Happy to be *home* with her man, she took off her hat and gloves. "A scrumptious meal?" she called out after him. "Oh my. I can't wait to see what you've been up to." Giving him a passing glance through the doorway to the kitchen, she walked into the bedroom and placed her purse, hat and gloves on the dresser. She slipped out of her shoes and kicked them close to the closet door. "Don't try and spoil me, I may never leave," she said walking back out of the room.

"I don't want you to ever leave," he said. Taking her hand, he led her over to a chair in the living room, sat down and pulled her onto his lap. Caressing her, nuzzling her neck and noisily smacking as he covered her with kisses, he said, "I don't mind if you stay here forever."

"I thought we were going to eat." Adeline laughed and tried to free herself from Melvin's arms.

"I'm filling up on you," he said between kisses.

"Well, you'll need to fill me up for me to survive this attack."

"Attack?"

"Yes, you assaulted me as soon as I walked in the door. And now you're holding me down, restraining my movements. Without some kind of nourishment, I'm sure I won't survive until morning. Especially if I'm going to have to keep fending you off."

"Kiss me first, and tell me how much you adore me, then I'll feed you."

"Tell you I adore you? I'd rather starve!" Adeline hopped up and made it no further than the couch before Melvin pounced on her. She landed on her back and he fell on top of her.

"Tell me if you want to eat." He brushed her hair out of her face and planted a kiss on the cheek. "Otherwise you *will* starve."

Adeline looked into Melvin's eyes and said, "I adore you, Melvin. You are my heart, my soul, and my love." Then parting her lips, she met his, opening her mouth slightly, she allowed his tongue to find its way inside. Slowly rolling against hers and sucking in on it, Melvin kissed her deeply and passionately. She bit his lip as she pulled away. "Now is that enough to get me food?"

Pushing himself off of her, he sighed and said, "I've fallen in love with a hopeless romantic. I give her sweet kisses and all she wants is food."

"I will be hopeless if I don't eat," she said, following him in the kitchen. "I'm starving. What did you cook?"

"A casserole."

"A casserole? What no neck bones or ox tail soup?"

"Uh-uh," he said, opening up the refrigerator and taking out a pitcher of lemonade.

"Not even a pan of cornbread? None of your southern cooking today, filling me up with all your 'blackness'"?

"Nope."

"A casserole, huh?" Adeline shook her head. "Aren't we just a Julia Child?"

"Yep. Just threw some chicken and rice in a dish, added some peas, some herbs, a roux, and sprinkled some breadcrumbs on top. Stuck it in the oven for an hour and we've got a casserole. I just needed something quick, all in one dish, so I could fill you up and get you to bed in the shortest amount of time."

"It's too early for bed." Adeline looked down at her watch. "I thought we'd curl up on the sofa, catch up on our soap operas or take a drive or something."

"It's not too early for what I have in mind." Melvin eyed her teasingly. Licking his lips he walked over to her, pulling her in to him, he moved his face close to hers.

She could feel his hot breath and closed her eyes as she inhaled the sensuous scent of him. He took in her lips and kissed her hard. His hands slid down her back, grabbing her buttocks. His lips still pressed against her, he walked forward, pushing her back to the wall, and started unbuttoning the front of her dress.

Adeline stretched her neck as he moved his mouth down it and onto her chest, she moaned softly. He squeezed her breast up out of her bra, caressing it with his hand and mouth.

"You know, baby," Adeline said, pushing back off his arms and taking in a deep breath. "All of a sudden, I just don't feel hungry anymore." She pulled from his embrace, put her breast back inside her bra, turned around and started walking out of the kitchen. "At least not for food," she said over her shoulder.

Melvin came to the doorway, leaned on the frame and watched as she made her way to his bedroom.

"You coming?" she said as she reached the bedroom door.

"You know once I come in there, I won't even be letting you up for air, let alone food, for at least the rest of the day. Are you sure you don't want to eat first? Go for that drive?"

"I'm absolutely sure."

Melvin covered up the casserole, put the pitcher of lemonade in the icebox and followed Adeline, who was already waiting with only a slip on.

He took off his shirt, and then looked at her as if he had forgotten something.

"What?" she asked.

Walking over to his chest of drawers, he picked up something from the top of it. "After you left I couldn't find my wallet so I was looking for it in the folds of the sheet. I found this." He held his hand out, cupping a copper penny. "No change was in my wallet, so I knew it was yours. Figure you're going to need another one, you know, before we get at it." He smiled at her. "I got one I can put in."

"Oh my, God." Adeline turned away and closed her eyes, covering her mouth with her hand. She'd place a copper penny in her uterus to keep from getting pregnant. If this was that penny it could be a disaster.

"I don't think it's anything to worry about, baby," he said.

Bringing her hand down from her mouth to her stomach, she cried out, "What do you mean? Nothing to worry about?" Her voice spilled over with panic. "I can't have a baby. I can't have *your* baby," she said through clenched teeth. "What would I tell my husband? He thinks I can't have children."

"You don't even know if you're pregnant. It could have fallen out after we finished. And if you are pregnant, just tell him that you love me and that its my baby." Melvin tried to put his arm around her, but she shrugged away. "Adeline, baby, I love you. You love me. It would be nothing wrong with us having a baby together."

"I'm going home." Adeline walked over to the closet, bent over, grabbed the one shoe and slid it on her foot, then grabbed the other as she hopped over to the dresser. There she picked up her hat, gloves and purse and reached over to grab her dress off the bed.

Melvin grabbed her wrist. "You're leaving in your slip? Come on, baby. Home? Sugar, you just got here." He stood up. "We never get to spend this much time together. Don't do me this way. I thought you were going to stay a few nights."

"I'm not your baby." She put her dress on over her head. "And I'm not having your baby." Her voice had gone up two octaves. Her fear coming out as anger. "If that is the case." She lowered her voice and looked down at her stomach.

"Would it be such a bad thing to have my baby? " He stood in front of her, lifting up her chin with his finger tips, and smiling down at her.

"Your baby would be black," she said, turning her head away. "And yes, that would be a bad thing."

Shaking his head, he walked back over to the bed and dropped down on it. He clasped his hands in his lap, and blew out his breath.

He looked up at her, she could see the sadness in his eyes.

"Melvin," she said, coming over and stooping down in front of him between his legs. "How would I explain having a Negro child to anyone? And how could I explain having a baby to my husband? I can't. And that's not the only reason. You know that. I *can't* have a baby. I could never have another baby."

"You'd have one for him," he said. "For white Walter."

"I would not. Do I have one now? I don't have a child by him even after thirteen years of marriage. You know I've told him I can't have one. Stop being like that. Why do you think I stick that copper penny up in me?"

"You mean, why I stick that copper penny up in you. I do that for you."

"Yes, my love. You do it. You take care of me. You help me not get pregnant. You make it so we can be together anytime we want. And, I do things with you that I would never do with, or for, Walter. But you are in the same boat with him when it comes to me having a child. And because of the color of your skin, maybe even more so, I can't do it."

"Do you not want to have my baby because you don't love me," he said, eyeing her.

"No," she said, her voice faltering.

"Tell me the truth, Adeline. Look me in the eyes and tell me the truth."

"I said no. I love you. If my life was different, if I wasn't with Walter, I would have your baby. I would have a gaggle of your babies. But I am married to Walter, and I avoid having sex with him as much as I can. He's mostly given up trying, but just the other night, I had to tell him I was on my period to keep him off me."

"You had a period?"

"If I had had a period you think I'd be so upset about that penny?"

"If you ever wouldn't want to keep a baby of mine because you're afraid to tell him, I'd tell him. You wouldn't have to face that alone. I'd walk right up to that great big house of yours on the Hill and say to him that you belong to me."

"I do belong to you," she whispered, "but, I'm married to him."

"Adeline, you need to stop living this lie."

"I can't."

"You mean you don't want to."

She stood up, smoothed the front of her dress with her hand, and said, softly, "I don't want to."

She walked over to the dresser, and stood watching his reflection through the mirror. She reached in her purse and pulled out her pack of cigarettes. Lighting one up, she started to feel his pain. She did love him. With all her heart. He was the only one that knew her secrets. Knew everything about her. The smoke curled and drifted up above her head. What she felt for Melvin she could feel for no one else. She trusted him. She needed him.

He was such a strong man, but when it came to her, at times he seemed vulnerable. Maybe even weak, and that was not him. This was taking a toll on him, she knew it. On his manhood, just like Walter said he felt sometimes. But she couldn't stand seeing Melvin like that.

The time she and Melvin spent together, their *life* together, was good. It was better than good. It was filled with laughter, soft kisses, and love. Exuding the kind of feelings she hadn't had since Joe. Maybe even more than what she had felt for Joe.

He was just sitting there on the bed, shirtless, with his legs spread and his hand folded down between them, staring blankly at the wall. She couldn't leave him like that. It would be too long before she saw him again. And while he was the one with the sad puppy face now, she knew it would be her pining away until she could see him again. She had to make it right with him before she left to go home – on Sunday, she decided. Yes, she would stay.

She put her cigarette out in the ashtray on the dresser, reached inside her purse and pulled out a shiny object. Snapping her purse shut, she turned to face him, a sensuous smile easing up the corners of her mouth. She held it up in her hand and in a sexy, pouty voice, she said, "A penny for your thoughts."

Chapter Twelve

Hildale, Utah

The next morning Beanie hopped down the stairs, taking two at a time and humming, *I'm Off to See the Wizard.* She strolled into the kitchen with a large grin plastered on her face. Last night Orson announced over dinner that he was going to Colorado City, Arizona the next morning to look at some property for the church, and asked if anyone wanted to go with him. When both Margaret and Dorothy said they'd like to go, Beanie realized this would be the perfect opportunity to get Miss Adeline's money from Western Union and catch a bus to Boston.

This was the day she was going to leave Orson.

"You're in a good mood this morning, Beatrice." Margaret flashed a smug look as she set a bowl of oatmeal in front of Orson along with a side of Libby's fruit cocktail.

"Something you want to share with the rest of us?" She placed a hand on Orson's shoulder causing him to look up from his morning paper and stare at Beanie.

Why does she always do that? Beanie thought with a scowl on her face. *She's always trying to get me in trouble.* "I don't know what you're talking about, Margaret. I just woke up feeling good. That's not a crime, is it?" She wasn't about to let Margaret deflate her bubble of enthusiasm. Today she would embark on an incredible journey, to what might as well be the other side of the world.

Boston, she thought, *I'm going to Boston, and I'm never coming back.* She thought about all of the sights, the history, the politics; everything that made that area of the country a hub of excitement. She had read about the Rockefellers and the Kennedys and the high society parties they gave and attended. She couldn't help but wonder if her new friend, Mrs. Adeline Garrison, might be involved with that crowd. She tried to hide the smile tightening her lips, but the thought of getting away from Orson and going to this magical place steeped in history and high society made the smile solidify. *Once I leave here, Orson, you'll never find me.*

"Hmph," said Margaret. She turned, walked over to the stove, flopped a heaping spoonful of oatmeal into a bowl and said as she placed it on the table, "Here. Sit down and eat before it gets cold."

Beanie readily sat down and took a big bite. She was going to need all of her strength as she traveled. Eyeing the bowl of bananas and apples centered on the table, she made a mental note to be sure to pack a few of each for the long journey.

Orson folded the paper and set it next to his empty dish. He looked at Beanie and said, "Are you sure you don't want to go with us to Colorado City?"

Beanie took another bite of oatmeal. "I really have too much to do today. I have to fix the holes in the children's jeans, do the laundry, watch the baby, and then make some apple pies for dinner tonight."

Orson looked at Beanie and said, "I've changed my mind. Margaret and Dorothy can stay home and do that and look after the baby. I'd like you to come with me today to look at the property."

Margaret snapped her head around, and said in a rather whiny voice, "But Orson, you said we could go with you." Only Margaret could get away with talking to him like that.

No! Beanie screamed in her head. *Not today. I have so much to do: pack, get to Western Union, pick up the money, buy a bus ticket to Boston, and then get far, faraway from here. No! No! No!* She pushed down her panic and said, "As much as I would love to go with you, I really think Margaret and Dorothy should be the ones to go instead of me. They know far more about the real estate business than I do." She offered Margaret an angelic smile and added, "Especially Margaret."

Right then Dorothy entered the kitchen, grabbed a bowl from the cupboard, filled it with oatmeal, and said with excitement, "When are we leaving? I was thinking we could take a picnic lunch with us. Wouldn't that be fun?" She set her bowl on the table, grabbed the second to the last banana and sliced it on her breakfast.

Margaret looked at Dorothy. "Orson wants Beatrice to go with him instead of us."

Dorothy dropped her spoon into the oatmeal. "No, Orson, please. I was really looking forward to going with you. You know how much I love that area."

Beanie scooted her chair back, stood, and chirped, "I'll make the picnic lunch for you." She went into the pantry and returned a moment later holding a wicker picnic basket, a bag of potato chips, and some rolls. "And don't worry about the dishes. I'll take care of them." She eyed the bowl of fruit, sighed, and placed every last piece in the basket. She would have to find something else to take with her on her long trip.

Orson shot Beanie a quick frown, then looked at Dorothy and grumbled, "Fine, but I'm leaving in five minutes."

Beanie could tell that Orson was upset with her for not going with him. She wasn't sure why he changed his mind and wanted just her to go, but the thought of being alone with him out in the middle of nowhere made her shudder. Casually she said, "When do you think you'll be back?"

Orson eyed her. "No later than four, why?"

"Oh, no reason. I just wanted to know when I should have dinner ready for you."

Dorothy looked at Beanie and said, "Are you sure you don't mind staying here by yourself?"

Beanie held up her hands, smiled and said, "Don't worry about me. I have so many chores, I'll be lucky if I finish them by the time you get back."

Orson glared at her. He had a knack for sniffing out Beanie's lies. So in her mind, she decided that she would bake the pies, mend all of the holey jeans, make the beds, wash the dirty clothes, and *then* go to Western Union. She looked at him and said, "It's true, Orson. I have enough things to do to keep me busy all day."

Finally Orson nodded and said, "We'll see you this evening."

Beanie spent the morning doing the chores she listed to Orson. But in the afternoon she packed for her trip. She stood by her closet and wondered, *what do they wear in Boston?* She pulled her lime green suitcase from the back of the closet and began stripping tops and dresses from their hangers. She pulled all of her underwear, socks, and most of her trousers from her dresser and packed them in the suitcase. *Shoes, I'm going to need some good shoes.* She pulled out three pair; her favorite saddle shoes, a pair of white Keds, and a pair of low black pumps. She looked at the full suitcase, slipped on the saddle shoes, and then wedged the other shoes in wherever they would fit. She pulled the suitcase to the edge of the bed, sat on top of it so that it would close, and then she snapped the latches shut. She groaned as she pulled it off of the bed. It weighed a ton. But nothing was going to stop her from walking the three miles to the Acme Market where Western Union was located. Worst case, if the weight became unbearable, she'd leave a trail of clothing behind, like fabric breadcrumbs.

All of the children, with the exception of the littlest one, were in school, and wouldn't be back for another two hours.

Beanie tiptoed into the toddler's room and peered into the crib. The child slept peacefully, with her thumb hidden in her mouth and her fingers kneading the blanket fringe like a kitten.

Beanie quietly exited the room and closed the door behind her. *I'll have to call Mrs. Weller to come and take care of her.* She grabbed the suitcase, carefully descended the stairs, and went outside to stash it along the side of the house. Going back in, she went to Orson's office, opened the door and stepped in. Though the room was not officially off-limits, Beanie still felt uncomfortable in there.

Rich red cherry wood paneling encased the entire room giving the office a cave-like feel. Floor to ceiling bookcases lined the far right wall, while an ornate mahogany desk sat facing the door. Behind the desk, a large picture window opened up to the manicured backyard.

Beanie stared out the window at the elaborate playground and meandering red brick walkway. This could have been a wonderful place to live if it hadn't been for Orson. But as much as she liked this house, as long as Orson lived there, it would never be a loving home for her.

She pulled her mind back to the present, sat down at the desk and opened up the top center drawer. When she saw the small black address book, she pulled it out and flipped to the W's. Using Orson's desk phone, she dialed the number. A moment later she said, "Hello, Mrs. Weller, this is Beatrice Peterson. I was wondering if you might do me a big favor."

Fifteen precious minutes later, Mrs. Weller stood inside the foyer. Beanie took the woman's coat, hung it on the coat rack and said, "Thank you so much for coming here on such short notice. The others aren't here, and I'd forgotten that I have a piano lesson this afternoon with a new teacher." She hated to lie to the elderly babysitter, but by the time everyone found out, Beanie would be long gone. She grabbed her coat and said, "They should be back here in a couple of hours, no later than four o'clock." Then Beanie walked out of the front door and stood on the porch facing Mrs. Weller.

Mrs. Weller smiled sweetly and said, "Don't worry, dear. I'm happy to take care of the little one." She said good-bye, and closed the door leaving Beanie alone on the porch steps.

Beanie quickly ran to the side of the house and grabbed the suitcase that she'd stashed earlier. Then she hurried across the lawn and ran down the sidewalk until she knew she was a safe distance away from the house. An hour later, Beanie stood in front of the Acme Grocery store.

"May I help you, young lady?" The gentleman behind the Western Union counter put down his pen and looked at Beanie.

She dropped the case to the floor. "Um, yes. I'm supposed to pick up some money here."

The man smiled at her and said, "Of course. What's your name and the name of the person wiring you the funds?"

"My name is Beatrice Peterson, and the name of the person sending me the money is Mrs. Adeline Garrison."

The gentleman looked at Beanie for a moment, then motioned to one of the chairs facing the counter and said, "Please take a seat. This will only take a moment." He slipped away into the back office.

Through the opened door, Beanie watched him thumb through the yellow pages, pick up the phone, dial, carry on a quick conversation, and then rummage around his desk.

A moment later the gentleman returned and said, "It should only be a few more minutes. I have to verify that the funds are available." He gestured to the coffee pot on the edge of the counter. "Would you like something to drink while you wait?"

Beanie smiled. "No thank you. I'm fine." She fiddled with the handle on her suitcase and said, "Do you know how far the bus station is from here?"

The gentleman eyed her scuffed piece of luggage and said, "Why? You going on a trip?"

"Yes, sir. I'm going to Boston."

"Boston? That's a mighty long way to travel. You going by yourself?"

"Yes, but I'm meeting a friend there."

The gentleman poured a cup of coffee for himself, stirred in some creamer and said, "Well, the bus station is downtown. You'll have to take a taxi."

Beanie frowned. "How much do you think that will cost?" She didn't know how much money Miss Adeline had sent her, but she prayed that it would be enough for the bus fare and the taxi ride.

Beanie wasn't sure how long she had waited, but it seemed like at least a half hour. Finally she said, "Excuse me, but have you heard anything yet about the money? I'm kind of in a hurry."

The gentleman looked up from his paperwork and said, "I'm sure it will only take a few more minutes."

Before Beanie could respond, a familiar and angry voice from behind her said, "Beatrice!"

Beanie swung around only to be met by Orson's deadly glare. Her face drained of blood "Orson! W-what are you doing here?"

He grabbed her by the arm, glanced at her suitcase and said, "I could ask you the same thing." He picked up the suitcase, looked at the man behind the counter and said, "Thank you for calling me. I appreciate it."

The Western Union man gave Orson a quick nod and replied, "Of course, Mr. Peterson. She said she was going to Boston. I just thought you should know she was here."

As Orson hauled Beanie out of the Acme Grocery store, she started to cry.

"Stop crying," Orson hissed through clenched teeth, "or I'll really give you something to cry about." He quickened his pace forcing Beanie to trot along next to him. "I've given you everything. A home -" He gestured with the suitcase as though it weighed nothing at all. "All the clothes you could possibly wear. Good food. You want for nothing, Beatrice." He weaved through the full parking lot pulling her behind him. "And this is how you repay me, by running away to Boston? You've embarrassed and humiliated me. Even mere acquaintances have more respect for me than my own wife does. Luckily, I stopped by my office on the way home from Colorado City. Otherwise, I would have never gotten the phone call letting me know what you were trying to do."

When they got to the car, both Margaret and Dorothy stared at her through the window. By their frowns, Beanie could tell that they were equally as upset with her.

Orson tossed her suitcase in the trunk and said, "Get in. I don't even want to look at you right now."

Beanie quietly slipped into the back seat and stared out the window as they drove home. This was bad. She had never seen Orson this upset before, and he had hit her for much less. When she told Miss Adeline that it would only be a matter of time before Orson killed her, she'd said it for a dramatic effect, never really believing that he would be capable of doing it. But watching Orson struggle to keep his anger from erupting, she realized that the idea was not so far-fetched, and that her time had, quite possibly, just arrived.

With tears brimming, Beanie leaned her forehead against the window and thought, *if he kills me tonight, nobody, including Miss Adeline, will ever know.*

Chapter Thirteen

August 1, 1959
Boston, Massachusetts

"That damn penny."   Adeline's voice was uneasy. She seemed close to tears, as she whispered into the phone.

"Sweetie, I can barely understand you." Melvin's voice was calm. He tried to coax her to be clearer. "You either have to stop crying or you have to speak above a whisper."

"I don't want anyone to hear me."

"Who's there?"

"Jean."

"Well, I'm sure she can see that you're crying. Just tell me what's wrong?" Melvin sat on the side of his bed. He'd just been ready to walk out the door to check on the jobs schedule for the day with his landscaping business when the phone rang.

"I think she knows anyway," Adeline said. "She asked me if I was, and I tried to laugh it off. I told her "No" and that she and I were just going to end up old women with no children, just the two of us. Why did I say that to her? She got so sad and told me that she had lost a child before. I felt so bad for saying it. I don't know if she meant her child died or if someone took it from her."

"*She* lost a child? Do you mean . . . . are you . . . are you pregnant? Is that what you're talking about? The penny?"

"Yes. The penny. It must have come out before we had sex. I'm pregnant."

"Are you sure? What did the doctor say?"

"I can't go to my doctor. He's friends with Walter and me. Dr. Randall. You know, my friend Cassie's husband. I can't go to him, he'd tell Walter."

Melvin didn't say anything for a long while. He didn't quite know what to say. The first thing he wanted to ask was, is it his, or is it Walter's? But the last thing he wanted was to make Adeline more distraught. He knew whatever he said, it would upset her. "What are we going to do, Adeline?"

"What do you mean, 'we'? I'm the one who's pregnant." She shrieked and started sobbing into the phone. "I don't know what I'm going to do."

"I'm in this with you, baby. You know that. Whatever you want to do." Melvin sat holding the phone wishing he could be there with her. To put his arm around her and tell her it would be okay. He would do whatever it took to make it okay. "You want me to come and get you? Where is Walter?"

"He's not here."

"Well what do you want to do?"

"I've been taking these tablets called Lydia Pinkham. They're supposed to make me miscarry. But nothing's happened."

Melvin could hear Adeline as she tried to catch her breath, to stop crying. "How long is it supposed to take for the tablets to work?"

"I don't know, I've been stuffing them down my throat by the handful. But I've been throwing up so much. I've had morning sickness so bad, that's probably what tipped Jean off. I don't know if I've gotten enough of them in me to do anything."

"Are you sure that they work? The tablets?" Melvin wanted to be helpful, but it was hard wrapping his head around what was happening and staying calm so he could keep Adeline the same.

"That's all I know to do," she hissed. "I can't have this baby," she said, her voice barely audible. "What else am I supposed to do?"

Melvin sat quietly. He ran his hand across his face and over his hair. The momentary silence over the phone seemed to mark the road of no return. Once he spoke, there was no going back. He'd do anything for Adeline. He couldn't see her suffer, even if it meant sacrificing their child's life. He took in a breath, "There is something else we could do."

"What?"

"I know of a woman . . ."

He heard Adeline sigh. It seemed like it was one of relief. He felt it in the pit of his stomach.

"I can make the arrangements and take you," he said, his voice low. "Wait for you. Take care of you afterwards."

"How do you know about that? How do you know someone who does that?"

"That shouldn't be a worry to you. All you need to know is that I will always be here for you. Always take care of you. You know that, don't you?"

"You'll need money," she said.

"I have the money. I'll take care of it. I'll make the arrangements and call you back."

"How long will it take for you to make the arrangements?" Her sobs seeming to ebb. "I can't wait much longer."

"I don't know how long it'll take. When it's done, I'll let you know. Stop taking all those tablets, Adeline. You might hurt yourself. And where would I be without you?"

Melvin hung up the phone and felt as if he wanted to weep. What he needed to do made his chest tight, his temple outwardly pulsate. He grinded his teeth and ran his hands over his knees. He'd sacrificed a wife - a normal life to be with Adeline, to be there for her whenever she could be with him. Now he was giving up family – a child. But he knew that life and love all too often meant sacrifice and loss. Adeline was the other half of his being. What she wanted and needed, so did he.

Melvin picked up the phone and set out to make arrangements for Adeline to have an abortion.

Chapter Fourteen

Jackson, Mississippi
1938

Hattie Jean was pregnant. The humiliation that was Charlie Ray just wasn't going to stop. And she knew, no matter how many times her momma told her differently, it was her fault. Her fault for not being black enough. Her fault for trying to fit in. Her fault for going in that barn with that greasy, knuckleheaded boy to prove to him that she was just like every other colored girl. But no matter how she tried, or what she did, she just couldn't – didn't - fit in.

She sat under her favorite weeping willow tree and cried as the branches swayed around her in the cool breeze. Hattie Jean pulled her knees up close to her chest, wrapped her arms around them and buried her head. She had missed two of her cycles and all the praying and church going she had done hadn't helped. Her momma had taken her, practically dragged her, to one of the midwives for colored people in Hinds County. That woman took one look at her and without even touching her, told Ophelia that Hattie Jean was pregnant.

How could she know just by looking at me?

After that news Hattie Jean had cried for a week straight. She couldn't go to school, she couldn't get out of bed, and she couldn't eat. Not just because she was depressed about her predicament, although that was a big part of it, but because she was so sick. Her morning sickness was worse than anything.

Her momma had gone and talked to Charlie Ray's mother, and she had said she "was right shamed about it." Even about him, saying that she hadn't "raised no child to act like that." But what good did that do now?

Hattie Jean's mother had made her go along with her to talk to Charlie Ray's momma. And no matter how bad she cried or protested, her mother insisted that she "needed to be there."

For what, Hattie Jean thought, *to endure even more embarrassment?*

And during that visit that's just what she felt – humiliation. She stood resigned, darting her eyes around the room, not wanting to look at anyone in particular and not wanting anyone to look at her the entire time they were there. She'd tried to block out the talk about her, and the steely glares Charlie Ray's mother kept throwing her way, but it didn't help. She wished she could just sink into the floor and disappear.

Hattie Jean's mother stood firm and made Charlie Ray's mother own up to her son's actions. Making sure she got what she came for, Ophelia didn't budge until she heard his mother confess that she wasn't gone to stand for such a heathen living in her house and that she was going to send him north to Cleveland to live with his uncles. Word round from people said that Charlie Ray was "right 'fraid of his uncles," and if anybody could make him "repent for what he had done to Hattie Jean," it supposedly was them.

That had satisfied Ophelia and she grabbed Hattie Jean by the hand, and stormed out the house so fast that Ophelia had to hold onto her 'Sunday go-to-meeting hat' while her pocketbook flew in the wind she created.

But nobody could tell by the way Charlie Ray was acting before he left for Cleveland that he was sorry for anything or that going to live with his uncles posed any great fear to him. He'd curl his lip, grin and smirk at Hattie Jean every time he crossed paths with her, sometimes, going out of his way to do it. And so did all his friends. They made hissing sounds, catcalls and heckled her.

How could she have such a horrible man be the father of her baby? That made her cry more.

Hattie Jean leaned her head back against the bark of the tree and wiped her tears with the back of hand.

I'll never be able to show my face again, she thought. *I know that Charlie Ray told everybody that I gave it up willingly.*

And her mother hadn't made it no better. While she had stood up for her in front of everyone else, she had been real quiet at home, only mumbling when she prayed to God for strength for her and her "wayward" child. Standing at the door of Hattie Jean's room she had said, "Well, now you have your reputation, for all it's worth, and a baby to boot."

Hattie Jean fidgeted under the tree and thought about what would become of her. She too, had to go up north. That's the way it was, her mother told her. Leastways 'til the baby was born.

What's the difference in everybody seeing me with a big belly and seeing me with a child? Those that know would know that a baby just didn't get there by magic.

Hattie Jean's exile was to Chicago. She'd stay with her aunt and uncle until she had the baby. They said there was a school up there where pregnant girls could finish their classes so they could still graduate and even learn how to take care of the baby. Hattie Jean figured she didn't need any help. She'd helped take care of enough white babies to know what to do. And if she could do something good enough for the white folks to trust her to do it, it had to be good enough for her colored baby.

Chapter Fifteen

Hildale, Utah

Almost two weeks had passed since Beanie's failed attempt to run away.

This morning she stared at her image in her bedroom mirror. The black eye was barely noticeable underneath the makeup. And the swollen right cheek looked almost normal except for the small scab where Orson's ring had grazed her when he hit her. She gingerly threaded her sore arm through the long sleeved shirt, covering up the purplish fingerprints tattooed on her upper arm. She couldn't stand to look at them - Orson's brand of ownership.

When she opened up her bedroom door, Margaret stood there with a deep-set scowl carved into her face and holding a sheet of paper. She shoved the paper at her and said, "Here's your list of chores for today."

Beanie clenched her jaw, but silently took the list and started to walk away.

Margaret grabbed her by her sore arm and said in a low threatening voice, "You're not the only one who's been imprisoned here, you know. Because of your little *stunt*, I can't leave you alone. So now, instead of going to the store or the park at will, I have to wait to run my errands until there is someone else who can *babysit* you just to make sure you don't run off again." She clamped down a little harder. "But today you are going to finish all of those chores on your own. And when you're done, you're going to come back to your room and stay there until I get back. Is that understood?"

Beanie stared at Margaret's wrinkled brow. "Where are you going?" Beanie asked her.

"You think I'm going to tell you so that you can gauge how long I might be gone? No, Beatrice." Margaret said. "I'm not going to let you ruin my life further by having to explain to Orson how and why you ran away again." She followed Beanie down the stairs. "You've destroyed Orson's trust in you forever, and that I can't change. But if you start proving to me that you can be left on your own, one day my trust in you just might be restored."

Beanie lowered her head and mumbled, "Thank you for the opportunity, Margaret." She didn't feel remorseful for running away. She only felt bad for getting caught.

As soon as Margaret pulled out of the driveway, Beanie ran to the kitchen and dialed the phone.

When a woman's voice answered, Beanie said, "Miss Adeline? It's Beanie. I'm sorry for not calling you earlier, but I didn't have a chance to get the money."

"Why? What happened?"

"Well, I left, just like we had talked about. But when I got to Western Union, the man behind the counter told me to wait. So I waited. I thought maybe you hadn't sent the money like you said you would. But then Orson showed up. Oh Miss Adeline, he was so mad." Beanie touched her sore cheek and winced. "He hit me again, and not just a slap across the face. I honestly thought that he was going to kill me this time." She poked her head outside the kitchen and glanced down the grand hall to make sure Margaret hadn't come back home just to check up on her. "This is the first opportunity I've had to call you. They haven't left me alone for a moment until now." She leaned back against the kitchen wall. "I'm really afraid of him."

"What are you going to do?"

Beanie took a deep breath and released the pent up angst, "I don't know. But I know I can't stay here."

"Do you want me to wire you more money?"

Beanie could hear the concern in Miss Adeline's voice and said, "It's no use. He'll find out. He told me there isn't anything that goes on in this town that he doesn't know about." Defeat filled her words. "I think my only choice is to try to be the wife that Orson wants me to be. " The notion of staying there under Orson's rule caused her to weep.

"Don't cry, Beanie, we'll think of something. In the meantime, I'm going to have my friend, you know, the private investigator I told you about, see if he can findCora for you. Give me their full names."

"Henry and Cora Hampton. Her aunt's name is Lynnie, but I don't know her last name. She lives somewhere in New York." Beanie wiped her dripping nose on her long sleeve."I know it's not much to go on, but it's all I've got."

"Don't lose hope. I'll keep trying to find her. In the meantime, do try to keep in touch with me so that I'll know you're okay." She gave Beanie her address and hung up.

Chapter Sixteen

As the seasons came and went, so did Beanie's dreams of leaving Orson and fleeing to Boston. But the phone calls to Miss Adeline helped restore her spirit. Whenever she wasn't under the watchful eyes of Orson, Margaret or Dorothy, Beanie would dial that same wrong number that she first dialed a year ago, and they would talk for as long as time would allow. The clandestine conversations with the lady from Boston evolved into an unlikely long-distance friendship. For the first time in Beanie's life, she felt like she had a true friend, a confidante, someone who she could tell her innermost thoughts to. They talked of jazz, politics, current events, Miss Cora, everything that was taboo in the Peterson household.

With each conversation, Beanie grew closer and closer to Miss Adeline, even so far as to consider her a mother figure since she was over twice Beanie's age. Beanie learned that Miss Adeline was opinionated and persuasive. She freely said what she thought, but most of all she seemed self-assured and Beanie needed to learn to be like that.

When she couldn't sneak phone calls to Miss Adeline, Beanie wrote letters instead. Even though she knew that she might not get a response back for a couple weeks, the idea of purging her heart and letting her words bleed onto the pages gave Beanie a sense of relief. It was a way for her to proclaim the things Orson kept hidden from the rest of the world without him ever finding out.

For two weeks now, Margaret and Dorothy took turns staying home, robbing Beanie of any opportunity for a long-winded, casual conversation with Miss Adeline. This morning, Beanie sat at her dressing table with pen in hand. She glanced out the opened window at the vivid, blue, cloudless, Utah sky and wrote:

July 14, 1960

Dear Miss Adeline,

I've missed talking with you these past few weeks. With Margaret and Dorothy monitoring my every move, I haven't been able to call as often as I'd like.

Please forgive me for bringing this up again, but have you found Miss Cora yet? It's been nearly a year since we first started looking for her. I fear that by now she has long forgotten about me. And the chances of finding her are slim. But I do appreciate all of your efforts. You've been so kind to me.

I'm sorry if my handwriting seems a little shaky, but my right index finger is bandaged. Orson hurt it when he grabbed me by the hand. He said it was an accident, but it's hard for me to believe him knowing the horrible things he's capable of doing. Consequently, I haven't been able to play the piano as often as I would like because it hurts too much. But I have been listening to a lot of jazz lately on the radio. I've found a station that plays it at night. So when I go to bed, I'll turn it on very quietly so that no one else in the house can hear it. I'm particularly fond of Miles Davis' song, So What. Have you heard it?

I'm trying to stay positive, but I miss hearing your voice, and your words of encouragement. Without them I feel lost, broken, and deprived of any hope for a better future. I will leave him one day. That is a promise. But whether it is on my own or in a wooden coffin is still to be determined. In the meantime, I will pretend to be that good and proper wife that is expected of me. But on the inside, I will curse him for all of the horrible things he's done to me. I believe there is a special place in hell for monsters like Orson. And he will, one day, be held accountable for the torment that he has caused me. My only hope is that his suffering lasts an eternity.

Beanie reread the letter and then added:

I thought you might find this amusing: Orson never found out about the second miscarriage, so at least I never suffered from his revelation of that secret. But his desire to have sex with me has not diminished. So to keep from having to have sex I use beef blood on menstrual pads to show Orson that I am on my period. (Yes, he requires that I show him the soiled pads.) So far it's worked beautifully. As far as he knows, my periods last much longer than most women's. I suspect he's beginning to think there's something physically wrong with me. For such a smart businessman with three wives, he's rather dumb about women. Don't you think?

Please write when you get the chance. I will try to call you again very soon.

Love,
Beatrice (Beanie) Peterson

P.S. I wanted to send you a picture of me so that you would know what I look like. Unfortunately, the only photograph I had was this one with Orson standing next to me. So I ripped it in half. I didn't want you to have to look at that horrible man.

Beanie stuffed the letter and the picture in the envelope and addressed it. She was just about to lick the back when she heard familiar whistling coming down the sidewalk. Beanie ran to her window and yelled out, "Hold on, please. I have another letter here for you. I'll be down in just a second."

The mailman stopped whistling, looked up at her and yelled back, "No problem, Mrs. Peterson."

Beanie ran out of the front door and down the sidewalk. She handed the letter to the mailman and breathlessly said, "Thank you so much for waiting."

"Of course, Mrs. Peterson. My pleasure." The postman took the letter, stuffed it in his bag and handed her a stack of mail. "You have a nice day, and please give my best to your husband."

The following day, at ten in the morning, Beanie walked out to the mailbox and opened it. When she saw that it was still empty, she thought, *hmm, the mail is late today.* She looked up and down the sidewalk for the postman, but he was nowhere to be found. *Oh well, I'll get it later.*

She busied herself with dusting and vacuuming, making the day fly by. She felt a little lighter after emotionally purging by writing that letter the day before and found herself smiling into the evening. She was just finishing with the final touches in the living room when Orson walked through the front door. He dropped his keys on the small wooden buffet in the foyer, along with the bundle of the day's mail. He set down his briefcase, stripped off his suit jacket and handed it to Beanie "Here, hang this up."

"Of course, Orson. How was your day?" When she reached for the jacket she nearly fainted. There on top of the stack of the day's mail was her letter to Miss Adeline with '*Postage Due'* branded over the area where the stamp should have been.

Beanie stifled a cry. *I forgot to put a stamp on it!* She reached for the stack of mail and said, "Here, I'll take this to your office for you."

But Orson intercepted her and said, "That's all right, I've got it. Just hang up my jacket, please, and let me know when dinner is ready."

Beanie could barely walk. She thought about what she had written in the letter and knew that Orson would soon be reading her most private thoughts only to discover what she really thought of him. She grabbed the wall to steady herself. *He's going to kill me when he finds out.*

"Are you feeling all right, Beatrice?" Orson picked up the stack of mail, stood beside her and placed his arm on her shoulder. "You look a little pale."

Beanie momentarily swallowed her panic, straightened up and said, "No, Orson. I'm fine. I think I just inhaled too much furniture polish."

Orson nodded. "Call me when dinner is ready. I'll be in my study."

Beanie's hand walked the wall, lending support to her shaky legs. She closed her eyes, fighting back the tears. In a matter of moments, Orson would be screaming for her. He would yell at her until he ran out of scathing words and insults, and then he would hit her until his rage subsided.

This incident might bring them both to the brink.

Ten minutes later, and the house still remained quiet. Beanie set the dining room table and thought, *why hasn't he yelled at me yet? Is he waiting until after dinner, or until bedtime where he can punish me in the way he knows will hurt me the most?*

"Go tell Orson that dinner is ready," Margaret told Beanie.

Beanie nodded and slowly walked down the hall to Orson's study. She tapped on the door and said, "Orson, dinner is ready."

From behind the door she heard him say, "I'll be there in a minute."

A few minutes later when Orson entered the dining room, he wore the same expression on his face as he had when he came home.

As they all sat and bowed their heads while Orson said the prayer, Beanie thought, *he hasn't read the letter yet. There's still time.*

That night after everyone had gone to bed, Beanie snuck into Orson's study. She tiptoed across the varnished wooden floor, careful not to make a sound. There, on his desk, sat the pile of mail. It was all there, except for her letter. She snuck around to the back of the desk, sat in his chair, pulled open the drawer and rummaged through the contents. It wasn't there either. She started to close the drawer when she noticed a small box full of coins and some folded bills. She grabbed the box, closed the drawer and tiptoed out of his study.

Once back in her bedroom, she quietly pulled on a pair of black stretch cigarette pants and a long sleeve mint green blouse. She carefully pulled her most comfortable walking shoes from the closet and slipped them on. Standing on her tiptoes, she reached for a shoebox that had been stashed in the back of the closet shelf. She opened the lid and stared at the contents - a year's worth of letters from Liddie and a small coin purse with a few dollars that she had been able to save. She removed the money from the shoebox then shoved the box back up on the shelf. Grabbing her coat and her purse, she snatched up Orson's money and dumped it, along with her coin purse into her jacket pocket.

She tiptoed down the stairs and down the grand hall. Carefully she unlocked the front door, opened it just enough to slip through, and then closed it behind her.

The cool night air made her shiver as she snuck down the driveway. But the adrenaline pumping through her veins caused her to break out in a sweat as she ran for her life down the dark and deserted street.

She was going to Boston, tonight. Or however far the twenty three dollars in her pocket would take her.

Chapter Seventeen

Boston, Massachusetts
July 15, 1960

Adeline sat barefoot in her gold plastic covered Queen Anne living room chair with her legs curled under her. She lit up a cigarette and tossed the pack on the coffee table. Holding it between tight lips, she picked up the album cover of Ella Fitzgerald's *Hello, Love* and flipped it over. Staring at Ella's smiling face, she whispered, "Sing to me, Ella."

Inhaling a long drag and blowing the smoke away from the cover, Adeline anticipated the next song with her eyes fixed on Ella. She reached inside the hi-fi console next to her and turned up the volume. Getting up out of the chair, she sat on the floor and laid back, lying face up. She blew a whiff of smoke out and watched it as it wafted up toward the ceiling. Closing her eyes, she embraced the feelings the song stirred in her. The words tantalizing her senses, tingling down deep in her soul as it flowed from Ella through the speakers of the hi-fi into the longing crevices of Adeline's mind.

"Willow weep for me. Willow weep for me. Bend your branches green along the stream that runs to sea . . ."

Adeline loved that song. She had loved it since the first time she heard it as a ten-year-old girl. But Ella's rendition was her favorite, with its violin and piano intro. The song reminded her of home. It reminded her about being strong on the inside, even when your countenance and all things around you looked low and sad, something she had learned after leaving home.

Adeline's mother had told her about the weeping willow tree - how the leaves were simple, feathery, appearing as if they couldn't withstand much. Sometimes they weren't even able to cling to the tree branch for the entire summer, like they were timid. But she had said, the roots of a willow were extraordinary. Unlike the fleeting leaves, the roots were tough and stubborn, giving the tree a persistent will to live. And those branches, as weak as they seemed, bending and swaying with the winds, were filled with a sap that could heal all kinds of pains.

Pains from the love of a man.

Pains from the loss of a child.

The musical interlude enveloped Adeline — the violins seemed to weep with her, and the lone trumpet floated into her heart, winding and slithering its way through the holes that had been left there by loss. Her body and soul ached for Melvin. She took in a deep breath and exhaled as her mind escaped to *him* - his face, his smell, and she longed for his touch.

Whisper to the wind, Adeline sang with Ella, *and say that love is sin . . .*

A tear rolled out of Adeline's eye and ran down her temple. She turned on her side, took a drag on her cigarette, and expelled the smoke through her nostrils. "Yes, I know Ella," she whispered. "It certainly is a sin." But Melvin was a part of her. She stretched out her hand in front of her and stared at it. She brought it back, ran it across her breast and down her stomach. He was as much a part of her as her hand, her breast, her breath. As life itself.

How she missed Melvin. She had been foolish to tell him she never wanted to see him again. And even more foolish not to attempt going – no *running* back to him.

He had taken her to that dark, red brick paved alley to see that woman to take care of her problem just as he had promised. The one light shining on the side of the building next to the fire escape had cast only a cloudy glow. He waited for her in the car. She had refused to let him go up with her. She had nervously climbed the steps, tears streaming down her face. The place was clean and neat enough, the woman's smile kind and understanding, and that made it hurt even more. Her hands shaking terribly and her legs spongy and weak, she turned the knob on the bathroom door where the woman had instructed her to change. Pulling the door shut she watched through the crack as the woman spread a white sheet over a brown wooden table and lay steel utensils on top of it. Adeline closed the door, leaned over the sink and prayed.

It's been a long time, God, I know. And my plea to you always seems to be the same— help me get out of this. You have let me down before, Lord. And I have let you down, too. But if you just get me out of this one . . .

She remembered how she almost fell, how the towel rack had held her up and steadied her when she had gotten off the toilet and looked in it. There in the toilet was the bloody remnant of the child she had come to abort, and she knew that the Lydia Pinkham tablets had worked. They had made her miscarry.

"Thank you, God," Adeline whispered.

Thanking the woman, and apologizing for the bloody mess in the bathroom she ran back down the stairs, into that dark alley. She found Melvin waiting for her in the car and once inside of it she screamed at him the entire way back. *I never want to see you again*, she had told him. *Never do I want to have to go through that again*, she said to his shocked and horrified face. She had him drop her off at a corner restaurant and called Cassie to come and get her.

She hadn't seen him since.

Yes, gone my lover's dream, Lovely summer dream . . . Adeline closed her eyes and sang the words.

Another tear rolled down her face and she knew her heart would never mend without him.

Instead she had buried herself in campaign activities for Jack and shopping. Both had been therapeutic, although the latter had caused Walter much angst. She smiled at that thought. But as another tear welled up in her eye, she thought, *not nearly as much as he causes me.*

Wiping the tear her mind drifted to Beanie.

Adeline's mother had a saying: *There was a man that was sad because he didn't have any shoes until he met a man that didn't have any feet.*

Beanie was the man that didn't have any feet.

Adeline got up off the floor, went over to the hi-fi, lifted up the arm and placed the needle at the beginning of the song to play again. Standing there staring at the record she thought about that house that Beanie lived in and the goings on there. Yet even with all that she had been through, Adeline would never wish for Beanie's situation.

Over the past months Adeline had come to believe Beanie's tale of plight. She felt for her, maybe even loved her like the love shared between a mother and child.

Adeline sat back down on the floor. She moved close to the hi-fi speakers, drew her knees up to her chest, wrapped her arms around them and leaned her chin atop of them.

Attempts at finding Beanie's friend, Cora, had proven futile. She had again followed her husband for his job after it had moved him to Florida, but there the trail stopped cold. He'd left his job soon after the move and they hadn't been there long enough to make friends and hadn't left a forwarding address. For all the PI knew, they could have moved back to Utah.

But that didn't matter to Adeline, she was ready to take Beanie in if need be.

"Someone's feeling awfully melancholy this morning." Jean stood in the archway that separated the dining room from the living room, her eyes showed a knowing look as she gazed on Adeline. Her light skin with freckles covering her cheeks was shiny. She was slim and her hair that she usually kept brushed back into a neat bun at the nape of her neck was loose and done up with curls. "Keep this up," she said, "and you'll be late for your flight this afternoon."

"Good morning, Jean." Adeline glanced at the clock over the mantel. "7:45, already?" She looked over at Jean. "You look nice this morning. I got up and made Mr. Garrison coffee and thought I'd listen to some music. He went into the office at 6:30 to take care of some business before we had to leave. I guess I just got caught up in Ella."

"I knew you did all that shopping yesterday for your trip out to California today. Thought I come to help you sort through it and see what you wanted to pack." Jean stuck her hands in the side pockets of her brown and orange plaid belted dress. "But soon as I stepped in the back door, I heard the sounds of Ella and knew you'd be in here being real quiet like. You usually only play that song when you feeling kind of low."

"Do I?" Adeline smiled. "I guess I did have a few things on my mind. I was thinking about that little Beatrice girl." Adeline paused and stared down into the hi-fi. Shaking her head thinking of Beanie's predicament, she reached in, stopped the record and turned off the record player. "She likes jazz."

"Does she now? She seems to like you too, ma'am."

"Yes, she does, doesn't she? I like her too. I told her she could call me Liddie."

Jean chuckled. "But you hate nicknames."

"I know, but people seem to feel closer to people when they use a nickname. She needed someone to feel close to. That's why I told her about jazz because it can talk to you, smooth out the hurt, and comfort your soul."

"Isn't she a little young to like that kind of music? For those kind of feelings?" Jean's narrow eyes watched Adeline.

"Maybe if you just looked at her age . . . ." Adeline laughed as she took the album off and placed it back in its cover. "It seems she had a passing interest in a John Coltrane song she learned at her piano teacher's house." Changing the subject, Adeline didn't want to share too much of Beatrice's troubles with Jean. "I told her how I enjoyed it and then recommended a few songs to her." She looked over at Jean. "I don't know if she plays much now, but she seems quite the little expert. I guess she has an ear for music."

"Well ma'am if she's to learn about it, or about anything, she'll do just fine to learn it from you."

"Do you think so, Jean?" The compliment made Adeline blush.

"Yes, ma'am I do. Excuse my expression, but you're one white woman that has it all together." Jean had a one-sided grin on her face.

Adeline reached down on the coffee table, picking up her pack of Pall Malls. She took one out and lit it up. "Let me slip my feet in some shoes and we can go out to the car and get those packages," Adeline said, evading Jean's comment and walking past her, she headed upstairs to her bedroom. "I left most of what I bought in the trunk of the car yesterday to keep it away from Walter's watchful eyes." She called back over her shoulder.

Adeline found a pair of beach shoes and put them on. She put out the cigarette in the ashtray on the nightstand and grabbed her car keys out of her purse. Going back downstairs, she found Jean waiting for her with that same grin on her face.

"C'mon Jean, let's get those packages in," Adeline said heading toward the back door.

"Mrs. Garrison, I hope you don't mind me saying . . ."

"Saying what, Jean?" Adeline looked back at Jean as she swung open the screen door.

"I'm real happy about Mr. Kennedy becoming the president of the United States. And I'm awfully proud that you're going to his convention."

"He hasn't won yet." Adeline eyed Jean. "But I'm excited about it too. And going to the Democratic Convention has just put me over the moon. I've never been out to Los Angeles before. Or California." Adeline opened the trunk of her Thunderbird and started handing packages to Jean. "But what's got you excited about it, Jean? You follow politics?"

"Well, no ma'am, but I just feel that if Mr. Kennedy got elected he might be more willing to help the Negro. I know he's a good friend of yours, so I figure he must be a good man and a fair person. And not being from the south and all, he'd be more likely not to have such a hateful attitude toward us."

Grabbing the last of the packages and slamming the trunk, Adeline headed back in the house.

Well, you know the nominee for the vice president is from the south," Adeline said. 'Jean set her lips firm and nodded her head. "Just put those packages down there next to mine, Jean." They'd gotten back to Adeline's bedroom, and she dumped her packages onto the bed. "But, it's not just southerners that are prejudiced. You know that don't you?"

"Yes, ma'am. You don't have to tell me that. I run into them every day."

She smiled at Jean and looked down at her watch. "You're right. If we don't get a move on, I will make us late for our flight. You know how I do everything at the last minute."

Adeline thought about Jean saying she runs into prejudiced people every day. She thought about Walter as she sorted through the packages on the bed. Glancing over at Jean, Adeline thought to herself, *yes Jean, you might even work for one.*

Chapter Eighteen

Hildale, Utah
July 15, 1960

Orson sat behind his desk staring at the scattered pile of opened letters, dozen's of them, all addressed to Beatrice Peterson from an *A. Garrison* that lived in Boston. After rereading the one that had been returned yesterday, he dropped it on top of the others, propped his elbows on his desk and lowered his head into his hands. "Why would she say all those terrible things to some stranger living in Boston?" he muttered. "She's made me out to be a monster." He leaned back in his chair and looked up at Margaret. "Everything I've ever done has been for the benefit of this family. If I caused her any physical harm it was only because she forced me to. I'm not a mean man, and I don't punish because I want to. I do it because I have to."

Margaret stood in front of the desk, tilted her head and offered her husband a comforting smile. "I know that Orson. You're a good man. She just didn't appreciate everything that you, Dorothy and I had done for her. She was an ungrateful child, Orson. This is not your fault."

"I'm sure the stranger in Boston thinks it is."

Margaret picked up some of the envelopes, thumbed through them and said, "Whoever this A. Garrison person is, they're not a stranger. Based on the postmarks, they've been corresponding for quite some time." She dropped them back on the desk, looked at Orson and said, "I knew that girl couldn't be trusted. Not after the first time she ran away."

A light bulb seemed to flash over his head and he said, "Of course. How could I have forgotten?" He pulled open his desk drawer and flipped through the files until he came to the one marked TELEPHONE BILLS. "Remember when I got the call from the man at Western Union? He said she was trying to get to Boston." He pulled out the file and began scanning the numbers on the bills. "I'll bet that this A. Garrison and the person who tried to wire Beatrice the money are one in the same." When he found a number that he didn't recognize, he circled it. When he finished looking over the year's worth of phone bills, he counted the calls, looked up at Margaret, shook them at her and said, "There are over fifty phone calls to this same number. You're in charge of paying the bills. How could you not have noticed it?"

Margaret drew in her breath. "Orson, I'm sorry, but how was I suppose to know that those numbers weren't dialed by you? I just assumed they belonged to one of your clients."

Orson glared at her and said, "You should have said something to me. And now I have to clean up this mess. " He grabbed the telephone, pulling it closer, he picked up the receiver. With his finger positioned on the rotary dial, he glared at Margaret and said, "Well?"

Margaret sucked in her breath and said, "Fine." Then she spun on her heels and walked out of Orson's office, closing the door behind her.

Once alone, Orson dialed the mystery number and waited in silent rage. When a woman's voice said "Hello," Orson said, "To whom am I speaking with please?"

A crisp voice replied, "To whom would you like to speak with?"

"My name is Orson Peterson."

"Oh, Mr. Peterson how may I help you?" The woman's voice turned curt.

"There seems to be numerous phone calls to this number from my house. May I inquire as to who has been calling you?"

The woman said, "I think, Mr. Peterson, that someone should inquire as to what *you've* been doing in that house."

"And what is that supposed to mean, Miss -"

"Mrs.," she said. "It's Mrs. Garrison."

Orson leaned into the phone. "Well, *Mrs. Garrison*, I would advise you to mind your own business and-"

"I think that what you've been doing is *business* for the Hildale Police Department, Mr. Peterson. And I have a good mind to call them , let them know what's going on over there and have them come out to investigate you."

"Let them know what, Mrs. Garrison?"

"You don't know what you've been doing, Mr. Peterson? Perhaps a little time behind bars will help you figure it out. Do not call this number again."

Before Adeline could hang up, Orson said, "She's gone, you know. Ran away last night."

"You couldn't think she's here already if she just left last night."

"Well, not unless you wired her money for an airplane ticket. Did you, Mrs. Garrison? I know about the other money. I know about the letters. I found them all."

"What I buy with my money is none of your concern."

"Maybe I'll just call the Boston police, give them your address and let them know that you might be harboring a runaway."

"Look, I don't have time for your threats. I'm late for a flight. You do what you must. But don't call my house ever again, Mr. Peterson," Adeline Garrison said coldly, and hung up.

Orson set the receiver down in its cradle and stared once more at the letters. He picked up t he one written by Beatrice and reread it for the fifth time, searing the incriminating words into his mind: *horrible man, monster, dumb.* He scrunched it up into a ball and threw it in the wastebasket. Then he picked up the torn picture of Beanie, stared at the long blond braid draped over her shoulder and said though clenched teeth, "You think I'm a monster now? Just wait until I find you. And I will. If it's the last thing I do, Beatrice Peterson, I will find you and bring you home."

He tossed the picture of Beanie on the stack of letters, picked up the phone again and dialed.

A moment later a woman's voice said, "Mr. Peterson's office. How may I direct your call?"

"Agnes, this is Mr. Peterson. I need for you to call the airport and find out if there are any flights from Hildale to Boston. If so, I need to know the flight schedule and the price of a one-way ticket. Then I want you to call the train station and the bus station. See what they have available to Boston." He stared at the place where his box of change used to sit and added, "And call me at the house when you've learned something."

"Yes sir, right away."

Orson sat at his desk staring at the picture of Beanie. With each minute that slowly ticked by he grew angrier and angrier.

"I just can't sit here and do nothing," he said. He grabbed his jacket, dropped the picture in his pocket and yelled to Margaret as he hurried out his office, "Margaret, I'll be back in a little bit."

Fifteen minutes later, when Orson passed the Greyhound bus station, he slammed on the breaks and came to a screeching halt. Turning around he pulled up into the parking lot, got out of the car and went inside. Orson stood in the bus terminal lobby staring at the bus schedule.

Denver, St. Louis, Kansas City, Chicago, St. Paul, New Orleans, Jackson, and the list went on. So many options for her, everywhere *except* Boston.

"May I help you, sir?" The man behind the counter smiled at him.

Orson fingered the picture of Beanie in his pocket and said, "I certainly hope so." He pulled the photo out and laid it on the counter. "Have you seen this girl? You see, she's my, uh, *daughter*." He forced tears to pool in his eyes. "She went missing last night, and Im so worried that something bad might have happened to her. We're checking out every option, the airport, train station, anywhere a young girl might go." He pushed the photo a little closer to the man behind the counter. "I would deeply appreciate any help you could give me."

The clerk picked up the picture and looked at it intently. A moment later he said, "You know, Mr.-"

"Peterson, Orson Peterson. And my daughter's name is Beatrice Peterson."

"I think I do remember her. Yes, I believe I saw her standing in the lobby early this morning. I remember her because of that long braid." He handed the photo back to Orson. "Your daughter sure has a lot of hair, Mr. Peterson."

"Would you, by any chance, know which bus she might have taken?" Orson looked back over at the bus schedule posted on the wall next to him. "There are just so many to choose from. She could be anywhere." He held the picture to his chest and sighed deeply.

The man behind the counter offered Orson a sympathetic smile. "I'm sorry, Mr. Peterson. She didn't buy a ticket from me, so I can't help you. But why don't you give me the picture, and I'll show it to the other two clerks? Maybe they know what bus she took."

Several minutes later, the man behind the counter returned with another clerk. "Mr. Peterson, I believe we might have found the bus, your daughter took this morning." He turned his attention to the young man standing next to him. "Tell him what you told me."

The younger clerk said to Orson, "I remember her, sir, because I sold her the ticket."

Orson wiped away his fake tears. "Oh thank God. Where did she go?"

"She said she was trying to get to Boston, but she didn't have enough money."

"So then where did she go?"

"Chicago. She bought a ticket to Chicago."

Orson slipped the picture back in his pocket, extended his hand and said, "Thank you both so much for your help. At least now I know where to find her."

The first clerk shook Orson's hand and said, "We're glad that we could help." He paused. "You know, Mr. Peterson, I can get you on a bus to Chicago this afternoon. You'd be going a different route than the one your daughter took, and you'd arrive a half a day later, but at least the two of you would be in the same city. Would you like a ticket to Chicago?"

Orson slipped his hand back in his pocket, wrapped his fingers around Beanie's picture and scrunched it. He smiled at the two clerks and said, "That's not necessary. I think I'm going to drive there instead."

Chapter Nineteen

Los Angeles, California
July 16, 1960

It felt like *déjà vu.*

Sitting in Los Angeles Memorial Coliseum at the Democratic Convention listening to Jack speak, Adeline was jerked back in time.

It was the same rumble of the crowd, the same cheering at the words of the speaker, the same platform of promises to be kept, prosperity to be had. The same Boston accent . . .

Adeline sat alone. Walter was off somewhere, she knew, somewhere shooting off his mouth to whoever would listen, trying to show how important he was. How important what he had to say was.

He drank on the flight over and kept drinking up until the time to leave the hotel for the convention. And once there, he couldn't sit still.

Her mind wandered back to that political convention in Chicago. Back to the point where her life took a wrong turn.

Was it there, she thought, *or was I somehow always on the wrong track?*

Adeline shifted in her seat, brushed her hand under her thigh to straighten out her dress.

"*. . . they all know that it's time for a change. We are not here to curse the darkness, we are here to light a candle.*" Jack's words wafted past Adeline and became muffled. The clapping mixed with the echoes of Jack's words, "*His party is the party of the past, the party of memories . . .*". They floated past Adeline, over her head, around her until they disappeared somewhere behind her. The cheers in the room and the bright lights seem to dim as her own memories flooded her mind. Memories laced with regrets. Not just about losing Joe. Not just about marrying Walter. Not just about walking out on Melvin's love for her. Or even taking on the worry of a sixteen year old whose husband was a cruel polygynist. It was everything, in all times. It was the lifetime filled with 'what-ifs' and the wrong decisions and bad choices. And it seemed as if they started at that Democratic Convention in Chicago so many years ago.

And now here she sat again.

They had flown in the last day of the convention only to hear Jack speak. But she and Walter were to make a vacation out of it. Stay over the weekend and possibly a few days into the next week. Go to Grauman's Chinese Theater. Shop on Rodeo Drive. Walter even hoped to visit Frank Sinatra at his home . . .

Adeline just couldn't sit with her thoughts anymore. She slipped out of her seat when Jack, it seemed, began to speak directly to her, "...*to all who respond to the Scriptural call: 'Be strong and of a good courage; be not afraid, neither be thou dismayed.'*"

Walking out of the Coliseum, she dug down in her purse for a cigarette. Pulling out her pack of Pall Malls, she reached up and wiped the single tear that ran down her face.

Puffing on her cigarette, Adeline wandered over to the rental car that they had picked up that afternoon after landing in LA and wondered how she would find Walter. She just wanted to leave. To go back to the hotel, climb into bed and stop her mind from churning. But with that crowd inside, finding him would probably be impossible.

As she neared the car she heard low grunting noises and laughter. As she drew closer she could see the silhouette of two people leaning up against a car where she remembered Walter had parked.

She dropped her cigarette on the ground, and twisted it with the point of her high heel shoe. Walking as quietly as she could she moved close enough to see who it was against the car.

"Walter! What are you doing?"

Walter was thoroughly inebriated and pressing up against a woman who seemed to thoroughly enjoy his attention. She leaned backwards over the car hood, with him leaning over her. They both sprang upright at the sound of Adeline's voice. The woman brushed her hair back off her face as Adeline walked in closer.

Walter's shocked expression quickly grew into one of anxiousness.

"Liddie." He said nothing more. He glanced from Liddie to the woman, back to Liddie and then down at his clothes. He brushed down the front of them, straightened out his tie, and fumbled with his pants.

"If you don't mind, miss," Adeline said looking at the woman, "I'd like for him to drive me back to my hotel."

Walter looked at the woman and said, "Um, this is my wife."

"Pleasure to meet you," the woman said, as Adeline opened up the car door and got into the passenger's seat.

Walter walked around the car, and got in. Turning the ignition and pulling out of the parking lot, he glanced at Adeline and said, "I'm not getting anything from you."

"So? What?" Adeline said calmly, staring straight ahead. "You were planning on having sex with her right there in the parking lot?"

Nothing else was said on the ride home, or in the hotel room. The shrill noise broke the silence nearly an hour after they had arrived back to the hotel. Adeline answered the phone, gave a pleasant greeting but then listened mostly before hanging up.

"That was a campaign worker. There's something at the Biltmore tonight. A celebration of sorts."

Walter jumped up from the couch in their suite where he had been sitting for the better part of an hour. "Do you want to go?"

"No. I'm really not up for it. You go, Walter. I'll stay here."

"If you don't want to go . . ."

"I think Jack wants you there," Adeline lied.

"You think?" he asked.

"Mmm hmm." Adeline looked at him and smiled. "So you should go."

As soon as Walter left, Adeline packed her bags and called down to the desk to get a cab to the airport. She was going home.

Sitting on the plane, Adeline wondered why it made her angry that Walter was making advances at another woman. After all she was having an affair.

Well, *had* an affair.

Maybe she wasn't really angry. Perhaps perturbed. If he had it in him to try to have sex in the parking lot of the Los Angeles Coliseum, why was he always bothering her for it? Surely he could get someone to go to a hotel with him on a regular basis.

Adeline looked out of the window at the blue sky and the white fluffy clouds just below and thought about how much she missed Melvin.

I wouldn't care if Walter did find someone else to have sex with, Adeline thought. *It would certainly be better for me. Wouldn't be a constant reminder of what I just threw away.*

Maybe I should just try to be a better wife. Do my duty, as it were. Seeing as I've decided to not see Melvin anymore.

Adeline scrunched her nose at the thought, and shook herself. Stretching her neck, she looked down and she saw the flat, brown land below.

I wonder if that's Utah.

I wonder is Beanie still there somewhere.

I wonder did she make it out of that hell hole this time.

And the nerve of that man. Adeline clicked her tongue. The infamous Orson Peterson himself calling her home and questioning her. She'd like to take him and Walter and...

Right Adeline, she had to stop herself mid-sentence, *you had the love of a good man, and you picked Walter.*

You picked living a lie over living with love.

"I hope Beanie makes better choices than I have," she whispered as she leaned back on the headrest.

Chapter Twenty

Chicago, Illinois

Beanie pulled the covers over her head when she heard him enter her room. She knew he'd read her letter and had come to kill her.

Orson closed the door behind him and walked over to the side of her bed. He stood silently for a moment and then said in a menacing voice, "You're going to pay for what you did, Beatrice. I'm going to teach you a lesson you won't forget." He reached for the cover and yanked it back.

Beanie felt her heart pounding into her ribcage as she clamped her eyes closed even tighter.

"Don't pretend to be asleep. I know you can hear me." He grabbed her shoulder and shook it. "I'm not as stupid as you think. Now wake up! Wake up, Beatrice!"

Beanie's eyes shot open when she felt his hand grab her and shake her.

"Wake up, Beatrice. We're almost here." The elderly woman who had boarded the bus two days ago with her was leaning over the aisle and nudging her shoulder. "We'll be pulling into the terminal shortly." She sat back down next to her husband, grabbed his hand and said to Beanie, "It's nice to go visit the grandchildren. But it's so much nicer to come home."

Beanie sat straight up in the seat. *Thank God, it was only a dream.* She relaxed, stretched her arms up over her head and yawned. She smiled at the woman and said, "Thank you for waking me." Not wanting to carry on the conversation any further, she stared out the bus window at the Chicago skyline. In the distant horizon, skyscrapers jutted up from the ground looking like rows of jagged teeth.

The woman leaned across the aisle again and said, "What are your plans while you're here, dear?"

"Oh, I'm not staying here. I'm going on to Boston."

"Boston? How lovely. You have family there?"

Beanie thought about Liddie. She had been more of a mother to her this past year, than her own mother had. She laughed with Beanie, cried with her, gave her advice, talked straight to her without mincing words, even if it wasn't what Beanie wanted to hear. She encouraged her and cared for her as much as any mother would. Beanie smiled at the couple and said, "Yes, I have family there."

Ten minutes later the bus exited Wacker St. and pulled into the lower level of downtown Chicago's Greyhound Bus Terminal.

Beanie stepped off of the bus after the elderly couple and stood by the side of the bus staring at the line of buses parked parallel in the underground parking lot.

"When does your next bus leave?"

Beanie smiled at the elderly woman. Both she and her husband had already retrieved their luggage from the bus driver. "I'm not sure. I need to check inside at the counter." She looked around again and then asked, "Do you know where I might find a telephone?"

The elderly woman's husband pointed to a set of glass double doors and said, "There are some inside the terminal. Just go through these doors and you'll find a bank of them on the far left wall of the lobby. But be mindful of pickpockets. There can be some unsavory characters loitering there."

"Thank you." Beanie waved goodbye to her travel companions, entered the terminal and walked across the lobby. She stopped at the row of telephones. All were occupied, with lines of impatient travelers stemming from each phone booth. And along the bare walls, several of those unsavory-looking characters she was warned about loitered. *I'll find a phone booth outside.*

She hurried across the lobby, past the information booth located right in the middle of the terminal, up the escalator to the street level and out the front doors. Standing under the big blue vertical Greyhound sign attached to the corner of the block-long, brick building, she scanned up and down the block. Arcades, markets and clothing stores lining the block enticed the passersby. Men wearing fancy suits and women dressed in pencil skirts, heels, and tweed waistline jackets traversed the busy sidewalks with purpose in their steps.

Not seeing a phone booth, she hurried across Randolph Street, carefully avoiding fast moving cars and delivery trucks. She followed Clark Street about a half a block until she stopped in front of a beautiful stone building with several sets of bronze colored doors and various flags perched above them, casually waving in the breeze. A bronze plaque mounted on the wall to the side of the door read "City Hall."

"Thank goodness," she said as she slipped into a phone booth that stood on the edge of the sidewalk across from the entrance. But a moment later she groaned when she saw the out of order sign hanging from the rotary dial. She stepped out, saw a man sitting on a bench on the left side of the building entrance reading a newspaper and said, "Excuse me, but do you know where I might find another telephone booth?"

The man set the paper down beside him, stood up and said, "I believe there is one by the Morrison Hotel. Just go down two more blocks and it will be on this side of the street, right before Monroe Street." Then he opened one of the doors leading into the building's lobby.

"Thank you," said Beanie to the man's back. She eyed the newspaper, picked it up and stared at the front-page story. A picture of four young black men sat at a lunch counter. The headline read, "Segregation Resistance

Continues." She tucked it under her arm and hurried down the sidewalk in search of a fully functional telephone booth.

Less than ten minutes later, Beanie found her phone booth right in front of the Morrison Hotel just like the man said. She was just about to step in when a familiar tune drifted out from the alley behind her and hit her in the face. "Blue Train!" she said. "I can't believe it." She followed the music to a little bar wedged in between the backsides of two large buildings. It looked like the city had sprouted around this small joint, leaving it stuck back in time. Looking up at the neon sign above the door that read "Jazz," she pulled open the faded red, wooden door and peeked inside. It took a moment for her eyes to adjust to the dim lighting. But when they did, she saw the room had at least a dozen small round tables with two to four chairs surrounding them, each facing a stage at the back of the room. A four piece band seemed to be practicing. They'd play a few notes and then stop.

"Welcome to Smoky Joe's. We're not open quite yet."

Beanie looked at the old man polishing glasses behind the bar and said, "Oh, I'm sorry. I heard the music from the street, and I just had to come listen."

He set the glass back down and grabbed another one. "How did it sound?"

"Really nice. I love that song. John Coltrane is one of my favorite jazz players."

The old man smiled. "You like jazz?"

"Oh yes, it's my favorite music. Count Basie, Duke Ellington, Benny Goodman, I love them all."

The man tossed the dishtowel on the bar and started wiping it down. "Have you been to the Blue Note across the street from the Morrison Hotel? Now that's the place to listen to the big names play. It's the biggest jazz club in Chicago. Don't get me wrong. I get some good talent playing here, but they ain't no John Coltrane." A dissonant chord interrupted their conversation. "See what I mean?" He looked over at the bandleader and yelled, "That's terrible. You better have that fixed by the time we open otherwise you'll be playing to an empty house."

The man playing the sax yelled back, "Sorry Joe, it's just not coming out right without our piano player."

Joe tossed the dishtowel over his shoulder and yelled back, "Well, you're just going to have to make it work." He turned to Beanie and said, "Sorry about that. They're having some difficulties reworking the set because their piano player called in sick at the last minute again." He wiped his hands on the towel, tossed it on the counter and said, "What can you do, right?"

Beanie looked at the gauze wrap on her right index finger, tugged it off, wiggled all of them and said, "I play piano."

The man raised his eyebrows, tilted his head toward the piano on stage and said, "Go give it a whirl."

Beanie grinned and began to weave through the garden of tables toward the stage.

"Hey, what's your name?" he yelled to her.

She turned around and said, "It's Beatrice, but everyone calls me Beanie."

"Hey guys, this is Beanie. Get her set up at the piano and let's see what she can do," he said as Beanie climbed the steps to the stage.

The man holding the saxophone reached his hand out to help her up the last step. "Hi Beanie. My name's Byron."

Beanie took the young man's hand and smiled. His caramel colored skin made his teeth gleam like perfectly polished piano keys. "Nice to meet you." She slid on to the piano bench, thumbed through the music perched on the fallboard and said, "I'm ready when you are."

Byron said, "Okay, let's start with, *Hello Little Girl*. The sheet music should be right there. Do you know that one?"

Beanie pulled the piece from the stack, quickly scanned the Duke Ellington song and said as she positioned her fingers over the keys, "No I don't, but I'm sure I'll figure it out."

Byron flashed his band a skeptical look and said, "Follow her lead. Ready? A one and a two and a-"

Beanie's hands attacked the keys, tickling them at a fast and furious pace. After the first few bars, the drummer jumped in, swiping at the symbols with his brushes, followed by the low melodic thumping of the base fiddle player.

After a full minute of Beanie's piano solo, Byron sang in a gravely voice, *"Hello little girl, don't you remember me. Hello little girl, don't you remember me. I'm the same little guy that brought you from Tennessee."*

Seven minutes later when Beanie played her final note, the band clapped and cheered.

"Wow, Beanie. That was terrific." Byron propped his sax on a stand, walked over to Beanie and leaned on the piano. "I can't believe that was your first time playing it. It was amazing, almost as good as the Duke's playing."

Beanie blushed, "Well, I don't know about that, but thank you."

"You want a job?"

Beanie arched her eyebrows. "You mean it?"

Byron nodded, "Sure do. You're really good."

"But what about your other piano player?"

"He's nowhere near as good as you, and he's unreliable."

"How much will you pay me?"

"Five dollars a night, six nights a week, closed on Sunday."

"Will you pay me nightly?" Beanie figured that thirty dollars would certainly be enough to get her to Boston. But if she agreed, she'd have to find a cheap place to stay.

He looked at his watch. "We open in fifteen minutes. What do you say, you up for it?"

After mulling it over in her mind for a few seconds, she stuck out her hand and said, "Deal."

Byron grabbed her hand, shook it, and yelled over to Joe. "Hey Joe, we got ourselves a new piano player."

Beanie stood up and said, "Oh, thank you so much. I won't let you down." She flew down the steps and yelled, "But I gotta make a phone call first."

"Just use the one in the office, now that you work here," Joe said smiling at the newest member of the band. "It's just down the hall."

Beanie trotted down the small hallway to the door marked "Office," found the phone on the desk, dialed zero, and gave the operator Liddie's number. She listened to her band practice while she waited for the operator to connect them.

When Liddie said "Hello," the operator said, "Collect call from Beatrice Peterson, do you accept the charges?"

"Yes, I do."

When the operator hung up, Beanie said, "Liddie, it's me. I just wanted to let you know I left. I ran away."

"Where are you?"

"I'm in jazz club in downtown Chicago."

"What are you doing there? And what is all that noise I hear in the background?"

Beanie closed the office door and said, "That's the band playing. And I'm going to be playing the piano with them."

"Why are you playing in a jazz club in Chicago?"

"Because that's as far as my money would take me."

"Why didn't you call me for more money? If Orson hadn't called me I wouldn't have even known you'd left. And if I hadn't gotten back from California early, I would have missed this call."

Beanie felt bad for making Liddie worry, but she was confused. "What? When? How did he even know about you? How did he get your number?"

"He found your letters from me, Beanie, and he found my number on the phone bills. That was almost two days ago, and I've been worried about you."

"I'm sorry, Liddie, I didn't mean to make you worry, but I had to get out of there quick." She paused, peeked out the door and looked back down the hallway. "It doesn't matter now. He can't hurt me anymore."

"So when are you going to get here? Do you need me to wire you more money? I could do that now."

"No, don't do that. I'll get paid every night, and I'll buy a bus ticket next week."

"Paid?"

"Yes, they're paying me to play the piano. Isn't that marvelous?"

"Oh Beanie, you don't know those people. Something bad could happen to you in that kind of place."

Liddie's motherly concern made her feel warm inside. She reassured Liddie. "Don't worry. It's just one week." She looked over and saw Byron standing at the end of the hall waving at her and said, "Oh, I gotta go, they're calling for me. I'll call you later. Bye." She hung up before Liddie could talk her out of it. And then, grinning like a jack-o-lantern, she hurried to Byron.

Chapter Twenty-One

Beanie opened up the curtains in her small flat above the club, while sipping from a mug of coffee. No horns honking, or delivery trucks rumbling by on Clark Street meant that today was Sunday, her day off. She plucked the two pieces of toast from the toaster, slathered butter and sprinkled cinnamon and sugar on them, and cradled them in a napkin as she walked over to the little dinette table nestled under the window and sat. *I can't believe I've already been here four months,* she thought as she took a big bite of the gooey toast. She hadn't planned on staying in Chicago more than a week, just long enough to earn money for some new clothes and bus fare to Boston. But after that first night playing with Byron and the boys, she knew that Boston and Liddie were going to have to wait a little while for her arrival. She took another sip of coffee and smiled, *I never thought I could be this happy.*

After she finished her breakfast, she grabbed a pen and a sheet of writing paper from the junk drawer next to the sink. She'd been thinking about Liddie lately. It had been close to a month since she actually talked to her. And she didn't really want to talk to her today either, because she didn't want to have to explain why she was still there in Chicago. At least with a letter, she could share news without having to justify her actions.

Beanie put the date at the top of the page and wrote:

November 20, 1960

Dear Liddie,

Hope you're doing well. I'm terrific. Playing piano at the club has been so much fun. Most nights we play to a packed house, which is incredible considering Chicago's premier jazz club is right across the street. Sometimes in between sets, I'll pop over to the Blue Note, just to see who's playing. I finally heard Duke Ellington play, "Hey Little Girl." Of course he plays it much better than I do.

What are you doing for Thanksgiving? I'm going to be spending it at one of my friend's family's house. I've been there several times, and they're very nice people.

Beanie paused for a moment and thought about the first time Byron took her on the El train to the south side of Chicago to meet his family. She'd been so apprehensive; a young white girl walking in the projects with a young Negro man. But now she had no problem with it.

Have you ever been to the Chicago Stadium? It's where they have sporting events and concerts. I thought you might find it interesting to know that it even held several republican and democratic political conventions. My friend and I are going there tomorrow. We saw in the paper where they will be filming a new movie there called, The Manchurian Candidate, sometime in the next few months, and they are looking for musicians to play during a political convention scene. So we are going to try out for the parts. Wouldn't that be exciting if we got selected? I understand that Frank Sinatra will be starring in it.

If I do get to be in the movie, I will try to come to Boston some time after they have finished filming. But Ill let you know for sure.

Please write when you get the chance.

Love,
Beanie

She folded the letter, tucked it in the envelope and then addressed it. She was just about to lick the stamp when she heard a *tap, tap, tap* on the front door.

"Beanie, it's me."

Beanie jumped up from the table, hurried to the door and opened it. Byron stood in the hallway wearing rolled up Levi's, a black leather motorcycle jacket, and looking like a milk chocolate James Dean.

"You ready?" he said as he walked through the front door and stood in the small area that made up the living room, dining room, kitchen, and entryway.

"I just need to grab my jacket. What time are we supposed to be at your aunt and uncle's house?"

"Not until three. So I thought we could take a little river cruise so you could see the Chicago skyline."

"That sounds fun." She glanced out the window at the washed out blue sky and said, "Do you think I'll be warm enough with just my jacket?"

"You'll be fine. But if you get cold, I'll give you mine."

Beanie mused as she closed and locked the door behind them, "My, such a gentleman, you are."

Once outside, they walked down Clark Street past the Greyhound bus station, and turned right on to Wacker Street. Ten minutes later they stood in line waiting to board the boat that would take them on a forty-minute architectural cruise up and down the Chicago River.

When Byron pulled his wallet from his back pocket and dug out enough money for two tickets, Beanie put her hand on his arm and said, "We talked about this. You need to save your money for school. After you graduate and become a big time doctor then you can pay for mine if you want to. But until then, we go Dutch."

"You sure you want to wait that long? At the rate I'm going, I'll be thirty before I even get my undergraduate degree, let alone go to medical school." He looked at Beanie and said, "Tell me I'm not stupid for wanting to become a doctor."

"You're not stupid, Byron. You're a dreamer, and you want to do more with your life than just play in a jazz club."

"I'm beginning to think that that's all it's ever going to be, just a silly dream. I'll never be able to pay for it with what I make at the club." He shoved his wallet back in his pocket and looked at Beanie. "School during the day, the club at night. What was I thinking?"

Beanie put her hand on Byron's arm. "Don't give up on your dreams. It may take awhile to get there, but you'll get there. And one day you'll be saving lives. Who knows, maybe even mine." She gave his arm a pat. "Now let's forget about it for awhile and just enjoy the boat ride."

From behind her, Beanie heard a woman whisper, "Did you see that? That white girl just touched that Negro boy. Isn't there some sort of law against that? I sure hope they're not getting on our boat. I don't think I could stand watching them."

The woman's cruise companion replied, "That's appalling. That girl should be ashamed of herself, associating with those people. Where are her parents?"

Beanie turned and glared at the two middle aged white women. She opened her mouth to say something.

Byron pulled her by her arm, turning her back around and said, "C'mon, Beanie. Let's go. We don't need to stand here and listen to a couple of old ladies jabbering on about something they know nothing about." He put his hand on her back and guided her out of the line.

As she passed the two gossipers, Beanie leaned in close to one of the women and said, "Shame on you -"

Byron grabbed Beanie by the wrist and pulled her away from the women before she could finish her sentence. He led her out of the parking lot and on to Wacker Street. "We don't need any trouble. Let's just go get a cup of coffee and forget about it."

This was not the first time that Beanie had overheard a derogatory comment about Negroes. She looked up at Byron and said, "Doesn't it upset you the way people talk about you?"

"Of course it does. But there's nothing that you or I can do that will change the way people think. We just have to ignore them." He shoved his hands in his pockets as they crossed the street."

"Those women back there were just plain rude."

As they stepped up on the curb Byron said, "I appreciate your sentiments, Beanie. Maybe one day things will change."

"I certainly hope so because wrong is wrong, no matter who is doing it to whom."

Byron held the door to the coffee shop open for Beanie. Just as she was about to enter, out of the corner of her eye she saw a familiar-looking blue Rambler slowly driving down Wacker Street.

Orson.

Could it possibly be, after all this time? Her face grew pallid. She hadn't thought of him in months. How could he have found her after this long? Did he force the information out of Liddie? How long had he been here? So many questions tumbled around in her head. And then another thought made her clutch her stomach. *If he knows I am in Chicago, then chances are he also knows I work at Smoky Joe's.*

"Beanie, are you feeling okay? You look terrible."

She hadn't told Byron anything about her life back in Utah. She felt no need to. But now that they were friends and seeing the growing concern on his face, she said, "There's something I need to tell you."

And as they ordered coffee and fries and ate, Byron had to continue to hand Beanie more napkins as she told him about Orson: the forced marriage, the miscarriages, the children, the sister wives, and everything else that made up her life back in Utah. She wiped her eyes and blew her nose, then dropped the napkin on the saucer plate where the French fries used to be.

"And you think that was him?"

"I don't know, but it sure looked like his car." She dabbed at her eyes with a clean napkin.

Byron looked out the coffee shop window. "And your friend in Boston hasn't mentioned him?"

Beanie shook her head. "No, but I haven't talked to her in several weeks." She felt the tears pooling up again and said, "If he finds me, he'll kill me. There's no doubt in my mind. I stole money from him. I ran away, and I've humiliated him in front of his family and the Church."

"Don't jump to conclusions. There are thousands of blue Ramblers around. And chances are that after all this time, he's given up."

Beanie shook her head. "You don't know him. He doesn't give up."

Byron laid some money on the table, scooted out from the bench and stood up. "C'mon. We gotta catch the train. We'll talk about it later."

Beanie sucked in a big breath and let it out. She forced a smile and said, "You're right, it probably wasn't him. I'm just being paranoid." But she couldn't help looking over her shoulder as they walked the few blocks to the El train. She couldn't wait to get on the train, go to his aunt and uncle's place, and forget about Orson.

That evening after helping his aunt wash the dinner dishes, Beanie joined Byron and two of his friends out in the back yard.

As she sat down on one of the metal lawn chairs, she said, "It sure is nice of your aunt and uncle to open their home to all of us."

Byron took a sip from a bottle of RC Cola and said, "They're my great aunt and uncle. But yeah, they're always feeding these guys."

One of Byron's friends said, "Course we keep coming back. Can't get collard greens and ham hocks like that at the university." He handed Beanie an opened bottle of soda. "Hey, Byron told us what happened to you guys at the river today."

Beanie took the soda. "Thanks, Marcus." She tipped it back and took a swig. "Yeah, I was pretty upset about it. In fact, I think I was more upset than Byron."

Marcus leaned back in his chair. "I'm getting pretty tired of all the racist shit, too. But at least we don't have that segregation problem here like they do down south."

Byron's other friend, Carl, cut in, "Man, Marcus. What's wrong with you? Look around you. We live on the south side with all the other Negroes. You got your Italians that live on the east side, the Jews and the Russians who live on the west side. And who do you think lives up on the north side in them big ole' mansions? The whites. If that aint segregation, then I don't know what is. Oh, we can work or go to school right along side them white folks, but don't think for one minute that we can just pack up and move to their neighborhoods. It don't work that way, brother." Carl looked at Beanie and said, "No offense."

"No offense taken, Carl. I agree with you. Segregation is wrong." She finished her soda and set it down by her chair. "I came from an all white place. I'd never seen Negroes before coming here." She said, thinking how Orson called them the devil. "And what I knew about them made Negroes out to be murders, rapists and thieves."

"Really? Why did you start hanging around us? Weren't you afraid," Marcus asked.

"No. I knew that anyone who could play jazz as good as Byron couldn't be all bad. Plus, I don't believe any of it. Negroes are the same as everybody else."

"That's what we've been working on." Carl said, handing Beanie another soda. "Equality. You know about the sit-ins in Mississippi, right?"

"No. What are sit-ins?"

"In the south, colored can't sit at a public counter to eat next to white people. But they've been doing it anyway, and it's causing a whole lot of waves. And, that's just the start of it. I've been talking with some of my college friends. And from what I hear there's gonna be a lot more of them, and demonstrations, too. We're all tired of it, so we're gonna fight back." He looked at Beanie. "We're taking our civil rights." He held his RC Cola out and said, "Here's to freedom."

Beanie, Byron and Marcus clinked his bottle and said in unison, "To freedom."

Chapter Twenty-Two

January 20, 1961
Washington, D.C.

It was snowy out. Twenty-two degrees, one of the coldest inauguration days in history. But even the nor'easter that fell the day before the inauguration and brought that cold along with eight inches of snow didn't stop Walter. Jack had won the election and Walter's vicarious friendship through Adeline brought out the rooster in him. Strutting around, sticking out his chest, shaking his tail feathers and crowing about his "friend," the President.

Walter drank in the success of the campaign as if it were his own. The pre-inauguration ball given by Frank Sinatra and Peter Lawford at the D.C. Amory made him act giddy even. And he may as well have pinned the two $10,000 tickets he bought for their entrance onto his lapel, because he made sure everyone knew what he had spent. But Adeline wasn't in the mood for his schmoozing, bragging or the cold weather. All she thought about was Melvin. And as the break from him increased with each passing day, the hole inside of her grew wider. His absence made her sullen and short-tempered, she was disagreeable to everyone and to everything. Even the bitter cold outside couldn't override the constant coldness she felt in her life without him. And even though she had looked forward to Jack's inauguration festivities she had found it hard to enjoy the star-filled pre-inauguration ball.

Walter hadn't helped with Adeline's attempt at a mood adjustment. Coming in from the second pre-ball given by Jack's father at 4 o'clock in the morning, Walter, drunk, climbed into the bed with her after she had been sure to reserve a room with two beds, wanting Adeline to "roll over, spread her legs, and do her wifely duty."

"It's been too long," he had mumbled. Three hours later, smelling like a nest of granddaddies, he wanted to have at it again, this time with a, "I need more," and she, too disgusted with it, could do nothing more than succumb. She lied still and let him have his way with her. Rising quietly after he'd finished and fell over on the bed snoring, she showered in the hottest water she could stand, put on a gown and crawled into the other bed. She turned on the television and stared at the news flashes of the new president and the almost unprecedented inauguration weather.

Now awake and, seemingly fully charged after the two sloppy, awkward, one-sided poundings he gave Adeline, and with less than four hours of sleep, Walter was full of steam.

Adeline thought he might even go out and help the U.S. Army Corps and the boy scouts clear the parade route down Pennsylvania Avenue, single-handily, pushing hundreds of the stalled cars abandoned in the wintery weather with his bare hands.

"It's clear out. Snow's stopped. Still cold, but it looks to be a beautiful day." Up and dressed, Walter was buttoning the cuffs on his shirt while Adeline, still in bed, tried to find some comfort in the warmth of the covers. "Have a look-see." He opened the curtains that covered the large picture window and looked at Adeline.

"Ugh," Adeline groaned and pulled the covers over her head.

"Did you hear that Jack asked Sammy Davis, Jr. not to attend that pre-inauguration ball last night because he's going to marry a white woman?"

"May Britt," Adeline said from under the comforter.

"What?"

"The woman Sammy's marrying is named May Britt." She spoke a little louder so he could hear her from inside of her hiding place.

"Whatever her name is," he said, "it makes me think that Jack won't be as helpful to the Negroes as they seem to hope he will be." Adeline peeked out from under the covers at Walter. He grinned at her, tucking his shirt tail into his pants. "Good thing, too. He had a lot of people worrying what he was going to do about that whole civil rights business when he and Bobby helped get that Negro preacher out of jail last year. You know the one spouting all that desegregation talk. Getting people riled up."

"Martin Luther King, Jr."

"What?"

"The Negro preacher's name is Martin Luther King, Jr."

"Yeah, that's it. How do you know? What do you know about this desegregation nonsense?"

"Nothing. But what I do know is that it wasn't Jack that didn't want Sammy there, it was his father. Mr. Kennedy asked Jack to tell Frank to keep Sammy away."

Walter shook his head. "I don't like it that you're keeping up with what these Negroes are doing. I'm not prejudiced. You know that better than anyone about me. But you have to be careful about making big waves with something that involves the whole country. People don't like change." He got quiet for a moment. "May Britt, huh?" He looked at Adeline. "I guess next you'll be telling me that you approve of interracial marriages."

"I was just tell . . ." Adeline didn't finish her sentence. She hid her head again. *Why even talk to him*, she mused. It'll just prolong his presence around her, and she didn't know how much longer she could keep up with this act of tolerating him. She wanted to be left alone.

"Well, whoever was responsible for keeping a colored man from arriving with a white woman on his arm," Walter kept talking, "I think it was a smart move. It was an even smarter move when Jack picked a southerner as his running mate. Jack needs to keep his nose clean if he wants to get re-elected."

"He just got elected." Adeline took the covers off her face and looked at Walter combing his hair in the mirror.

"Never too soon to start planning for the next four years," he said. Adeline flipped over onto her stomach and pulled a pillow on top of her head. "Come on, Liddie. Get up. I got the name of a restaurant that a lot of the who's who will be eating in this morning. No telling who we might run into. Don't you want to get up and join me for breakfast, honey?"

Adeline peeked out from under the pillow and saw Walter tying his tie and looking at her through the reflection in the mirror over the dresser. "No," she moaned.

"Well, that means I'll have to try and make it back here to pick you up for the inauguration at the Capitol. It'll be hard enough making it one way through all the chaos in the streets because of that snow storm last night. Now I'll have to make two trips through it. Getting back here to get you, and then back out to the proceedings. We'll need to get there early."

"I'm not going," came muffled from under the pillow.

"What do you mean you're not going? Jack expects you there."

"I'm sure Jack hasn't given a second thought on whether I would be there or not," Adeline said.

Obviously upset over her decision, Walter barked at her. "We have to make our appearance there. How would it look for us not to be there? Not be at the inauguration of our friend."

"Walter." Adeline turned over and sat up in bed. "Jack cannot see you out in that crowd of thousands of people from the platform at the portico. Nor will anyone else. No one will know I didn't go. You go. Tell me what he said, and we'll be able to keep up 'our appearances', whatever that means." Adeline fell back on the bed, pulled up the covers, and nestled her head back into the pillows. Closing her eyes, she hoped that that would be the close of the conversation as well, and Walter would leave so she would be left alone to wallow in the painful throngs of her broken heart.

"What about the luncheon, he'll notice you're not there."

"I'll meet you there. How's that? That'll work won't it? I'll be there at noon and none will be the wiser that I wasn't at the speech."

"Liddie, I don't know what is wrong with you as of late. But I won't have you embarrassing me in front of this crowd. These are important people. They're my friends. They could help my business and that would help you be able to spend more of my money on shopping and trips to the Cape or whatever it is you do. I need you at my side."

Adeline threw back the covers, sat back up, this time with more force, and tilted her head. Speaking slowly, she said, "Walter, I think that you must have forgotten that I am the one that introduced you to 'this crowd'. It's *my* friendship that keeps you in the loop. And if anything, you'd embarrass me," Adeline hissed. "Salivating all over them with your power-hungry tongue dangling out of your mouth, wagging away at them."

Adeline, seeing Walter's face grow flush, thought perhaps her harsh words might start an argument which would prolong his leaving. She wanted him gone, whatever that took. She couldn't make him mad. So she took in a breath and switched gears.

"It is not my mood, honey," she started again, speaking more softly this time. "And I apologize if that's how it seemed," she said. "I'm just sore from our lovemaking." With that lie tumbling from her lips, she rubbed her hands down her thighs, forced a smile and tried to look coy. "It reminded me of our younger days, you were so forceful and virile. Twice in a few hours, my goodness, Walter." She fluttered her eyes at him. "And each time with such intensity, it made me almost explode inside, it has just drained me. I couldn't move if I tried." She brushed her hand across her chest and sighed. "I know *you* know what you did to me." Adeline raised an eyebrow. "It would seem as if you'd give me some time to rest so that I'll be fit for tonight's festivities."

Walter stood motionless and stared at Adeline. The anger that his face showed at her first words seemed to be fading into an arrogant, proud smirk. He seemed to instinctively rub his groin and broke the momentary silence with a grunt.

"You want to have at it again?" he offered, his voice low, a poor attempt at making it sound sultry. "I could skip breakfast."

"No! No. No." Adeline laughed. She held out her arm, palm forward wanting to stop him in his tracks. "This trip has turned you into more of a man than I can handle. Really, honey. I won't be able to walk if you do. Just leave me be and let me rest. Please?"

"Okay. But you better be ready tonight." He walked over to the bed and bent down for a kiss. Adeline turned her cheek. Not seeming to notice, Walter kissed it, squeezed Adeline's breast and said, "I have more of last night to offer." He smiled at her, walked over to the rack and retrieved his overcoat and hat. "Yeah, I think you're right. You do need your rest. I'll see you later this evening." He grabbed his cock through his pants, pushed out his hips toward her, gave that same little smirk then opened the door and left.

"Ugh. Finally." Adeline plopped back down on the pillow and made spitting noises pretending to spew the sickeningly sour taste from the lies she had told out of her mouth.

Yuck. I'll be damned if I go through that again, she thought. She decided that she'd have to get him so drunk that he'd come home after the inauguration ball and be able to do nothing more than pass out. She pulled the covers up over her face and let out a small scream. She just couldn't endure anymore of his jerking, gyrating antics, which he couldn't think pleased her.

What was I thinking about when I decided to get over Melvin and be a better wife? Surely that couldn't include what Walter had done to her earlier.

Adeline tossed and turned for the next three hours. Instead of out of sight out of mind, the longer she was away from Melvin, the deeper and stronger her yearnings for him grew. And the less she could tolerate Walter. It had been more than a year since she'd broken it off with Melvin and she needed him more now than ever.

Adeline kicked the covers off and padded off to take a shower. The warmth of the water might help relax the tension she felt entangled within. Stepping inside the steamy flow, she let the water beat down hard on her. Running over her bare skin, down her hair, over her breasts, she followed against the water's flow with her hand. Rubbing up from her inner thigh to her stomach, her hand worked in circles slowly moving up to her neck. Then sliding it back down she stopped right below her navel and started to cry. Her mind and body ached for Melvin.

Stepping out of the shower, she wrapped a towel around her body and swiped the condensation off the mirror. Leaning in she stared at herself.

"What is wrong with you?" She spoke to herself as she watched tears flow down her cheeks. "Beanie was a sixteen year old child who had the sense to run away from the things that tormented her and embrace her love of music and find happiness in a strange place. Yet you," she pointed at her reflection in the mirror, "stay with Walter, the tormentor, and push Melvin, the one thing that makes you happy, away." Adeline sat on the floor, her back against the tub, and held her face in her hands and sobbed.

After what seemed like more than a half an hour, Adeline pulled herself off the floor and got dressed. Pulling her hair back, she clipped it tight at the nape of her neck, slid on a silk babushka and her mink coat. She too had heard talk about where certain kinds of people would be and that's where she wanted to go.

The doorman of The Mayflower where she and Walter were staying hailed a cab for Adeline.

"Take me to the U Street Corridor," Adeline instructed as she entered the taxi.

"Ma'am, you sure you want to go there?" The black faced driver turned and looked at her warily.

"I'm sure. You can drop me off near 13th Street." While she had never been to the area she'd heard that it had been known as the Black Broadway and was in the Shaw neighborhood.

Shaw. A black neighborhood.

And she knew that Duke Ellington had been born on 13th Street. That, she figured, would be as good a place as any to start.

"It's your dime." The cabbie started the meter and took off down Connecticut Avenue, making a right on Rhode Island. After about five minutes, he spoke again. "You know with it being Inauguration Day and all, most folk is down on the Mall. Not too many savory people around up this way today."

"I just thought I'd get me something to eat," Adeline answered, not altering her stare out the window.

"I could take you to a restaurant, instead of dropping you off. Might be a little safer." He glanced at Adeline through his rearview mirror.

Adeline broke her stare and looked back at him, smiling at his worried eyes. "I'll be fine."

"How about Ben's Chili Bowl? It's on U Street. Right up here." He pointed toward the street with his finger.

"Chili? No. I wanted something different."

He met her eyes in the mirror. "Different," he asked. "Like what?"

"Oh, I don't know. Maybe some oxtail soup. Some cornbread, or maybe some pig's feet and black eyed peas."

The driver turned all the way around and looked at Adeline. "Pig's feet and black eyed peas?" He chuckled. "That's what you want to eat?"

"Mmm hmm." Adeline nodded.

"Ma'am, did you come here for the inauguration?"

"Yes I did."

"If you don't mind me saying, I think a better way to experience Washington D.C., especially since you seem to like politics, seeing you braved the cold to attend today's goings on, is to go to see the monuments. You know, like the Washington and Lincoln memorials. Or even get out of the cold and go over to the Smithsonian. You'd be much safer and probably find them more to your liking."

"My liking includes ox tails and black eyed peas and if you know a restaurant where I could find that, you can take me there. Otherwise, you can let me off just up there, " Adeline pointed ahead, "and I'll find something myself." Adeline started digging down in her purse to find money to pay her fare.

"No. I'll take you. I know just the place. The Florida Avenue Grill. It's at Florida Avenue and 11th Street. I'll take you there." He glanced up in his mirror. "And I'll come back and get you in an hour. How's that? Then you'll have a ride back."

Adeline smiled at him. "I'll be fine, you know. But not having to walk a long way in the cold is a good idea. You think an hour will be long enough?"

"Oh, yes ma'am. And I'll be back in one hour exactly. You keep inside and stay warm if you finish early. I'll be back to get you."

"Okay. I will." Adeline pulled the door open after the cab stopped in front of the restaurant. Leaning forward she handed him a twenty dollar bill before she got out the cab. "I'll see you in an hour."

Once inside the restaurant, memories of Melvin flooded her mind. It seemed her eyes found every dark-skinned man and tried to transform him into Melvin. She was finding it difficult to think, to breathe. She felt sad and sick, her stomach fluttered and her head ached.

She propped her head up with her hand and barely looked up when the waitress came over to take her order. Adeline did notice the cock-eyed look she got from the waitress when she told her that she'd have the fried catfish, macaroni and cheese, and a side of collard greens and cornbread. She ordered sweet tea to go with her meal and with the tears that she hadn't ordered, yet persistently fell down her cheeks.

After bringing Adeline her meal, and stealing glances at her as she spoke with one of the other waitresses, Adeline's waitress came over to fill up her water glass and said,

"Honey, whatever it is, just don't fight against it so hard. Give into those feelings, let it go and it'll get better."

"Thank you," Adeline said, lifting up her watery, red eyes to meet those of the waitress. Adeline didn't know quite what *she* meant, but she took it to mean something profound. She took it to mean that she should give in to her feelings for Melvin. Not to fight them, not push him out of her life. That was all it took. Just those few words from a stranger, who didn't know what was wrong with her, had made her know what she had to do.

She took the palms of her hands and swiped them across her face, wiping away her tears. She opened up the paper napkin and blew her nose in it.

That was it. She decided she was going back to Boston. Tonight. She was going back to Melvin. She was going back to being a part of his life, back to his arms, back to his bed.

She'd have that cabbie take her back to The Mayflower alright, but he'd have to wait for her. She was only going to stay there long enough to pick up her things, leave a note at the desk for Walter . . . hiding her face in her napkin, she giggled at that idea. What would she write to her husband on that note, *"Gone home to be with my man, see you when you get back"?* Because her next stop after leaving the hotel was going to be the Washington National Airport.

It wouldn't be the first time she just up and left Walter while they were on a trip.

Beaming with a broad smile on her face and not giving a care in the world to who saw the dramatic change in her demeanor, she all at once felt good. Thinking she'd need all her strength to do the things she wanted to do to Melvin to show him what he meant to her, she picked up the hot sauce, and sprinkled it all over her collard greens and catfish, and took in a mouthful.

Chapter Twenty-Three

May 16, 1961
Boston, Massachusetts

The lights were low, a lamp resting on each end table that flanked the sides of the white French provincial couch illuminated the living room. Smoke interlaced with the sweet, flowery smell of whiskey and rum permeated the air. And the conversations and laughter that filled the room was louder than the record player playing the 45 of Elvis Presley and the Jordanaires singing *Are You Lonely To-Night.*

"I'll call your five and put in another five."

"I'm out."

The girls' Tuesday Bridge Night had turned into Tuesday Party Night for everyone. There was more drinking, arguing and eating than there was playing cards, and as of late it wasn't the women playing Bridge but the men playing Poker.

The four men sat around the card table, smoking cigars with a bottle of Bacardi white rum in the center of the table. Cassie stood behind Glenn, and Helen had pulled up a chair and sat next to her husband, both close by as they watched their husbands lose game after game.

Walter was the winner tonight, but Adeline didn't fuss over him. He patted himself on the back enough. He didn't need her help. She sat on the couch with Arlene.

Although it started out as the girls' night, the four men of the couples that met every second Tuesday of the month, had invited themselves and had become a permanent addition.

There was a card table for the actual card playing, and the dining room table was used for the spread of food and the liquor. It was Adeline's turn to have it at her house. Jean had set up a feast that rivaled anything done by a professional caterer. It was still early for the group. Even though it was a weeknight, the "bridge" playing usually ended late.

The next record dropped and it was, Chubby Checker's *Pony Time.*

"Oohh," Cassie screeched. "I love this dance. C'mon Adeline, dance with me." She went to the couch and pulled Adeline up by the arm."

"*It's pony time, get up,*" Cassie sang with the record and beckoned for Arlene and Helen to join. "Let me see you do the pony, Liddie."

Boogety, boogety, boogety, boogety, shoo . . .

Adeline slid her feet back one at a time, alternating between hops on each foot. She shook her shoulders, like a pony prancing, and flipped the imaginary reins she held onto back and forth. Smiling she snapped her fingers and shook her head to the rhythm of the beat.

"Yeah, go Liddie!" Cassie called out, then sang the next words to the song, *"Now ya turn to the left when I say 'Gee.' You turn to the right when I say 'Haw.' Now gee' ya ya baby. Now haw . . ."*

Adeline turned to the left on cue, ponied over to Helen, grabbed her and at "haw" turned Helen to the right, but Helen's pony got twisted up and fell over into Adeline. Cassie reached over to catch them both and they all got tangled up, falling into the hi-fi, making the record skip.

Boogety, boogety, boogety, boogety, shoo . . . Chubby cried out.

The four of them doubled over with laughter and stumbled into the dining room.

"Oh Liddie, you're such a good dancer," Arlene said.

"Yes you are," Helen chimed in, "How did you learn to dance so well? I just can't get my feet right."

"That's because you've got two left feet," Cassie said. And they all broke into laughter again.

"Ladies! We can't hear ourselves think in here," came a booming voice from the living room.

"Well that's a surprise," Arlene winked and leaned into the others, lowering her voice, "I didn't know they knew how to think."

They all giggled at that, which brought Jean out of the kitchen.

"You ladies doing okay in here? It's a lot of commotion going on for a card game."

"Oh Jean, Liddie was just dancing circles around us." Cassie went over and put her arm around Jean's shoulder. "She's such a good dancer. Can you dance like that?"

"No ma'am, Mrs. Garrison's got me beat." Jean smiled at Adeline. "Now how about I get you ladies some fresh ice and you try my little sandwiches before they go bad?"

The ladies fixed plates for their husbands and nibbled from the table on the sandwiches and fruit salad Jean had made. Eventually, they all went back into the living room.

"Have you heard from President Kennedy, Liddie?" Arlene asked.

"Oh sure," Walter spoke up, "he called just last week, said he was in the neighborhood, was wondering if we wanted him to pick up our dry cleaning."

All the men laughed. "Oh Walter," Arlene said. "Liddie knows what I meant."

"What do you think about that space program your President is keen on, Walter? He's looking to put man on the moon."

Before Walter could speak, Helen asked, "Did you see the launch last week? I know you couldn't have missed it."

"It was May 5th, dear," Helen's husband answered. "Freedom 7 lifted off from Cape Canaveral making Alan Shepard the first American in space."

"Of course we saw that, Helen," Walter answered, looking at everyone giving a laugh. "No one would have missed that. It was history in the making. Did you think you were the only one that saw that?"

"Walter, leave my poor wife alone. She's trying to get more involved with current events. And I think she's doing a mighty fine job of it."

"I do too." Liddie smiled at Arlene.

"Is that the phone, honey?" Walter looked at Adeline.

"Yes, it is. Kind of late for phone calls." Adeline looked down at her watch. "Wonder who it could be. Ill go and get it in the bedroom. I'll never be able to hear down here."

Adeline hurried up the stairs and down the hallway to her and Walter's bedroom, and plopped down on the bed. As she pulled off her clip-on earring, she picked up the phone and put the receiver to her ear. "Hello."

"Hi Liddie. It's Beanie. Did I wake you?"

Liddie glanced over at the clock sitting on her nightstand. It was close to 10:30 pm. "Well, hello stranger," Adeline said, a smile crossing her lips. "No you didn't wake me. We're having Bridge night. I've been waiting for you to call. How is everything? You at work?" Putting her earring on the nightstand she spied a pack of cigarettes and took one out and lit it.

"No, not at work tonight. Im really good, though. Playing at the club is great. I'm learning so much and having so much fun."

"That's nice. I'm glad you're able to keep up with your piano playing. And I have a surprise for you once you get here. We're going to get you a piano."

"Piano? Liddie, really you shouldn't."

"Don't get so excited, you have to get here first. When are you coming?"

"I had planned to come this month, remember? But now something's come up."

"Now what?" Adeline said, leaning over to flick the ashes off her cigarette into the ashtray on the nightstand.

"Have you heard about the demonstrations that are going on?" Beanie asked.

"What demonstrations? What are you talking about?" Liddie felt her stomach flutter, and a warm rush seep out from her skin, she licked her lips.

"The things that are going on in the South - the sit-ins, the boycotts . . ."

"Oh my goodness, Beatrice, are you talking about all this stuff with the Negroes? I hope you're not getting involved with those people. How would you even know about that? Really Beanie that is none of your concern."

"But it is. It's all of our concern. And it's too late, I'm already involved."

"You're involved? What do you mean? You can't do anything about that. I thought you've just been playing at a jazz club."

"Yes, I am, but I got to meet a lot of Negroes working at the club."

"Beanie. You just need to stick with your friends, the ones you work with. Play your music, and get enough money together to come here to Boston. I can still send you the money if you want me to."

"No. Don't send me money. Really, I'm okay. And I am coming to Boston, I just have to go to Mississippi first."

"Mississippi? Beanie - "

"Liddie, I have to go, our ride to the bus station is here. I'll see you soon."

Liddie pulled the receiver down from her ear and stared at it. Beanie had just hung up on her. But that didn't worry her as much as Beanie's announcement that she was going to Mississippi to be a freedom rider.

Adeline placed the receiver in its cradle, slid her shoes off and rubbed her feet together. Playing back the conversation with Beanie in her head, Adeline acknowledged to herself that Beanie hadn't actually said the words *freedom rider*, yet Adeline knew that's exactly what was happening. Beanie was boarding a bus heading south to protest segregation.

Adeline's mouth went dry. She took a long drag on her cigarette and then smashed it up in the ashtray. A sense of dread came over her. Swallowing hard and running the tip of her tongue over her lips, Adeline retrieved her earring and clipped it back on.

Didn't she know that people – black and white – were getting killed in the South in these so called "non-violent" protests?

Adeline drew in a breath, let out a long sigh and unconsciously reached over for the pack of Pall Malls and the lighter. She placed the stick of tobacco between her lips and tried to steady her hand as she drug down the flint wheel. She stopped, hand midway to the end of the cigarette and flipped the lid of the lighter shut, extinguishing the flame.

Why would she risk her life to help a cause that doesn't even affect her?

Adeline flipped the lighter open again, lit the end of her cigarette, took a long drag, let it out and watched the smoke dissipate into the air.

"Are you okay?" Cassie came into the bedroom, sat down on the bed. She rubbed Adeline's shoulder. "You were taking a while on that phone call. I thought maybe something was wrong."

"No. Everything's okay. That was Beatrice. You know, my young friend."

"Is she okay?"

"Yes. She's fine." Adeline smiled at Cassie.

"Good. We don't want you drifting back into the blue funk you were in the past year. The only time you seemed happy was when you got a postcard or letter from Beanie."

"I'm okay now."

"You've been better than okay these past few months. Ever since you got back from the inauguration you've been nothing but smiles and sunshine. I think that trip really did you some good. I was so happy to have my best friend back."

"Yes. You're right, Cassie. That trip did me a world of good. More good than you could ever know." Adeline took a drag on her cigarette and smiled at Cassie.

Chapter Twenty-Four

May 17, 1961
Chicago, Illinois

"You sure you want to do this? You don't have to, you know." Byron paused at the door to the Greyhound bus and looked back at Beanie. "We'll understand if you don't want to go with us."

Beanie tucked a rolled up poster board under her arm and pushed on Byron's back, forcing him up the bus steps. "I said I'm going. Now get on the bus because you're holding up the line." Beanie looked back at Marcus and Carl right behind her, combed her fingers through her newly cropped shoulder length hair and said, "We're in it until we win it, right?"

Carl smiled showing a streak of white teeth against his dark skin. "Yep, we're in it 'til we win it." Behind them, a small group of people waited patiently to board the bus.

Some were fellow Freedom Riders, but the majority of the passengers were simply travelers trying to get from Chicago to destinations down south. It wasn't clear whether or not these people knew that they were about to become part of the Civil Rights Movement. But once they crossed the Mason Dixon Line, history would be made, and Beanie, along with all of her traveling companions, would be right in the middle of it.

A third of the way down the aisle, Byron stopped and stood so that Beanie could slide into the window seat next to him. She propped her rolled poster board against the back of the seat in front of her and leaned back in her seat. Both Carl and Marcus, each carrying similar posters, slid into separate seats toward the middle of the bus.

Byron leaned in and whispered, "So what did Liddie say when you told her you were going to be a Freedom Rider?"

"I didn't actually tell her that. I just said I was going to Mississippi first, and that I would come to Boston afterwards. She wasn't too happy about that. And I can't blame her. I've been telling her for over a year now that I would come to see her."

"It's not too late, you know. You can still change your mind."

Beanie looked at Byron intently. "I told you that I wanted to do this with you guys. It's important to me."

"Even if it's dangerous?"

"Don't worry about me, Byron, I'll be fine."

Byron leaned back in his seat. "All right then, I won't ask you again."

"Good, because the answer would be the same. We're in it 'til we win it." Beanie settled back in her seat and watched as a mixture of young Negro and white people carrying posters quietly boarded the bus. She thought about what Liddie said, *"I hope you're not getting involved . . . that's none of your concern"*. Liddie was probably just worried about her, and for good reason. Just this morning Carl got word that Freedom Riders were hurt three days ago in Anniston when a mob of angry people stoned the bus and slashed the tires. The bus was able to get away, but when the driver stopped to change the tires, the mob firebombed them. She hadn't had time to find out more about the attack, but made a mental note to ask Carl later what else had happened.

As the bus pulled out of the underground parking structure and turned left on to Lower Wacker Street, she prayed, *please don't let that happen to us.*

Watching the Chicago skyline grow smaller and smaller out Beanie's window, made her think of the first time she saw the jagged skyscrapers, almost a year ago to the day. Oh, how much her life had evolved during that year. She never thought that she would still be in Chicago, nor did she ever imagine that she would be sitting on a bus with a group of students ready and willing to make a stand against segregation. But here she was, sitting on a bus next to her best friend. The world only saw him as a Negro. But she saw him as an intelligent, kind, caring man who played a mean sax and would one day become a great doctor. She reached over, touched his right hand and said, "I'm really glad we are doing this together. It's important to me."

Byron looked at her and smiled. "I'm glad you're here, too. I really didn't want to spend two weeks alone with those knuckleheads back there." He tossed his head in the direction of his friends. "They can get pretty rowdy. And now that we've all graduated college, they're extra anxious to sow some wild oats."

Beanie glanced back at Carl and Marcus. "They'll be fine. It's a peaceful demonstration. We're not going there to fight. We're just trying to make a statement."

Byron pushed up his right sleeve and scratched at a scarred splotch on his forearm. "Let's just hope the authorities agree with you once we cross over into Kentucky."

Beanie looked down at the scar on his arm. "What happened there?"

"Oh that?" He rolled down his shirtsleeve. "I got burned when I was two. I was playing by the stove and accidently some hot water got dumped on my arm."

"Looks like it hurts."

"Not so much anymore, but it itches sometimes. I guess it was pretty bad at the time. My grandmother said that my mother cried and shook so hard when it happened that you would've thought she was the one who got hurt."

"Where is your mother now?"

"She's dead. Died when I was little."

"I'm so sorry." Byron didn't offer more, so Beanie didn't pursue the subject.

They talked some and napped some, making the long bus ride enjoyable.

Somewhere along the rolling green hills of Kentucky, Byron asked, "So why do they call you Beanie?"

Beanie pulled her eyes away from the dark pink redbud trees and white dogwoods dotting the changing landscape. "It's kind of silly, really. When I was little, I stuck a jellybean up my nose. My parents had to take me to the doctor to have it removed. When he got it out, the doctor shook it at me and said, 'No more beanies up the nosies.' So from that moment on, everyone called me Beanie." She looked at Byron. "How about you? Did you ever have a nickname?"

Byron scrunched his nose. "Nah, just Byron."

Sometime later, Carl leaned over the seat in front of Byron and Beanie and said, "Hey, you two, wake up. We're pulling in to Nashville." He had changed seats during the nine-hour bus ride. "We're gonna pick up a few more riders here, and then we'll be on our way to Birmingham."

Beanie yawned, "Shall we use our signs here?" She nodded to the poster still rolled up and leaning against the seat.

"No, we'll wait until we get to Birmingham, and then we'll all stick them out the windows at the same time." Carl leaned down a little closer to them. "Let's just pray we don't run into the same situation as the others did."

"Do you know if any of the riders were hurt in the Anniston attack?" said Beanie.

Carl lowered his voice. "Most got away with only minor injuries. But some on another bus about an hour behind them were nearly beaten to death with metal pipes."

Beanie whispered. "That's horrible. What happened?"

Byron leaned in a little closer. "From what I understand, the mob stopped their vehicles in front of the bus, forcing it to stop. They kept pushing on the door of the bus until it broke, and then they rushed inside and started beating people."

Marcus walked up the aisle, leaned on Byron's seat and joined in on the conversation. "I heard that some of the mob laid down in front of the bus to keep it from moving forward."

"If I'd been driving, I'd a just run 'em over," whispered Carl.

Beanie swallowed. "And we're headed right into that?"

"No, we'll be some sixty miles away from there," Carl told her.

That small amount of distance did little to comfort Beanie. She thought about their final destination in Jackson, Mississippi, a little over two hundred miles from Birmingham. "What about Jackson? Has there been any trouble there?"

"I haven't heard about any. But, remember, we're going to be one of the first buses to arrive, so . . ." Carl's words trailed off as he shrugged his shoulders.

Beanie stared at all three of them and thought *maybe I should have listened to Liddie . . .*

The three hours from Nashville to Birmingham gave Beanie ample time to think. She cared a great deal for Byron and his friends. And she truly wanted to help them in their fight for equality. She looked out the window, hoping their short layover in Alabama would be uneventful.

Though she tried to sleep, her anxiety over what may come in Mississippi made it difficult. But she closed her eyes, forcing rest until they got to the next stop. As they pulled into the Birmingham bus terminal, Carl said, "We're here. Get your signs ready."

Beanie, along with seventeen other Freedom Riders, slid their windows open. But before they could unroll their posters and hang them out the window, three policemen boarded the bus with their hands positioned close to their pistols and their batons drawn.

The first officer wearing a gray uniform, mirrored sunglasses and a dark blue policeman's hat strolled down the aisle tapping the baton in his palm. He stopped in front of Byron and Beanie and looked down at them for a prolonged moment. Then he turned and slowly walked back up to the front of the bus, turned back around and said with a deep southern drawl, "Y'all are under arrest for violating the Jim Crow law. So Im gonna need ya to follow these gentlemen off this here bus and head on over to that paddy wagon." He nodded in the direction of a police van with bars on the windows. "And I don't want no trouble from anyone, ya hear? We don't wanna shoot ya, but we will if we have ta."

Beanie grabbed hold of Byron's hand and whispered through the side of her mouth, "What are we going to do?" She tried to force the panic out of her voice.

Byron stared straight ahead. "We're going to do just as the officer says."

When Beanie got off the bus, she nearly cried. An angry mob, just like the one Carl told her about, stood along side the road carrying rocks, sticks and shotguns. They screamed obscenities and hurled rocks at the riders as Beanie and the others followed the policemen toward the waiting van.

From a few feet behind them, Beanie heard Marcus scream. She turned and saw a big gash across his forehead and a large rock at his feet. She started to pull a tissue out of her purse, but Byron stopped her. "But he needs it, Byron. He's bleeding."

"He'll be fine. Let's just get to the van before it happens to us."

An hour and a half later, the riders had been booked, mug shots taken, and placed in a large holding cell.

That night Beanie sat on the floor of the jail and leaned against the wall with Byron on one side of her and Marcus and Carl on the other side. Old tears had stained her cheeks hours ago, but they still kept coming as if she had an endless supply of them. "What's going to happen to us?" she sniffed. "How long are we going to have to stay here?"

Carl stretched his arms up and rolled his neck around. "It depends. We'll have to be arraigned first, go to trial, and if we're found guilty, we'll be convicted and sent to prison."

"Prison. I can't go to prison." Beanie started to cry again.

Byron put his arm around her. "Shut up, Carl. We're not going to prison just for riding a bus for crying out loud We may get a fine or we might even have to spend the night in jail. But we're not going to prison."

Marcus felt the tender lump on his head and said, "If we were in Chicago, I'd say you're right, Byron. But down here, the rules are different. So it's hard to say what they'll do with us."

Carl leaned over and said, "Did you see all those reporters out there when we got off the bus? There must have been at least a dozen, plus television cameras. I'll bet we're in the news, maybe we'll even get our picture in Life Magazine."

"Well a lot of good that's going to do us in here," said Beanie as more tears dribbled down her cheeks.

A few moments later, the policeman who had arrested them walked up to the cell and stood by the door. "Listen up, y'all. Today's your lucky day." He unlocked the door, opened it and said, "Remember that mob out there? Well, I've just been informed that they're a comin' back tomorrow with reinforcements, too many for my boys to handle. So y'all are leaving my city tonight. Now git up off your Negra asses and let's go."

Beanie and the others stood up. They clustered together but didn't move. She grabbed Byron's hand, pulled him closer and whispered, "I'm scared. What if there's a lynch mob outside just waiting for us?"

Carl leaned in. "Could be a trap. Maybe he's going to take us out back and kill us."

Beanie gasped and squeezed Byron's hand tighter. Byron turned to Carl and hissed, "Shut the hell up. What's wrong with you?"

"You willing to just follow him out into the black of night? What's wrong with *you*, Byron?" Carl asked.

The two friends glared at each other until the policeman said, "C'mon, let's go. We ain't got all night."

Not sure of their fate, the group reluctantly followed the officer down the dimly lit hall to the back door of the jailhouse.

He unlocked the door, opened it and pointed to the same police van they arrived in. "So here's what we gonna do. Ya'll gonna get back in that there paddy wagon, and Im gonna drive ya to the border of Tennessee and drop ya off there. You're gonna go home, and you ain't never coming back here. Cuz' if I see ya, I'll arrest ya. And the next time, I won't be lettin' ya go. Understand?"

Beanie was about to walk out the door when the policeman leaned in to her and said, "You best mind the company you keep. I'd hate to see that pretty little white face of yours splattered all over the road somewhere." His eyes traced her body, and then he grinned. "Or worse."

She hurried through the door before he could say anything else to her.

All eighteen Freedom Riders wedged back into the police van and huddled together as the vehicle pulled away from the police station and lumbered down the road. Though Beanie couldn't know it for sure, she surmised that all of them were frightened and thinking the same thing: *God, please don't let us die tonight.*

Three hours later, they all stood along side the deserted road watching the red glow of the van's tail lights get smaller and smaller. He dropped them off on the state line, just like he said he would.

As the group walked the fifteen miles to Fayetteville, all Beanie could think about was how she was going to break the news to Liddie.

Dear Liddie,
Guess what? My friends and I were just arrested in Birmingham, Alabama for being Freedom Riders . . .

Chapter Twenty-Five

Hildale, Utah
May, 1961

Orson sat at his desk staring at the grainy black and white photograph on the front page of the Salt Lake City Tribune. It looked like her, but the hair was different, shorter. She and a bunch of coloreds were being escorted off of a Greyhound bus by several armed police officers. At first he passed over the story because of the title: Freedom Riders Arrested in Birmingham, Alabama. He had no interest in what the Negroes down south were doing. *Trouble makers,* he would say to Margaret and Dorothy. *They're nothing but troublemakers. They're the devil and they should all be put behind bars.* But when he saw the vaguely familiar face among them, he picked up the paper and read the story.

"Why?" he said to the image of his wife. "Why would you shame me like this, Beatrice?" *Beatrice.* He hadn't said her name in nearly a year. He'd thought about her, but he never spoke of her to the family. After all, she had shamed them too. When she ran away, and he found out that she took a bus to Chicago, his first instinct was to go after her. And he did. But sixty miles down the road, he pulled the car off on to the shoulder, pounded on the steering wheel, and then turned the car around. He realized that trying to find her in a city the size of Chicago was a ridiculous idea.

But this time, he knew exactly where Beatrice Peterson was hiding - in a Birmingham, Alabama jailhouse.

He ripped the story from the newspaper, folded it into a small square and tucked it into his jacket pocket. He yelled out his open office door, "Margaret! Margaret!" When she didn't respond, he yelled louder, "Margaret, my office."

Margaret rushed into his office, her hand still holding on to a dishtowel. "Goodness, Orson, what's wrong. Is the house on fire?"

"I'd like you to pack a bag for me, enough for at least a week."

"A week? Where are you going?"

Orson stood up and stared out his office window. "I'm going to Alabama. I have some unfinished business to tend to."

Chapter Twenty-Six

Jackson, Mississippi
1961

Beanie sat at the small kitchen table drinking a cup of coffee, while Byron, Marcus and Carl sat with the other riders in the living room. She could hear them arguing about whether or not to split up or continue on as one group. Now that they had reached Mississippi, some wanted to go through Georgia and some through the Carolinas. She looked at the Negro woman standing over by the counter holding a coffee pot and said, "Thank you so much for letting us meet here tonight. We really appreciate you opening your home to us."

The woman walked over to Beanie, topped off her cup and said, "When my nephew first told me he was doing this, I warned him that this wasn't gonna be no simple thing. People just don't change overnight, ya know? It takes time, especially when things been a certain way for a long time. Just because a bunch of young folk decide to sit on a bus, don't mean that people are gonna accept Negroes and whites as equals." She smiled at Beanie. "But I admire you for trying." She walked out of the kitchen with the pot of coffee and said, "Anybody want more coffee?"

Beanie looked down at the small stack of blank postcards in front of her. She had promised herself to write to Liddie as often as she could. She hadn't written in a long time and she had so much to say she decided to write a letter instead. Taking a sheet of stationery from the box she carried with her, she wrote:

June 15, 1961

Dear Liddie,

You'll be happy to know that the freedom ride from Fayetteville to Jackson, Mississippi went much more smoothly than our ride to Birmingham. However, we did encounter some resistance as we neared Jackson. Our bus was followed by a group of men in pick up trucks. They shot out our back window, but the driver just kept going until he met up with a line of sheriffs on the outskirts of Jackson. They escorted us right to the bus station.

We went to the First Baptist Church in Montgomery a couple of weeks ago to listen to Dr. Martin Luther King Jr. speak. Since he is such a supporter of the Freedom Riders, we felt it was our duty to support him. There were at least fifteen hundred worshippers and activists stuffed into that church. During Dr. King's speech, people outside the church threw bricks and tear gas through the windows. My friends and I were very scared, but we made it out of there unharmed.

We've decided to go to Georgia to listen to Dr. King speak again. I'll come to Boston sometime after that. Will write more later.

Love,
Beanie

As the months progressed, Beanie, Byron, Carl and Marcus continued to travel the Deep South with fellow freedom riders spreading their message of equality. Beanie finally sent a postcard to Joe apologizing for not returning to Smoky Joe's as promised after two weeks, but that there had been a change in plans. She hoped that the band had been able to replace her and Byron with acceptable musicians. She asked Joe if he wouldn't mind boxing up her few belonging and keeping them in the office until she could return for them. And then she apologized again for leaving him in the lurch.

And for the most part, Beanie kept her promise, informing Liddie of their travels and adventures, but leaving out details. She hadn't told Liddie about being attacked by the Klu Klux Klan outside of Montgomery. Nor did she tell her about some of the riders being arrested and sent to Parchment Prison in Jackson. She figured that all Liddie would have to do is read a newspaper to find out about those stories. And if Liddie happened to mention them the next time they talked, then Beanie would give her all the details.

The late September weather remained unseasonably hot and muggy in Jackson, Mississippi. And it looked like today would be no different. Only nine o'clock on this Saturday morning, and already the temperature had shot past eighty degrees, making Beanie long for the cool crisp breezes that came down from Salt Lake's Wasatch Mountain Range. She missed the weather there, but nothing else. She looked down at her stack of blank post cards and thought: *maybe I should send one to Mama just to let her know where I am and that I'm okay.* She pulled out one of the cards, fanned herself with it for a moment and then wrote:

September 23, 1961

Dear Liddie,

Yesterday we had our first real victory. The Interstate Commerce Commission issued an order stating that all the 'whites only' signs must be taken down at every bus and rail station across the South.

My friends and I have been staying with the families of fellow riders, sleeping in sleeping bags on the floor. It's not very comfortable and not very private, but at least we're safe.

I miss talking with you.

Love,

Beanie.

As soon as she set the pen down, Byron walked into the kitchen and said, "Hey, we're going for a walk. You wanna come?"

Beanie looked up from the postcard and said, "Where you going?"

"Marcus, Carl and I are going to take a walk around the neighborhood before it gets too hot, maybe stop at Bailey's Drugstore for a soda."

"Sure. I've got to mail this postcard to Liddie anyway."

"Great. Here, I'll keep that." He took the postcard and slipped it in his back pocket. "I'm pretty sure there's a mail box inside of Bailey's. At least I think I've seen one in there. Things seem so different than they did when I lived here."

Beanie pushed the screen door open and stepped out onto the porch. "I didn't know you lived here before."

"Yeah, when I was little. I lived about a mile from here." He looked back at Carl and Marcus and said, "Hey, you guys want to go see the area where I used to live?"

"Sure. Might as well. I'd love to," the three said in unison.

Meager, neatly kept houses lined each of the blocks they walked. Children played and laughed in their yards while the adults congregated on porches. The houses reminded Beanie of her parents' place back home. But the stares thrown at Beanie as she walked by confirmed that she was out of place.

After a twenty-five minute walk, Byron stopped in front of a vacant lot. A wild garden of weeds weaved in and out of a sagging wire fence that lined the back and sides.

"I thought somebody would have rebuilt here by now," said Byron.

Beanie stood next to him. "Is this were you used to live?"

"Yes, with my grandmother."

"What happened, man?" Marcus wanted to know.

"I don't remember all of the details because I was only four or five. But I remember waking up in the middle of the night. Smoke was everywhere, and I started coughing. I got scared, ran out of the house and hid. My grandmother and a boy died in that fire."

"Oh my goodness, Byron. Who was the child?" Beanie said.

"My grandmother was keeping another child – babysitting for a couple who had gone out of town." He looked back at what remained of his childhood. "For a long time, people thought it was me who died in the fire because it took them a couple of days to find me and then I left from around here after that. I went to live with some relatives down in Decatur."

"Isn't Medgar Evers from Decatur, Mississippi?" Carl asked.

"Yeah, he is. I found out that my mother was good friends with him when they were little," Byron said and nodded. "She used to go down there and visit with the same aunt who raised me. That's how she met him."

Beanie reached over and gently touched Byron's arm. "I'm really sorry. It must have been very difficult for you, losing everyone at such a young age."

Byron patted her hand and smiled. "What do you say we go get that soda?"

Fifteen minutes later, as they started to cross Raymond Street, Carl stopped and said, "You guys go ahead. I think I'm going to go down to Woolworth's instead."

Byron looked at him and sighed. "C'mon, Carl. Can't you forget about it just for one day?"

"Forget about it? You think Dr. King forgets about it for even one minute?" Carl sounded indignant.

Byron and Carl glared at each other for several seconds. Finally Byron said, "Fine, but take Marcus with you just in case there's trouble. We'll meet you back at the house in a couple of hours."

The foursome crossed the street, split up, and walked in opposite directions. When Byron and Beanie reached the drugstore, Byron motioned to the wooden bench by the door and said, "You stay here. I'll be back in a minute. What do you want to drink?"

"I don't care, just something cold."

A few minutes later, Byron returned, sat down next to her on the bench and handed her an opened bottle of Fresca "I mailed your postcard to Liddie."

"Thank you." She took a big gulp. "I miss talking to her."

"So why don't you call her?" He pointed his bottle of soda down the block. "There's a phone booth right over there."

Beanie smiled. "Good idea. I'll call her when we're finished." Then she took another long sip, and they sat and talked for a while longer.

Byron leaned on the outside of the phone booth while Beanie stepped in, leaving the door open, and dialed the operator. A moment later, Beanie heard Liddie's voice.

"Hello."

The operator said, "Do you accept a collect call from Beatrice Peterson?"

"Yes."

When the operator hung up, Beanie said, "Hi Liddie, how are you?"

"Beanie, where are you?"

"My friends and I are still here in Jackson. I just mailed you a postcard. But I wanted to hear your voice."

"Tell me who these friends of yours are. Are they Negroes?"

Beanie was taken aback by her directness. "Yes, some of them."

"Beanie, you need to stop this and come to Boston right now before you get hurt."

Beanie grew quiet for a moment, and then said, "So what are your plans for Thanksgiving?" Before Liddie could answer, Beanie heard shouting. She looked up and saw Marcus and Carl running across Raymond Street toward them. As they got closer, she saw blood dripping from Carl's nose and staining the front of his shirt. "Liddie, I've got to go. My friends are in trouble." Then she hung up.

Back at the house, when Carl went into the bathroom to clean up, Marcus whispered to Byron and Beanie, "When we saw those white guys standing by the door at Woolworth's and holding baseball bats, I told Carl it wasn't a good idea, that we should just turn around and catch up with you guys. He said that he wasn't doing anything wrong, just going to Woolworth's, that's all. I could tell he wanted to push it."

"Is that when they gave him the bloody nose?" Byron asked.

Marcus nodded. "They were egging us on, calling us *boy*. And when Carl tried to get past them, one of them punched him in the face. So I grabbed Carl by the shirt, pulled him away from them before they could do anything worse. And then we ran."

Byron glanced at the bathroom door, the water still running. He shook his head and whispered, "I sure hope he's not becoming a loose cannon."

Chapter Twenty-Seven

July 25, 1942

Hattie Jean was happy when she hopped down the steps off the city bus and started the fifteen minute walk to her aunt and uncle's house. She had been in Chicago nearly two years, finishing school, thinking about starting college there, but this was the first time in those two years that she had gone out to have a good time. Even in the sweltering 101 degree heat that had plagued Chicago since the day before, Hattie Jean practically skipped along.

She had met a man - handsome, well-educated man, the week before. She had gone downtown for the first time and wandered around and stumbled upon him. She smiled. "What are the chances?"

She pictured going out on a date with him. She doodled their names on her writing paper. He had sent her a letter just as he promised and she slept with it under her pillow every night since. Maybe, she dreamed, maybe he would even marry her. Those dreams seemed to drown out her reality.

Her aunt and uncle were so gracious to help her and the baby. They'd watch him while she had gone out on her excursions, even encouraged her to "Get out. See the city."

When she got enough money, she had decided, she was going to move her mother to the North. Things were so much better here. People were kinder and colored folk had a better chance. Plus, she didn't know if she could face those people in Mississippi ever again.

Hattie Jean bounded into the house, expecting her little toddler to come running up to her. Instead, she was met by her uncle's solemn face.

"You need to go to the hospital, baby." Her uncle put his arm around her. "I waited here to tell you and drive you over."

"Tell me what? Where's my baby?"

"Your aunt went with him. She stayed with him the whole time."

"My baby?"

"He had an accident. He's hurt pretty bad."

Hattie Jean's knees buckled under her and she dropped toward the floor. Her uncle grabbed her and took her and sat her in a chair. He went in the kitchen got her a glass of water and said, "We should get there as soon as we can." Hattie Jean looked up at him, he nodded his head. "C'mon, I don't know how much time we have."

Hattie Jean's uncle had to hold her up as she walked down the hallway to her son's room at the hospital. When she walked in the room, she saw him, little and helpless lying in the bed, gauze covering him up. Her aunt stood up when she came in the room and walked over to her.

"Baby. Come on over here and see him. They don't know if he gone make it or not."

Hattie Jean looked at her with terror in her eyes. "He was fine when I left home this morning."

Her aunt looked over at her husband. "I know, baby. But you know, God works in mysterious ways. We don't know what He might have in store for us."

Hattie Jean pulled away from her aunt's embrace. "Not my baby. He can't have my baby. I refuse to let him go."

Hattie Jean sat at the hospital all day, every day. Praying, crying, and begging the doctor's to "Do something more. Do something to help my baby." But no day did they offer much hope.

Ophelia came up from Mississippi to be with her daughter and grandson, sorry now she had sent them away. And once Hattie Jean's mother got there the two of them prayed twice as much, and twice as hard.

It only took six months for God to answer their prayers.

And as soon as the toddler was well enough to leave the hospital, Hattie Jean packed up her things, got her baby and boarded the bus back to Mississippi. Back to her mother. Back to where she knew her baby would be safe.

And all the dreams she had of having a life with the man she'd met in Chicago got packed away, too.

When she got home, she clung to her son. Never letting him out of her sight, hovering over him every minute.

"You can't stay here, you know," Ophelia told Hattie Jean one day, just out of the blue.

"If you want to make something of yourself, you got to leave from down here. All you do all day is chase after that boy. Give him some breathin' room and go make something out of your life."

Hattie Jean looked at her mother and then at her son. Then at the scar from the accident that covered nearly his entire right arm. "I'll do fine down here. I couldn't leave my little buddy with nobody to watch while I went to school."

"He's not your buddy, you know. That's your chile and if you gone be able to care for him, you got to get an education. Lessen you wanna clean white folks' houses all your life like I done."

"It's hard, momma, taking care of a baby and going to school."

Ophelia laughed. "You think I don't know that? What you think that I did with you after your daddy died. God rest his soul. I had to take care of you all by my lonesome."

"I just don't know, momma."

"Well I do. Couldn't have felt no prouder of you when you was up in Chicago going to school, actin' like them big city girls. Made me feel like I was gone be somebody. You gone back up to Chicago, and get that college degree you was telling me about. I'll keep the baby here with me."

Hattie Jean stared at her son. "C'mere, my little buddy." She picked him up. "Would you miss your momma if I went off to school?"

"Momma. Put me down," he cried out.

"See there," Ophelia said. "He don't even want to be bothered with you none."

Hattie Jean put him down and he ran off into the other room, squealing with laughter.

"Maybe, I could," she mumbled.

"Ain't no maybe to it. I got a little money saved up. We can go down to the bus station and get you a ticket."

"Whoa, Momma. I didn't say I'd do it. I'd miss the baby so much."

"He'll be here when you get back."

Hattie Jean decided to go. Maybe she could have a life. Just maybe. She knew her mother would take good care of the baby. But just thinking of leaving her buddy brought tears to her eyes.

Her mother didn't give her a chance to back out. She made her dress in her Sunday best, white gloves and bought Hattie Jean a new hat and a new pair of shoes. "You might have to do a lotta walkin'. You gone need a good pair of shoes," she had said. And then Ophelia rolled the money up in a handkerchief and pinned it to the underside of Hattie Jean's dress.

"Now," Ophelia said. "This a'way you won't lose it." She smoothed her hand over Hattie Jean's dress. "When you get to the bus station, get your ticket and don't say nothin' to nobody. Get on the back of the bus and just stay there, even after you cross the Mason-Dixon Line. That way you won't run into no trouble."

"I know, Momma. It ain't like I never rode a bus before." Hattie Jean turned around and found her son playing with a truck on the floor. "C'mere, Buddy." She picked him up. "Momma gone call you when I get to Chicago. You stay he re with your grandmother and be good. Give your momma a kiss." The toddler puckered up and gave Hattie Jean a kiss and then tried to get down out of her arms.

"Put him down, Hattie Jean. He gone get you dirty. Here." She handed Hattie Jean a brown bag. "I packed you a lunch. It's a long trip so don't eat it all at once."

"Yes, ma'am."

"Now git!"

Hattie Jean went down to the bus station, and gazed up at the "Ticket" sign. In the background she heard "Last call, for Boston, Massachusetts via Nashville, Frankfort and all points north. Now boarding for Chicago, Illinois via Memphis at Gate 5."

Hattie Jean walked up to the ticket counter to get her ticket out of Mississippi and to start her new life.

Chapter Twenty-Eight

Jackson, Mississippi
February 1, 1962

Byron stuck his head into the kitchen. "Hurry up, Beanie. We gotta go."

"Be right there." Beanie grabbed a hand full of NAACP brochures from a large stack sitting on the kitchen table and shoved them into her knapsack. As she walked past him she said, "I just finished reading the new brochure."

"What'd you think of it?"

"Compelling, especially that picture of the NAACP president's wife being dragged down the street by two white policemen." She put on her jacket, threw her pack over her shoulder and said, "I was surprised to read that more than a thousand demonstrators have already been arrested in the south. That means the Movement is growing."

Byron opened the screen door and stepped onto the porch. "And it's spreading. Oklahoma, Kansas, Texas. People are finally beginning to realize that this isn't some college fad that will fade away like panty raids or telephone booth stuffing. It has deep motivation and purpose."

Carl stood on the sidewalk with Marcus. He shoved his hands in his pocket to keep them warm and said, "Hurry up, you guys. If we miss this bus, we won't make it to Maryland in time." He turned to walk briskly in the direction of the bus stop.

Beanie trotted to keep up, pulling her jacket tighter to keep out the frigid morning breeze. "When's the sit-in?"

Without breaking stride, Carl pulled up his collar to block the wind and said, "It's scheduled for the 3rd in Chestertown, Maryland. And we're all supposed to meet at Bethel Church on College Street at eleven o'clock."

"Have you heard if they chose a location yet for the sit-in?" Marcus asked, moving alongside Carl. "I know they had several different locations picked out."

Carl shook his head. "We won't know until we get there. They don't want the location leaked. Less chance of a mob attack that way."

Beanie brought up the rear. She scooted up next to Byron and said, "What about all of the other riders? Are they going to meet us there?"

Carl looked back at her but didn't slow his pace. "We're all splitting up this time. There are sit-ins and demonstrations scheduled in Huntsville, Nashville, and Greensboro. They're all over the place. And there are probably a lot more that we don't even know about. People are just joining in and making a stand for equality. We're no longer being called Freedom Riders. They're calling us Freedom Fighters."

I miss Chicago, Beanie thought as they hurried to the bus stop. She missed playing the piano at Smokey Joe's, and she missed listening to Byron play his sax. Those were simpler days back then. And at times she yearned for them. Like now. But the desire to be a part of the Civil Rights Movement and the conviction to win the battle for equality, no matter the cost, remained steadfast in her heart. They'd made such great strides since their first Freedom ride last May. People were starting to take notice. They were beginning to listen to the plight of the Negroes. And more supporters were joining the Movement every day. But the battle to end segregation was far from over. Hopefully it would be, one day soon. And if she ever found herself back in Chicago, sitting at Joe's old piano, then it meant that it was over, and they had won.

It took the foursome two days to travel the thousand miles to Chestertown, Maryland. But when they got there, they were met by fellow freedom fighters who accompanied them on foot the few blocks to Bethel Church. Though it was Friday, the swarms of people moving from the parking lot, up the steps and through the sanctuary doors made it feel more like Easter Sunday.

Once inside, a low excited murmur coming from the nearly two hundred activists seated in the pews resonated through the church. Beanie slid in to one of the pews in the back, followed by Byron, Marcus and then Carl. She leaned over to Byron and whispered, "I was thinking that after this I might just head up to Boston to go see Liddie. It's not that far from here, and since I've never made it there, I thought this would be a good time. What do you think?"

"I think it's a good idea. You've been talking about going to see her for as long as I've known you. This is as good a time as any. How long do you think you'd be gone?"

Beanie shrugged, "I don't know, a week, a month, a year? We're not very good at keeping to a schedule, you know." She looked at Byron, making him chuckle.

"Well, you're right about that." He leaned back in his seat. Then a moment later he leaned over again and said, "Just drop me a postcard from time to time."

Beanie flashed him a mock scowl. "You making fun of me?"

Byron smiled. "Wouldn't dream of it."

From the pulpit a deep voice said, "Thank you all for coming. My name is Reverend Frederick Jones."

Beanie peeked in between heads to get a better look at the man behind the voice. An older gentleman wearing a dark blue suit smiled at the crowd. His skin was dark against the stark white of his shirt collar and the gray tight curls on his head. He pulled a pair of gold wire rim glasses from his breast pocket and put them on. Then he held up a pamphlet and said, "For those of you who haven't seen the new NAACP brochure, we have a bunch of them on the information tables along the back walls. Please take them with you today and pass them out."

Beanie recognized the pamphlet to be the same as the ones in her pack. A picture of a large group of Negroes and whites wedged in around a Woolworth's lunch counter was on the front cover with the slogan, "The Day They Changed Their Minds" in bold lettering across the bottom.

Reverend Jones set the brochure down and picked up a piece of paper. He seemed to study it for a moment and then said, "This is the list of target locations that we believe are known to use trespassing laws to maintain racial segregation. The place that we've chosen for today's rally is Bud Hubbard's Bar."

Murmurs caused the reverend to raise his hands and say, "Please, everyone. Quiet down. I know that this may come as a surprise to some of you. And for those of you who are not familiar with Hubbard's Bar, Mr. Hubbard is notorious for refusing to serve Negroes."

A man sitting in the middle of the church stood up and yelled, "Hubbard is an instigator. Last time he called the cops on us."

Someone else stood up and said, "Yeah, man, it was a bad scene. He filled the bar with his buddies, gave them free beer, and tried to get them to fight us. We had to beat feet before any of us got hurt."

Another voice yelled out, "Let's go tear it up down there."

The Reverend raised his hands and said, "People, may I remind you, this is a non-violent demonstration. We will speak softly and politely. And we will enter and leave the premises in a peaceful and orderly manner. There will be no fighting, no exchanging of bad words, nothing that would give reason for the law to come and arrest us. Is that understood?" He gripped the pulpit and looked around the church. "We are not here to fight with our fists. We are here to enlighten this nation about the humiliating, one-sided access to life that this callous practice of segregation dramatizes. We are here to change minds and notions. And today with the good Lords help, we will succeed."

The church erupted into applause and shouts of solidarity, including Beanie and her three friends.

The demonstrators were divided into groups of twenty and instructed to arrive at Bud Hubbards bar at thirty-minute intervals. Beanie and her friends had been assigned to the first group. As soon as they neared the bar, Beanie felt apprehensive. The loud laughter, shouts and cheers of the crowd inside caused her to lean into Byron and say, "I have a bad feeling about this. I think they knew we were coming."

"If they stop us from entering, we'll leave and the next group will try. And we'll do this again and again until they let us in."

Though it didn't ease her angst, she nodded and followed her group to the bar's entrance.

The place was jam packed with people drinking beer. Beanie could barely hear over the loud ruckus. But as soon as they stepped over the bar's threshold, the crowd grew quiet. They turned and stared at the demonstrators for what seemed like forever. Then someone shouted, "Let's get 'em!"

Suddenly, a stampede of angry white men descended upon them, pushing them out onto the sidewalk and into the street. Beanie lost her footing, tripped over the curb and fell. When Byron reached down to help her, two white men grabbed him, threw him to the ground and started hitting him.

"Byron!" screamed Beanie. She wanted to help him, but the crowd pinned her to the street. Then she saw Carl and Marcus run to Byron's aid. But the crowd swallowed them up, too.

Baseball bats and fists swung freely until sirens forced them to stop. When the crowd scattered, Beanie scrambled to her feet and cried out at the sight in front of her. Five fellow demonstrators lay bleeding in the street. Among them lay Carl and Byron.

An hour later Beanie sat in the emergency room of Chestertown's hospital. Instead of taking the wounded demonstrators to a Negro hospital in Annapolis, some fifty miles away, they brought them here. Though predominately white, the hospital had designated eight beds strictly for Negroes. And Byron and Carl laid in two of those beds.

Wadded and shredded tissues littered her lap. They'd been there for three hours with no word from the doctors regarding the state of Carl and Byron's conditions.

Marcus walked up and handed Beanie a Styrofoam cup of coffee. He sat down on the chair next to her, leaned on his elbows, with his head cradled in his hands and said, "This wasn't supposed to happen."

"Well, it did. And now they're lying in a hospital bed fighting for their lives." She took a sip of the lukewarm coffee, looked at Marcus and said, "What are we going to do?"

Marcus leaned back against the chair, his foot tapping with nervous energy. "There's nothing we can do except wait."

Beanie was tired of waiting, and she was upset that no one had given them any new information. She looked over toward the admittance counter. "Surely they must know something by now."

"I'll go check." Marcus stood up and walked over to the desk. He spoke to the woman seated behind the counter who, in turn, called for a nurse.

Beanie watched as the nurse spoke with Marcus for a moment, and then gestured toward an empty seat close by. Once Marcus sat down, the nurse hurried through double doors into some other part of the hospital.

Another fifteen minutes passed with still no word from the nurse.

"I can't take this any longer," muttered Beanie. She stood up and walked to a public phone that hung on the back wall. Then she dialed the operator.

A moment later a familiar voice said, "Hello?"

The operator asked, "Collect call from Beatrice Peterson. Do you accept the charges?"

"Yes," said Liddie.

When the operator hung up Beanie said, "Liddie." Her voice began to crackle. "Oh Liddie, something terrible has happened."

"What happened? Are you okay?"

"It all happened so quickly. People had baseball bats. And they were hitting us for no reason at all." She started to cry. "Oh Liddie, it was horrible."

From behind she heard Marcus call her name. She turned around and saw him walking toward her with a grave expression on his face. "Liddie, hang on a second." She let the receiver hang from its cord and hurried to Marcus. He whispered something in her ear, hugged her, and then they both began to cry.

When Beanie returned to the phone, she picked up the receiver and said through unstoppable tears, "One of my friends just died."

Chapter Twenty-Nine

Boston, Massachusetts
February 4, 1962

"You sure you don't want me to cook, baby?" Melvin peeked over Adeline's shoulder as she stood at the stove.

"No, I came over here early this morning, as early as I could, so I could fix you breakfast."

"I'm kind of worried. In all the years we've been together, I've always cooked. I don't want any poached eggs, or eggs Benedict."

"I'm not cooking that." Adeline had arrived early to what she now called her and Melvin's place, with a brown bag full of food and announced she had come 'home' to fix her man a good breakfast before he had to go off to work.

"Should I be afraid to ask what exactly it is you are cooking?" Melvin pulled out a kitchen chair and sat down. Sliding the brown bag she came in with across the table, he peered inside of it, finding nothing other than a bottle of orange juice.

"I am cooking grits, eggs – sunny side up, smoked sausage, bacon and toast so you can use it to sop up the yolk."

"What restaurant did you pick that up from?"

"I didn't pick it up from any restaurant. I went to the grocery store. What makes you think I can't cook? I can cook."

"You can?" He let out a chuckle.

"Yes I can. Now put that in your pipe and smoke it, mister." She swatted the dish towel at him. "Now let me cook and you go and get ready for work."

"What are you giving me for dessert?" Melvin asked.

"There's no dessert with breakfast."

"I can think of something that's sweet and yummy that I could have after every meal. I could even have it before every meal. Instead of every meal."

"Melvin. Stop it. After we eat, you are going to work, and I am going to stay here and clean up and fix something for your dinner. Then I'm going home. And after you get home from work and eat your dinner, you are to call me and tell me how absolutely fabulous I am and how tasty my cooking is."

"And where does making love come in on that list?"

"It doesn't. Now go and get ready for work."

Adeline was very happy with her morning as she thought about it on her drive back to the house on Beacon Hill. She thought that once Walter left in the morning for work, perhaps she could come most days to take care of Melvin like she had done that morning. Feed him, encourage him, and help his day start out right. Maybe even let him have a "dessert" on some of those mornings.

Why not, she mused. No one would ever know.

And she was happy all around now that she was back with Melvin. She had committed herself to him, despite being married to Walter, the day she came back from the inauguration. It was Jack's first day of a new life as President of the United States, and it was a first day of a new life for her, too. For her and Melvin.

She was still afraid of what giving up her life would mean. The ridicule she'd get from leaving Walter. The shame. She didn't know if she would be able to live through something like that. And the lifestyle. Buying whatever she wanted, when she wanted. Melvin had a good job. He owned his own landscaping business. Had a crew of men that worked under him and made his own hours. But a life with Melvin didn't compare to the one she had with Walter.

Adeline pulled up into the driveway and grabbed a box out of the backseat of the car. She had stopped to buy a new dress on her way home. Melvin was going to take her out to lunch the next day and she wanted to look nice.

It was cold and snowy as she climbed out of her car. She pulled her coat up close around her, juggling her purse and the box, she crunched though the ice on the ground and made her way into the back door. She had told Jean not to come in until one. She wanted her morning free and unencumbered from questions. And Jean needed some time off, maybe she even had a man she needed to tend to. Adeline smiled at the thought. She'd have to ask Jean about her love life, even though she couldn't share hers with Jean, she thought, she should find out more about Jean, about her life, about that child she said she'd lost.

As soon as she walked in the door, Adeline heard the phone ring. "Hello." She listened as the operator queried her. "Yes, I'll accept the charges." It was Beanie. Adeline's face and happy demeanor faded. The last thing she'd heard from her the night before was that one of her friends had died. Adeline hoped that it wasn't more bad news. She had warned Beanie that what she was doing could get her killed.

"Hello, Beanie," she said when the line clicked in.

"Hello." Beanie sounded sad.

"Where are you now?"

"I'm still at the hospital."

"At the Negro hospital?"

"No Liddie, it's not a Negro hospital. It's a small white hospital with a few beds designated for Negroes."

"I don't understand. What are you still doing there?"

"My one friend died, but the other one is still here. He's hurt pretty bad."

What are you doing?" Liddie sounded disgusted.

"What do you mean?"

"I mean this foolishness of riding on buses and going to sit-ins that you fill your postcards to me with. You can't make a difference doing this. You can only bring harm to yourself."

"It's not a foolish thing. And I can make a difference . . . well, I'm trying to. A difference in the world just like you told me I could."

"Yes, I did tell you that, Beanie. And that is admirable. And I'm happy that you took my advice and that you're trying to help others. But there are different things you can do. Things that won't get you killed."

"Like what? What else is this important?"

"Like the Peace Corps. President Kennedy is looking for young people - college graduates – to come and help promote peace in the world. The *entire* world, Beanie. All you have to do is finish school. Then you can really make a difference."

"I'm not going overseas to some place I don't know. This is where I belong. Doing this."

"You don't belong in the South. You don't know anything about the South, or about Negroes. Haven't you seen those signs that read "White Only" and "Colored Only"? Negroes are kept separate from whites down there. That's the way it's always been and that's the way it'll be. It won't change because you take a ride on a bus."

"It doesn't have to be that way."

"Beanie - "

"I know more about Negroes than you do."

Taken aback, Adeline lowered her voice, "How do you presume to know what I know? And what is it that you think you know about them?"

"I know that they've been treated unjustly. I know that those "white only" signs need to come down. That the Negro deserves the right to drink out of the same water fountains, and use the same restrooms as white people. They can do more than clean white people's houses, you know."

"My concern is for your safety. People are getting killed. I don't want you hurt for a cause that even if it's won won't affect you now or ever. The Peace Corps will help the world as well as other nations and your place in it. You have your priorities mixed up, Beanie. Im sorry about your friend, but I don't want to have to come and get your body from down there so I can bury you."

"If I die fighting this cause then at least my life will have meant something."

"Who will remember the poor little white girl who got herself killed over a cause that hasn't been resolved in over four hundred years? No one. You need to find a way out. Out of your presumed obligations. Out of Mississippi."

"Liddie, you just don't understand."

"There you go again, thinking you know what I know and how I feel. Beanie, you do what you must, but don't count on me to approve of your actions."

"You sound like a racist, Liddie."

A long silence went across the line while Adeline calmed herself. When she spoke, she spoke slowly, incredulity showing in her voice. "Are you calling me racist, Beanie? Are you saying that I am against the Negro achieving equality?"

"I don't know, Liddie, if the shoe fits."

Chapter Thirty

Chicago, Illinois

Sunday mornings usually brought churchgoers to Burr Oak Cemetery on the south side of Chicago. Dressed in nice trousers and skirts, families walked the gravel pathways to visit the graves of their loved ones.

This morning Beanie and Byron stood on either side of Carl's memorial plaque. It had been two months since Carl's passing. Beanie bent down and placed a small bundle of golden daffodils across the base of the plaque. She touched the embossed bronze letters and read the inscription, "Carl James Gaines. April 7, 1941 - February 3, 1962. Beloved Son and Freedom Fighter." She ran her fingers over the line of small italics at the very bottom of the plaque that read *May the Gates of Heaven be Open to All.* Then she stood up and quietly stepped back so that Byron could have a moment alone with his friend.

As she walked away, Beanie heard Byron say, "I'm sorry, man." She meandered down the path, stopping periodically to read the names of the people buried underneath the headstones and calculate their age at the time of death.

When he was ready, Byron joined her. They walked in silence until Byron said, "I still feel bad that I survived the attack and he didn't."

Beanie saw the pain and guilt in his face and said, "You can't blame yourself, Byron. Carl knew what he was getting into. He knew the dangers and the risks, we all did. And in spite of them, he was always the first one to step in and make a stand." She stopped walking and looked at him. "You once said that you hoped Carl wasn't becoming a loose cannon. He wasn't a loose cannon, just a passionate activist."

Byron gave her a weak smile and said, "He certainly was. There's no segregation in Heaven. But if there were, I'm sure Carl could get it resolved."

Beanie offered him a warm smile. She touched his arm and said, "You can be sure of that."

They continued to walk through the cemetery with quiet reverence, nodding to fellow mourners that passed by clutching fresh flowers for the graves they intended to visit.

When they came to a fork in the path, Byron said, "Come this way, I want to show you something." Halfway down the row of memorial plaques, Byron stopped in front of a simple engraved, marble square. "This is where Emmett Till is buried."

"You mean the fourteen year old who got murdered in Mississippi?"

Byron nodded. "Yeah, for touching the hand of a white woman. I remember when it happened back in the summer of '55. His face was so beaten up and mutilated that he was unrecognizable. When they brought his body back here, his mother decided to have an open casket funeral so that everyone could see what those two white men did to him."

Tears swelled in Beanie's eyes. Being involved with the Negroes' fight to end racial prejudice made her feel deeply for anyone who suffered this kind of injustice, especially an innocent young boy.

"The worst part," Byron said, "is, the two men who did it pleaded innocent and were acquitted by a jury of white men. After the trial, they admitted during an interview that they had killed him. But because they had been found not guilty, they couldn't be tried again." He looked over at Beanie. "Emmitt's death was pivotal in the Civil Rights Movement."

Beanie allowed the tears to fall. This boy's story touched her in a profound way. She remembered something Liddie had said to her over the phone: *You can't make a difference.* Maybe she couldn't make a difference by herself, but by being a part of something much bigger she knew that she *had* made a difference. The protests and the demonstrations over the past year brought small victories, but at a great cost to people like Carl and the others who had died for this Cause. She looked down at Emmitt's name and said, "We're working hard so that your death will not have been in vain."

As they exited the cemetery and walked toward the bus stop, Byron said, "I don't think I ever said thank you for coming back here to Chicago with me while I recovered. You didn't have to, you know. You could have gone back to Jackson with Marcus, or you could have gone to see Liddie. I would have understood."

Yes, Beanie could have gone to see Liddie. Maryland was less than four hundred miles from Boston. But she had been so angry with her for the things she'd said, and she didn't want their first face-to-face meeting to be tainted with animosity.

"I didn't need to go to Jackson to help with the Movement. There was plenty of stuff for me to do here. Between working at the NAACP and at Smoky Joe's, I've got a lot going on."

When they first arrived back in Chicago, Byron went to live with his great aunt to finish healing. Beanie stayed busy playing at the club and working for the NAACP. The Chicago's chapter wasn't far from Clark Street, and they needed an assistant to the secretary. She worked two hours in the morning for them, worked at Smoky Joe's at night, and on Sundays she would take the El train to the South side to visit Byron. She still sent postcards to Liddie but kept them short and benign.

"So how's it going at the NAACP?"

"Busy. Between fundraising for the Student Nonviolent Coordinating Committee and launching the new Voter Education Program, they've had to increase my hours to four a day." She looked down at the approaching bus. "Oh, I forgot to tell you. Guess what? I've decided to go back to school to get my high school diploma. It's always bothered me that I never graduated."

"Beanie, that's terrific. But how will you be able to handle working during the day, plus school, plus playing at the club at night? That'll be an awful lot on your plate."

"Don't worry. I'll figure it out."

"So when do you start?"

"Next week."

The following week, Beanie started back to school. She took classes in the morning, worked for the NAACP in the afternoon, and played at the club in the evenings. She handled the load well at first, but within a month the burden of trying to manage all three began to wear her down.

"So just tell Joe you need to cut back a few nights a week. He'll understand." Byron sat at her little dinette table sipping on a cup of tea. "I can talk to him if you want."

Beanie poured the hot water from the kettle into her cup. She dunked the tea bag several times, and then threw it in the trash. "I hate doing that to him again, especially since he gave me such a good deal on the apartment." She pulled out the other chair and sat. "I just can't leave him in the lurch again."

"Look, we all know how important it is to you to get your diploma. And I'm sure Joe would understand. I can still call my old buddy to help out."

"You mean the one who kept calling in sick all the time?"

Byron laughed. "He's grown up since then. Got a kid now and everything. So he could use the extra dough."

"I don't know, Byron."

"Well, what are your other options, quit school? Quit the NAACP?"

"No." she said. "I'll never quit the NAACP. And I *am* going to get my diploma. I can manage all three."

"Sure, right up until you keel over from exhaustion." He took another sip, and then set the cup on the table. "You know you can't keep this pace up for too long."

Beanie stared out the window at the soot-covered building across the alley. Receiving her high school diploma fulfilled a desire, working for the NAACP fulfilled a need, and playing at the club fulfilled a passion. She wanted all three, but the reality was, she couldn't have them all, not right now anyway. "You're right. Maybe I can play three nights a week instead of six. It'll be tight, though - the rent, groceries. I won't have much left for anything else."

"Why don't you ask Liddie for some money? She'd help you, wouldn't she?"

Beanie shook her head. "I don't want to ask her."

"Why? You still mad at her?"

Beanie thought about it for a moment. "No, not mad. I think I'm more disappointed than anything." She took a sip of the Lipton tea and looked at Byron. "You know, I asked her if she was a racist."

"What'd she say?"

"She didn't. And I didn't push it." Beanie set the cup down on the table. "I guess I didn't really want to know."

Joe gladly gave Beanie the extra time she needed. With her workload lightened, Beanie doubled up on her classes, cutting her schooling from two years down to one. And on Friday, May 3, 1963, at four o'clock in the afternoon, Beatrice Mae Peterson received her high school diploma.

"Congratulations, Beanie. You did it." Byron sat on the bar stool next to her, held up his can of RC Cola as a toast and took a swig.

Joe stood behind the bar facing her as he washed glasses, dried them, and stacked them on the counter next to him. "Yeah, Beanie. We're really proud of you for graduating."

Beanie laughed. "It only took me until I was twenty." She lifted her cup of tea, clinked Byron's can and took a drink. "But at least I did it."

"You surely did," said Joe as he slyly slid a large flat, wrapped package across the counter to Beanie.

"What's this, Joe?"

He winked at her. "Guess you're gonna have to open it and find out."

Beanie picked up that flat square package and shook it next to her ear. "Is it a toaster?" she laughed.

"Just open it," Joe wiped his hands on his dishtowel, flung the towel over his shoulders and put his hands on his hips. "I hope you like it."

Beanie ripped the package open and stared at the backside of a record album.

"Turn it over," he urged, his words laced with anticipation.

Beanie squealed when she saw the cover. "It's Duke Ellington's Jazz Party."

"Yep, it's got *Hello Little Girl* on there. And here, look." Joe pulled the album from her hands and pointed to the signature scrawled below the face of the man on the cover. "Look who signed it."

"No." She couldn't contain her excitement. "But how did you get him to sign it?"

"I went over to the Blue Note, told Mr. Ellington it was for his number one fan, and he signed it for me, right there on the spot. Do you like it?"

"Like it? I love it." Beanie stood on her tiptoes, reached across the bar, and planted a kiss on old Joe's cheek.

When she sat back down, Byron slid a card next to her and said, "Here."

"Byron, you didn't need to get me anything." When she opened the card, a piece of paper fell out into her lap. She picked it up, looked at it and said, "What's this?"

Byron said, "It's a coupon."

"A coupon?"

"Yeah. I didn't know what to get you, so I thought I'd give you a coupon. That way, you can pick out something that you really want, let me know - redeeming the coupon, and I'll get it for you."

Beanie gave him a big hug, thanked him, and tucked the coupon in her wallet.

For two months Beanie carried that coupon around in her purse. She stopped by jewelry stores, clothing stores, music stores. She even stopped in an art gallery. But nothing seemed to catch her attention. Then one day, while at work, she noticed a letter lying on the secretary's desk. It was addressed to the president of the Chicago NAACP branch, and it was signed, Dr. Martin Luther King, Jr.

That evening, before they started their shift at the club, she handed the coupon back to Byron and said, "I know what I want for my graduation present. I want you to take me to the March on Washington."

On August 28, 1963, Beanie, Byron and Marcus joined the busloads of demonstrators from all over the country that descended onto the streets of the nation's capital. They walked from the Washington Monument to the Lincoln Memorial linked arm in arm with the other peaceful demonstrators.

The three wedged through the crowd, pushing their way up closer to the steps. "I can't believe we're here, making history. This is so exciting," said Beanie latching on to Byron's hand so she wouldn't get left behind. "I've never seen so many people in one place. How many do you think are here?"

"A lot." Byron yelled back over his shoulder. He started to say something else to her, but the crowd erupted into thunderous applause and cheers, drowning him out.

A moment later, Dr. Martin Luther King, Jr. stepped in front of the podium and began to speak. He spoke of life, liberty, and the pursuit of happiness. "We must rise to the majestic heights of meeting physical force with soul force." He stopped for a moment, looked over the crowd and said, *"I have a dream. . ."*

Chapter Thirty-One

Washington, D. C.
August 28, 1963

"... *a dream that one day this nation will rise up and live out the true meaning of its creed:"We hold these truths to be self-evident: that all men are created equal . . ."*

Adeline stood still listening to Dr. Martin Luther King Jr.'s speech in complete reverence. She stood by the reflecting pool on the mall having marched in the sea of people - the thousands that had come, the ones that believed in bringing the law of the land in line with the words of the founding fathers of our nation. Standing, her arm linked in Melvin's, Adeline felt Dr. King's words as they moved inside of her and stirred her very being.

"I have a dream . . ."

His words reverberated from the speakers stacked high at Lincoln's Memorial and made the skin on her arms rise with goose bumps and a tingle run from her neck down the middle of her back.

"... *that one day even the state of Mississippi, a state sweltering with the heat of injustice, sweltering with the heat of oppression, will be transformed into an oasis of freedom and justice.*"

Mississippi. A place Adeline hadn't thought of in a long time. It was the place that Beanie had chosen to go instead of coming to Boston. A place she went to push for freedom for the Negro. Risking her life for it.

It was in Mississippi that Medgar had been killed in the driveway of his home just two months ago and only a few hours after Jack had made the speech about civil rights being a moral obligation of the American people. In a speech where he asked if a man, because he is dark, couldn't enjoy a full and free life, "then who among us would be content to have the color of his skin changed?"

Adeline looked over at Melvin through her sunglasses. His dark skin glistened with the sweat that beaded on his face. He wore a short brim, straw hat, and a short sleeve linen shirt. He stood, his arms folded across his chest, solemn, listening to Dr. King speak. She knew that inside him a hope burned hot that he could live his life free of the color of his skin and not to be subjected to the rails of hate and prejudice. A life where he needn't worry about being seen with a white woman.

"*Who among us would be content to have the color of his skin changed . . .*" Jack's words haunted Adeline, ever since she had first heard them more than two months ago.

They and Medgar's death set off a flicker inside her. And today it was Dr. King's words that fanned that flicker into a flame. His words moved her. She stood in the heat, fanning herself and knew, in spite of what she told Beanie, it might just be this one person, this one man that will make a difference for the Negro.

Dr. King's speech reached a crescendo, *"Free at last. Free at last. Thank God Almighty, I'm free at last."*

"Yes, free," Adeline said, looking over at Melvin as he took his handkerchief and wiped his forehead. He glanced down at her and smiled.

"Free." Adeline knew that every person there - black and white, just for the moment, felt just that.

Chapter Thirty-Two

Boston, Massachusetts
November 22, 1963

Two police officers came to Adeline Garrison's door at
10 o'clock on a Friday morning. It was chilly out. Jean was
in the basement doing laundry and couldn't get the door.
When Adeline pulled it open a feeling of dread overcame her.

"Mrs. Garrison?"

"Yes." Her voice was barely audible.

"You were listed as the next of kin for a -" the officer
looked down on his notepad, "Mr. Melvin Chambers. Did you
know him, ma'am?"

Adeline's knees buckled and she had to hold on to the
door frame to keep from falling.

"Uhm." She took in a deep breath, but couldn't say
anything more.

"Liddie, who's at the door?" Walter had gotten a late start that morning and was still at home. He came up behind her and looked at the police officers.

"May I help you?" he said. "I'm Walter Garrison. This is my house. This is my wife."

"Mr. Garrison, we have your wife listed as next of kin for a Melvin Chambers. He was killed this morning. Struck by an automobile while unloading equipment off of a truck. We need her to come down and identify the body and pick up his property."

Adeline felt dizzy. Her knuckles lost all color as she held on tightly to the frame of the door.

"I don't think she knows anyone by that name. Do you ̶" Walter stopped mid-sentence when he saw Adeline's face. "Liddie. You alright?"

Adeline nodded and fought to keep down the wail that was trying to escape from her throat. Things seemed to dim, and spin around, her eyes closed involuntarily. She felt hot and flushed.

"I'm sorry, officers. I need to take my wife in the house. Maybe call a doctor. I don't know what's come over her."

"Well, if she does realize she knows him, she'll need to come down to the Suffolk County Sheriff's Office. We can leave you the phone number."

"That won't be necessary. We know the number. But I doubt if we can help you."

"Well, thank you for your time, sir. Ma'am." The officer put his hand to the brim of his hat and tugged at it. They both left down the drive.

Adeline stared at them walking away. She wanted to speak, to call out to them to wait. To please take her to Melvin. But no words seemed to be able to escape from her throat.

Walter, trying to get her into the house had to pry her hands from their grasp on the door and practically carry her to the couch. She hadn't said a word and all the blood had drained from her face. She was pale and her breathing seemed shallow and forced.

"Sweetheart. What's wrong? Can you tell me what's wrong?" Walter laid Adeline on the couch and kneeled down beside her. "Do you need me to get the doctor? You want me to call Glenn?"

It took all of Adeline's strength to look over at Walter. The room had turned cold to her and she felt as if some force was holding onto her, dragging her down. Down inside the couch, to a place of utter despair and darkness. She felt heavy and her body felt numb.

"Honey." Walter looked at Adeline pleadingly.

Adeline swallowed and drew in a deep, ragged breath. "Go to work, Walter."

"I can't leave you here like this. I don't know what's wrong with you. Did you know that man? Is that what's wrong?"

"No," she said. "I didn't know him. I just all of a sudden felt dizzy. Lightheaded. But I'm okay now."

"You don't look okay."

"Just ask Jean to bring me some water." Adeline tried to sit up. She scooted down into the couch and pushed up on her elbows.

"Here, let me help you," Walter said. "What are you trying to do? You want to get up?"

"No. I just want to sit up. I'm okay now. Just tell Jean to bring me a glass of water."

"I'll tell her. But I'm staying home with you. I'll just call the office."

"No," Adeline practically screamed. Walter looked at her startled. "I told you I'm fine." Not lowering her voice, she said. "Please, just go."

Walter seemed at a loss. "All right," he said standing up. "I'll get Jean to bring you some water and tell her to look after you. I'll come straight home. Is that okay?"

Adeline stared at Walter. She didn't answer. She let out a deep sigh, closed her eyes and rolled her head back to lean it on the back of the sofa.

"Okay then, I'm leaving."

Adeline's heart seemed to flutter, her chest ached and she couldn't seem to catch her breath. She opened her eyes and saw Jean standing over her with a glass of water.

"I don't want that, Jean. If you could go and get my purse and car keys from upstairs off my dresser for me. And help me get into my coat."

"Are you okay, Mrs. Garrison?"

"Jean, I don't think I will ever be the same."

When Jean brought Adeline her purse and keys, Adeline instructed her to go home. "And if Mr. Garrison asks you anything, just tell him you put me to bed."

"What's wrong with you? Don't you want to tell me? Maybe I can help you."

"You can't help me. I'll see you tomorrow."

Adeline drove in a daze to the Suffolk County Sheriff's Office. When she told them she was there for Melvin she got the same stares she always did when it came to the two of them.

When they pulled the sheet off of his face for her to see him, he looked as if he was sleeping. She wanted to reach over and touch him. Shake him. Tell him to get up and come home with her. That she was there to take care of him, and she would never leave him again. But he didn't move. He didn't say, "Hi, baby."

Tears rolled down her face. She tried not to falter because there were too many eyes on her. Too many eyes would see a white woman crying over a black man.

"Yes, that's Melvin Chambers." Adeline sniffed back the tears. "Where do I pick up his things?" Adeline was led to an office with a sign that read "Property." She picked up Melvin's keys, his watch and wallet. She opened up the wallet and saw the note, in his handwriting that read, "In Case of Emergency," with her name and address listed. On the line that read "Relationship" he had written: "Next of kin."

"I'll have the funeral home pick up his body," Adeline told the officer at the desk, unaware if he was who she should tell or not.

She got into her car and drove to Melvin's apartment. *To their apartment.* She took out as many of Melvin's clothes as she could pull from the closet, threw them on the bed, lay down and wrapped herself in them, and then she started to scream. She wailed like a banshee, sobbed and cried. She pleaded to God for it not to be true. To please bring Melvin back to her, or to take her so she could be with Melvin. She cried until she could cry no more.

Sometime around one o'clock, she got up off the bed, and stripped down to her underwear. She then put on several of his shirts and pants, laying one over the other. Wrapping herself up in his overcoat and putting on his shoes, Adeline dragged herself out to the living room. She turned on the television and curled up on the couch to watch one of their favorite soap operas, *As the World Turns.* It was just coming on.

Then the show was interrupted and a black screen with white lettering reading "CBS NEWS BULLETIN" appeared. Walter Cronkite's voice said, *"Here is a bulletin from CBS News. In Dallas Texas, three bullets were fired at President Kennedy's motorcade in downtown Dallas. The first reports say that President Kennedy has been seriously wounded by this shooting."*

Adeline sat up and stared at the television. "Not you, too, Jack," she whispered. "I can't take any more grief today."

But less than an hour later Cronkite was back . *"From Dallas, Texas, the flash apparently official, President Kennedy died at 1 pm Central Standard Time. Two o'clock Eastern Standard Time. Some thirty-eight minutes ago."*

"Oh my, God."

Chapter Thirty-Three

Boston, Massachusetts

Both Jack and Melvin lived the same amount of days after the inauguration. 1,036.

Adeline told Walter that when those two police officers came to the door, it felt like a portent. She knew something bad was going to happen. It was like she foresaw Jack's death, she had told him. It's like she knew it was going to happen when the officers told them someone had died. She just didn't know who it would be.

Walter believed her.

Good thing because she couldn't very well tell him that the way she acted was because the love of her life had just died.

For the next few months Adeline went to Melvin's apartment every day she could and spent the morning there. She collected some of his things and took them home with her, but everything else she left like it was. Just as if he would come home at any minute and resume his day. His razor on the bathroom shelf, his bottle of pills in his medicine cabinet, his insulin in the refrigerator – he had gotten sick during that year they were apart. High blood pressure. Diabetes. Probably all stress-related she surmised because she had treated him so badly. She had vowed she would never leave him again.

Now he had left her.

She kept the kitchen stocked with the things he would have bought and kept his shoes shined just as he liked. She paid the rent and utilities every month. And she prayed every night to God that He would help her get through her loss. Sometimes she could smell Melvin and see him, standing in the doorway smiling at her. But for the most part the apartment and her heart were empty.

It was a cold day when Adeline drove up the driveway to the house on Beacon Hill right after noon and saw Walter's car parked in the driveway. She had told him she was going up to the Cape, but she had really planned to spend the night at Melvin's apartment. Perhaps it would be one of the nights that he would come and visit her. But the furnace for the apartment had blown and there was no heat. Even wrapped up in Melvin's clothes it was too cold to stay.

When Adeline walked in the house she heard voices. One sounded strained, fearful, the other menacing. Adeline put her purse on the kitchen table, followed the voices upstairs and then into her bedroom. She could smell alcohol as soon as she stepped into the room. And then she saw them.

Walter had his hand over Jean's mouth. Her eyes big, her hair a mess, and she was trying to break free of Walter's grip. Trying to scream out from beneath his hand. Her shirt was unbuttoned and her skirt pulled up. Walter was between her legs, his pants around his ankles, his hips thrusting into Jean, and with every thrust Jean squealed, tears running down her face. She must have been in the room changing the linen when Walter found her, because it was strewn all over the floor.

"You know you wanted this. You know you wanted a white man," he was saying. "Open your legs."

"Walter!" Adeline stood at the door, shocked at the sight. Walter jumped up as soon as he heard her voice. "What the hell do you think you're doing?" she asked.

Jean rolled over on her side. Straightening her clothes and whimpering, she curled into a fetal position. Walter reached down and pulled up his underwear.

"Oh my God," Adeline said and went over to Jean to help her up off the bed. "Come on, honey. Let's go get you cleaned up." Adeline walked with her arm around Jean into the ensuite bathroom. Turning back looking over her shoulder she glared at Walter. "You pull your goddamn pants up and get out of my sight."

"This is my house." Adeline heard him hiss.

"Jean, you stay in here as long as you need to," Adeline said, brushing Jean's hair down with her hand. "You fix yourself. Then come down to the kitchen and see me. I'm going to take care of Walter."

Adeline left the bathroom and found Walter sitting on the side of the bed.

"I thought you were going to the Cape," he said, not looking up at Adeline.

"So then, you thought it would be a good time to rape Jean?"

"I had a couple of drinks . . .". he mumbled the words. "She was in here sashaying all around. She's been eyeing me for years. A man can't live without it, you know. Any colored woman is glad to have a white man inside of her."

Adeline glanced toward the bathroom and saw that the door was ajar. She went over and shut it completely and walked back over to stand in front of Walter.

"Jean has never given you one iota of an indication that she wanted to have sex with you. You are not only a dirty old man, you are a dirty liar." She stood fiercely over him, making him look up at her. "I can't even form the words for what I want to say to you. You need to leave."

"I told you, this is my house. I'm not leaving."

"Oh yes you are. You acted like some wild, depraved animal forcing yourself on her. Don't flatter yourself, Walter. One time with you and no woman would ever want to have anything to do with you again. I don't have anything to do with you because you are pitiful at it. You can't satisfy a woman, you don't know how. And that . . ." Adeline pointed between his legs, "that little, scrawny, piece of . . . you'll be lucky if I don't castrate you with the kitchen shears in your sleep tonight," Adeline hissed. "Oh, yes, you are leaving here. Your house or not, at least until I've calmed down. And you'd better believe if Jean wasn't a Negro I'd call the sheriff on you. I just don't want to put her through that humiliation. Now get out!"

Adeline stood back, allowing him to be able to stand. Fire in her eyes, fists at her side, it took Adeline all the strength she could muster not to take the table lamp and smash it against his head.

Walter straightened out his clothes, grabbed Adeline's pack of Pall Malls off the nightstand, and kept his eye on her as he left the room. Adeline stood in the same position until she heard the door slam and the roar of the engine from his car leave from the driveway.

Getting to the kitchen, Adeline sat at the table trembling. "That bastard," she said. She put her elbows up on the table and buried her head in her hands. She didn't want to cry. She didn't want Jean to see her being weak. Not in control. Plus, what she had to do would hurt Jean, and she needed to be strong.

She dug down in her purse and found her checkbook. She opened it up and had just finished writing when Jean walked in and stood in the doorway.

"You want to sit down, Jean?"

"No. I'm fine."

"Has he ever done that to you before?"

"No. I mean he's done things like touch my breast, or my backside, but he always acted like it was an accident."

"I'm so sorry that happened, Jean. And you know with you being a Negro, and him being so prominent in the city, any attempt at legal action would only hurt you."

"Yes. I know that."

"Here." Adeline tore the check out of the holder.

Jean walked over and leaned across the table. "What's this?"

"It's a check for you. To help you out until you find another job. I have to let you go."

Jean looked up from the check and searched Adeline's eyes.

"I'm sorry," was all that Adeline could say.

After Jean left, Adeline picked up her keys and purse and went to Melvin's house. She stayed the night wrapped up in Melvin's clothes.

The day that Walter died was even colder than the day Adeline found him raping Jean. But the sun shined so brightly that one almost needed sunglasses.

That night after both had gone to bed, he had stumbled into the bedroom they had shared before the day he forced himself on Jean. Since that day she had made him sleep in a guest bedroom. The light from the hallway illuminated his face, shadows falling across the floor. She could see his eyes rolling back in his head. He was holding on to the door, trying to stay upright. He called out Adeline's name. She was already sitting up in bed, waiting for him. When he had said her name, she reached up and turned on the table light. But she didn't say anything.

"Adeline," he called out again. And then he started to convulse. He fell to the floor and writhed, his tongue wagging about, his eyes bulging from his head. Adeline picked up the phone and made a call.

"Cassie," she said calmly. "You need to get Glenn and come over here. I think Walter's dead." Adeline looked over at him and Walter looked back at her. She hung up the phone and watched as Walter began to shake uncontrollably on the floor, his eyes begging for help. He began making a gurgling noise, and after a long guttural moan his eyes closed.

By the time Glenn and Cassie got to the house, Adeline was sitting at the kitchen table, smoking a cigarette.

"Oh Liddie," Cassie came in the back door and hugged her. "What happened?"

Glenn walked in and looked at her, waiting for her answer.

"I don't know, we were in bed sleeping and he woke up choking and convulsing. I tried to hold him down, so he wouldn't swallow his tongue." She glanced up at Glenn. "I don't know if that was the right thing to do or not. Is what I've heard to do. And then he just stopped, closed his eyes and the last sound he made was a gurgling sound and a moan. It was just awful. I just couldn't stand to be up there. . . in our bed with him any longer." Adeline buried her head in her hands.

"I'll go up and take a look. It's all that stress and drinking he does," Glenn said. "I've been warning him for years."

"I'll go up with you, Glenn," Adeline said. "Cassie will you come, too?"

"Of course, dear."

The three went upstairs to Adeline's bedroom. When they walked in, Walter was across the bed, his feet dangling over the side. The covers were jumbled up and the pillows were on the floor. Adeline shrank into the wall and started to sob.

"You'd better get her out of here, Cassie." Glenn said. "This is too much for her. I've got to get an ambulance."

Cassie took Adeline downstairs while Glenn called the ambulance. By the time they got Walter to the hospital he was in a coma. He died three days later.

Cassie stood by Adeline the whole time. Helped her make funeral arrangements, pick out the casket and the plot and notify everyone. Adeline told her she was just too sick to do it.

Taking out the bathroom trash in Adeline's ensuite bathroom the day after Walter went to the hospital, Cassie approached Adeline. "Sweetie, I found these insulin bottles in the trash in your bathroom. You're not diabetic are you?"

"No," Adeline said, glancing down in the wastebasket. "I had to throw a lot of Jean's things out when she left. I called her several times to come and get them, but she never picked up the phone."

"They're empty."

"Yes, I know. She must have used those. Her other bottles are in the fridge, you can just throw them out, too."

"Okay. I will. Poor, Jean. I didn't know she was sick."

Adeline waited one day after Walter's funeral before she called her.

"Jean," Adeline said. "Walter is dead. Dead and buried. I want you to come here. Come and stay with me."

"I don't know."

"And I want to go to church. I want to go to church with you. I need to make a confession."

"They don't take confessions at my church. I'm Baptist, Mrs. Garrison. You'd need to go to your Catholic church for that."

"Don't call me Mrs. Garrison. Call me Adeline. And I don't want a priest or a preacher. I want to confess to you. Tell you all my dirty little secrets."

"Me? Oh my word. Where are your friends? Mrs. Randall and Mrs. Moore? Can't you talk to them?"

"I know you lost your house, Jean." Adeline couldn't make out anything decipherable coming from Jean. Just some grunting sounds. She knew that Jean found the conversation hard and heartbreaking.

"I don't know, Mrs. Garrison . . . What happened with your husband . . ."

"I wasn't on his side, Jean. I was never on his side. I just wanted you out of here so you could be safe. Be away from him. I didn't know the money I gave you would run out so soon. I went to the bank after I heard your house was going into foreclosure and tried to pay off the mortgage. But it was too late."

"Still . . . he-he . . ."

"I took care of that problem. You don't have to worry about that anymore."

"*You* took care of it?"

"It's been taken care of. Is that better? The problem has been taken care of and I want you here with me. This house is too big for me to be here all by myself."

"Wasn't ever anybody there but you and Mr. Garrison anyway."

"Well, he and his hot air took up a lot of space. You live by yourself, I live by myself. We should live together."

"I don't know if I could work for you anymore."

"Who's asking you to work? I said come live with me. I'll take care of you. You can take care of me. We'll take care of each other. I need you, Jean. I can't do this without you."

"Do what, Mrs. Garrison?"

"Live."

Chapter Thirty-Four

Washington, D.C.
March, 1964

It had been nearly seven months since the March on Washington, but the experience stayed at the forefront of Beanie's mind. Images of Joan Baez and Bob Dylan strumming their guitars played out in her head, making her relive that momentous and unforgettable event. She found out later that nearly a quarter of a million people attended the march, making it the largest peaceful demonstration in America's history. But it wasn't until Dr. King finished his moving speech that she clapped and cried out, *I want to move here.*

So when Byron showed her the acceptance letter from Georgetown University and asked her if she wanted to move there with him and Marcus, she said, "Absolutely."

Beanie skipped down the steps carrying her lime green suitcase, set it down by the bar, and stood next to Byron.

Joe walked around the bar and grasped Byron's hand. He shook it and said, "Congratulations on the scholarship, Byron. I knew you'd get into medical school. It was just a matter of time." He stepped over to Beanie and gave her a hug. "I'm sure gonna miss you guys."

"We're gonna miss you too, Joe. But we'll keep in touch," she told him.

"You better. It'd be nice if you two came back to visit once in awhile. Georgetown isn't that far from here."

Beanie glanced at Byron, and then looked back at Joe. "Well, I don't know that he'll have a lot of free time once classes start in August. But I'll try. Of course it will depend on my work schedule."

"So you already have a job lined up? How about a place to live? Do you have money?"

Beanie rolled her eyes playfully. "Yes, *Dad*. I'll be working at the Washington D.C. branch of the NAACP. And we're going to be sharing an apartment with our friend, Marcus. He's already there, he came up from Jackson."

Joe hugged her again, discreetly slipped a twenty-dollar bill in her coat pocket and said, "I'm just so darn proud of you guys."

Once again heading out on a bus, Beanie stared out the window at the diminishing Chicago skyline with a sense of anticipation. She was embarking on another journey, a new chapter in her life, and with her best friend beside her. She reached over, grabbed Byron's hand and squeezed it.

"What?"

Beanie grinned. "Oh nothing." But she couldn't contain her excitement. "I just can't wait to get there."

Byron squeezed her hand in return. "Me either." He let go, stared at her and said, "Have you told Liddie that you're moving to Washington?"

She knew that he wasn't really asking if she'd told Liddie. He was saying, "Tell her!"

"Fine." Beanie grabbed her knapsack from beneath her seat, rummaged around in it until she found a pen, and pulled out one of the postcards tucked in the side pouch. She grabbed the Time Magazine sticking out of her pack, used it as a desk and wrote:

March 15, 1964

Dear Liddie,

I just wanted to let you know that I am moving to Washington D.C. to work for the NAACP. I'm so excited about this move. I will be sharing an apartment with two other people. I don't have my new address with me, but I will send it to you once I get there.

Living so close, I hope to finally make a trip to Boston to visit you soon.

I've missed talking with you.

Love, Beanie.

Twelve hours later, when the two arrived at the D. C. bus station, Marcus was there to meet them. He hugged them and said, "Welcome to Washington D.C." He grabbed Beanie's suitcase and said, "The apartment is only a few miles from here, but we'll need to take a city bus to get there."

When they reached the apartment, Marcus opened the door, stepped in and said, "It's not much but the rent is reasonable and we each have our own bedroom."

Beanie took a quick tour of the sparse living room, the tiny outdated kitchen and bathroom, and the equally small bedrooms. When she returned two minutes later, she clapped her hands together and said, "Are you kidding? It's absolutely perfect. I'm going to love it here."

When springtime hit D.C., Beanie realized she had never seen anything quite as beautiful. Trees with pink clusters of cherry blossoms lined some of the streets, giving the capital a feeling of pageantry. Even more so that day because it marked the beginning of the annual Cherry Festival.

While some spectators sat in chairs lining Constitution Avenue waiting for the parade to begin, Beanie and Byron meandered through the festival booths looking at the homemade crafts.

Byron had been rather quiet this morning when they left the apartment. And he hadn't said more than two words since. He picked up a handmade leather belt, looked at it for a moment, and then set it back down on the stack.

Beanie hadn't been very talkative either. She had something on her mind, something that she'd been thinking about for a few weeks now. She set down the hand made leather purse she was looking at and said, "Is everything okay, Byron? You seem distracted."

Byron picked up a leather wallet, examined the stitching, and said, "Everything's fine. How about with you? You're pretty quiet yourself."

"I'm okay."

Neither of them elaborated.

They continued to silently walk through the booths and peruse the merchandise. Finally, Byron said, "There's something I want to talk to you about."

Beanie let out a breath. "Good, because there's something I want to talk to you about, too."

Byron smiled. "You go first."

She took a deep breath and said, "I want to go back to school."

Byron looked surprised. "School?"

"Yes. I want to go to law school."

"Beanie, I think that's a great idea. But have you thought this through? You've got to go to college first. Have you checked into any of the universities? How will you pay for it? What about your job? If you did do this, when would you start?"

Beanie knew he'd ask questions that she didn't have answers for. That's why she hadn't told him earlier. "I don't have all the answers yet."

"Well, what type of law were you thinking of getting into?"

"Civil rights. I want to be a civil rights attorney."

For a moment Byron said nothing. Then he hugged her and said, "I think it's a great idea. Maybe Liddie can give you some advice on what to do."

As they continued to walk through the booths discussing her options, Beanie said, "So what was it that you wanted to talk to me about?"

Byron shrugged. "I don't remember."

That evening, Beanie wrote a letter to Liddie telling her of her plans to go back to school. She even told her that she wanted to become a civil rights attorney and represent the Negroes.

. . . So I was wondering if you might have any advice for me. Maybe you could recommend a good college to apply to. My grades are very good, maybe even good enough for a scholarship. I know it will take me a long time to complete my schooling because I'll have to split my time between work and school. But it's important to me to get a law degree, and I won't give up until I've exhausted every last option.

If I do get to go to college, I wouldn't start until the fall. Maybe I can come visit you beforehand.

Love,
Beanie.

Two weeks later, Beanie was sitting on the couch reading Sylvia Plath's, The Bell Jar, when Marcus walked in, handed her a letter and said, "This was in the mailbox. It's from your friend, Liddie."

"Thanks." She opened it up, read the letter and then yelled, "Byron, come quick. Byron, hurry! You need to see this."

He rushed into the living room. "What's wrong? Did somebody die?"

Beanie handed him the letter and said, "Read this."
Byron read it out loud.

Dear Beanie,

I am so happy that you have finally put down roots long enough to get a college education. You know how important I think that is. I wish that you were here in Boston to attend my alma mater, Simmons College, but D.C. does have quite a few good, quality colleges. I know that you told me you had good grades, but I'm not sure how they would measure up with others that finished on time. But if I was picking a college for you, I would pick Georgetown University. It is an excellent school and there's a law school there, so I'm sure they have a great pre-law program. I've included a check that should cover your tuition and books for the first quarter if you choose Georgetown. It'll probably cover two or three quarters at one of the lesser expensive schools. If you do decide to go to Georgetown, I have a few friends there that could speed up the application process for you and then, I'd forward the rest of the year's tuition to the school. If you keep your grades up, I'll take care of all your college expenses – tuition and books.

I'm so proud of you!

Love,
Liddie

When he finished reading the letter, Beanie held out the check, squealed and said, "I'm going to college!"

For the next five months, Beanie worked extra hours at the NAACP office to make more money. She knew that once she started classes in the fall, her hours would be cut almost in half, making it more difficult to pay her share of the rent. The good news was that her boss assured her that there would always be a place for her there, especially when she earned her law degree and passed the bar.

And when August 29th rolled around, Beanie was ready for it.

That morning Byron handed Beanie a brown paper bag and said, "I put hard salami with no mayonnaise on Wonder Bread, just the way you like it. And there's an apple and Ritz crackers. You sure you don't want me to go with you, maybe walk you to your first class?"

Beanie took the bag out of his hand. "No thanks. I think I've got it. I already know my way around the campus." She clutched her lunch bag in her teeth as she slipped on her sweater. She pulled her hair out from under her collar and let it fall down her back. "Wish me luck, and thanks for making me lunch."

"You're welcome. Now go get 'em," he said.

A new school brought new friends, and new experiences. Beanie and Byron's life were filled with trips to the library, Friday night pizza parties, and group outings to the football games in the fall, but not necessarily with each other.

Beanie's friends tended to be pre-law students and Byron's people from the medical school. Their hangouts were different, they spoke a different jargon.

One night after one of the school's football games, Beanie and a few of her friends sat around one of the tables in the student lounge talking and laughing.

One of Beanie's friends, a wiry boy with blonde hair said, "Hey, I heard a funny lawyer joke the other day, you want to hear it?"

"Sure." They all chimed in.

"Okay. Someone said to a lawyer, 'You're a high-priced lawyer. If I give you five hundred dollars, will you answer two questions for me?' Then the lawyer said, 'Absolutely. What's your second question.'?"

Everyone had a blank look on their face and no one laughed. When Blondie didn't get the response he was looking for, he threw up his hands and said, "C'mon, guys. It was funny." He looked at Beanie. "You thought it was funny, didn't you, Beanie?"

"Well . . ." She was happy when she saw Byron enter the lounge, so she could duck answering that question. "Byron!" she shouted. She stuck her hand up and waved him over. When he got to the table, she said, "Everybody, this is my friend, Byron. Byron, this is everybody."

They greeted him with "hey," and "hi."

"Come sit with us. Just pull up a chair," Beanie said.

Blondie scooted his chair closer to Beanie, leaving the only open area on his other side. Then he leaned back and draped his arm around the back of Beanie's chair.

Byron eyed Blondie. "Nah, that's okay. I was just passing through, thought I'd come over and say "hi." I've got to go study. Nice meeting you all." He looked at Beanie and said, "I'll see you later."

That evening when Beanie got home, Byron was sitting at the kitchen table studying. Beanie dropped her knapsack next to the door and kicked off her shoes. "Why didn't you sit down with us this afternoon?" she said as she pulled out the chair next to Byron and sat down.

"You were sitting there with your friends, and I didn't want to intrude."

Beanie arched her eyebrows, "What do you mean? You're my friend."

Byron set his pen down, looked at her and said, "Do you like that guy?"

"What guy?"

"Blondie."

"Sure he's a nice guy, but he tells bad jokes."

"No, I mean *like him*, like him."

She threw him a crooked smile, and titled her head and said, "Why?"

He lowered his head. "I was just wondering."

"There has to be more to it than 'you were just wondering.'" Her eyes sparkled.

Lifting his head, he smiled and leaned in close to her. "I was wondering because . . . Because . . . Because *I like you*, like you."

Chapter Thirty-Five

December, 1964

Beanie sat on one of the benches next to the frozen rectangular, reflecting pond that connected the Washington Monument with the Lincoln Memorial. A dusting of fresh snow covered the lawn making the place look like one of the postcards in her knapsack. She'd spent all morning walking in Constitution Gardens thinking about what she should do. Things had been awkward at the house since Byron told her that he *liked* her.

His confession didn't require a response, but she knew that she needed to do, or say something to him.

And it wasn't that she didn't *like* him, because she did, very much. She just hadn't thought of him in that way. Maybe it was because of what she had learned in the last four years during their time in the south. Even though there had been great changes in segregation, people frowned upon whites and Negroes being together. She thought back on Emmitt Till's horrific murder only ten years ago, bludgeoned just for touching the hand of a white woman. Though she didn't see Byron as a Negro, the rest of the world still did.

But thinking about it now, watching the skaters glide on the glassy blue ice, she realized she liked him, too. And she was willing to take that risk.

"I thought I might find you here." Byron walked over and sat down on the bench next to her.

Beanie looked up. "Byron, I was just thinking about you." She glanced at him. "How'd you know I was here?"

"Because you weren't at your other favorite spot."

Beanie smiled. "So how was anatomy class?"

"Fine. We worked on cadavers."

Beanie wrinkled her nose. "That doesn't sound like much fun."

They remained quiet for several minutes, watching the skaters whirling their partners around. Finally Byron said, "Beanie I've been thinking, and I've decided to move out. There's an opening in one of the dorms on campus."

"Oh, Byron, why?" She felt her stomach clutch.

"I just think it's for the best."

Beanie put her hand on his arm and said, "Well, I don't. I think it's a terrible idea."

"Why?" he said, looking at her.

She got up and stood in front of him, blocking his view of the skaters. And when he looked up at her she said, "Because *I like you*, like you, too."

As the months progressed, so did Beanie and Byron's relationship. Friday night pizza parties and football games now included each other. And when Byron joined Beanie's pack of friends, Blondie moved on.

Beanie sat at the kitchen table with a post card and a pen. She hadn't written to Liddie in almost a month. She'd been too busy with school, her friends, her committees, and her new boyfriend. She wrote:

April 10, 1965

Dear Liddie,

How are you? I've been very busy with school and everything. Two weeks ago, some of my friends and I took three days off from school to attend a march with Dr. Martin Luther King, Jr. We walked fifty-four miles from Selma to Montgomery, campaigning for Negro voting rights.

I finally got to meet Dr. King and shake his hand. He thanked me for being part of the demonstration and I told him that the honor was all mine.

Thank you again, Liddie, for paying for my schooling. I would never have been able to do it if it hadn't been for your generosity.

I love you,
Beanie.

Byron walked into the kitchen, kissed Beanie on the forehead and said, "You ready?"

She smiled up at him. "Yep. Just got to put a stamp on this. Is Marcus ready?"

Byron hesitated for a second. "Um, he decided not to go with us."

"Why? I thought he liked the Cherry Festival?"

"He said he has too much homework to do."

"But it's Saturday."

Byron shrugged. "I don't know. That's just what he told me."

As they walked through the booths, Beanie picked up a leather purse and said, "A lot of the same things as last year." She sighed, "I'm not seeing anything interesting. You want to go get some lunch?"

"Um, lunch? I, uh, I'm not very hungry right now. Can't we just keep looking through the booths?"

Beanie raised her eyebrows. "Since when do you like to shop?"

"Well, I noticed a new booth over there. I thought we could go over and take a look." He took hold of her hand and led her over to the crafts booth. "Then we'll go to lunch afterwards."

"Okay, if you say so."

Byron's pace increased the closer they got to the booth. He stopped in front of it and said, "This is what I wanted to show you." He pointed to a row of handmade wooden jewelry boxes.

Beanie looked down at them. "They're nice. Do you want one?"

"No. I wanted you to have one." He picked up a small cherry wood box with a pink inlaid heart on the lid and handed it to her. "What do you think about this one?"

She took it, looked at it, ran her finger over the heart and said, "It's very pretty. Thank you."

"Open it." He smiled down at her.

Beanie opened the lid. She glanced at Byron and then pulled out the small box that had been hiding inside. When she opened the lid, she squealed, "Oh Byron. It's beautiful." Inside, nestled in a bed of fluffy cotton lay an engagement ring with a quarter karat diamond perched on top. She opened her mouth to say something, but Byron cut her off.

"Wait." He grabbed her by the hand, gave a nod of thank you to the man behind the table for helping him, and then led her away from the booth. He stopped under a cherry tree in full bloom, got down on one knee and said, "Beanie, you're my girl, and I love you very much. So Beatrice Mae Peterson, will you marry me?"

With tears in her eyes, Beanie looked at Byron.

"Well," he said. "Don't keep me in suspense."

"Oh Byron, I'd love to." Beanie hesitated, allowing the tears to fall. "But I can't."

"Why not? You love me, too, don't you?"

"Of course I love you."

"Then why can't you?"

"You know why." Beanie touched Byron's face, urging him to his feet. She took hold of his hands, looked into his eyes and said, "I can't marry you now because I'm already married."

That night Beanie and Byron sat on the couch. Beanie took ahold of Byron's hand and said, "It's not that I'm not going to marry you. I just have to get a divorce first."

Byron threw his hands up in the air and said, "Polygamy is not legal in the United States, so you are not really married to that man."

"But I am in the eyes of my Church."

"A church you never go to."

"It doesn't matter that I don't follow Mormonism any more. I'm telling you, I can't marry you until I iron this out."

"So does that mean you're going to have to go back to Utah?"

"I'm not sure. I'll call first."

"So you're going to call him? And say what? 'I want a divorce so I can get married again?'"

Beanie softened her voice. "Just let me take care of this."

"And what if you do have to go out there and see him again? He might try to hurt you."

Beanie smiled at him. "Well, then I'll take my big boyfriend with me and sic him on him."

"If I have to deal with him, I'll make sure he never hits another young girl."

For a week, Beanie thought about what she would say to Orson. She hadn't talked to him since that May night five years ago when she ran away. Would he even talk to her? Just thinking about him made her nervous. She played out the conversation in her head

Where have you been, Beatrice?

All over.

Where are you now?

Washington D.C.

What's your address?

And that's when she stopped. She didn't want him knowing where she lived. She never found out if he was the one driving that blue Rambler back in Chicago that day. But she wouldn't put it past him to come to D. C. to try and talk to her face to face, or rather, *intimidate her* face to face. He was the type of man that didn't like to lose, especially to a young girl who defied him. And what would he do to her or Byron for that matter when he found out she was marrying a Negro? The color of Byron's skin didn't matter to her. But she knew that it did to Orson, and that might be the one thing that would keep him from releasing her.

Maybe it was her Mormon upbringing, or that they were sealed according to the church. But she had been his wife for almost two years, and she just couldn't marry Byron without properly severing her ties to Orson first.

That night when Byron and Marcus went to see the Charlton Heston movie, *Major Dundee*, Beanie made a call. A familiar voice said, "Hello."

Beanie hesitated and then said, "Mama?"

The line went quiet for a moment and then her mother said, "Beanie? Is that really you?"

"Yes, Mama. It's really me. How are you? How's Daddy and the boys?"

Her mother started to cry. "I thought you were dead. We all thought so." Through broken sobs she cried, "Why Beanie? Why did you run away? Do you have any idea the pain you've caused your father and I, not to mention Orson and your sister wives? How could you do this to us, Beanie?"

"Mama, how could *you* have done that to me? You forced me to marry a monster. Do you have any idea what that man did to me? How he hurt me and humiliated me? I was a child, Mama. I had no business being married to a man twenty years older than me. I don't understand why you and Daddy did that to me? Please, Mama, help me understand."

The line went quiet except for the sporadic sobs coming from the other end.

"'I'm so sorry, Beanie. I'm sorry those things happened to you," whispered her mother. "But it's not unusual to marry that young. You know that. And we didn't have a choice."

"What do you mean you didn't have a choice?" When her mother didn't answer, Beanie said, "Tell me what you mean by that. I need to know."

"The Church held the land that our house was built on in trust. Orson threatened to take the land if we didn't allow him to marry you. If he took the land, we wouldn't have had a place to live. You'd marry soon anyway, and we thought it would be better for you to marry a man with means. Beanie, I never thought he would hurt you."

Beanie couldn't find any words. Her mind flashed back to her wedding day when Orson handed her father that envelope. She asked her mother, "Mama what was in the envelope that Orson gave to Daddy that day at the church?"

"It was a copy of the deed of trust with our names added to it. Your name's on it, too."

Beanie remained quiet for a moment. Thinking they had traded their only daughter for a piece of land, she felt hurt and betrayed by her parents. But she loathed Orson more and said, "He truly is a vile man and should be punished for what he's done."

"He's already been punished, Beanie."

"What do you mean?"

Her mother said quietly, "Orson died in a car accident on his way to Alabama in 1961."

Chapter Thirty-Six

Washington D.C.
March, 1967

When Beanie and Byron got engaged, Beanie insisted that she find another place to live. So she moved to one of the dorms on campus. She couldn't stand the thought of living in sin. She knocked on the door to Marcus and Byron's apartment and waited for one of them to answer.

When Marcus opened the door, she handed him a green envelope and said, "Happy Saint Patrick's Day."

"Hey Beanie, thanks. Come in. How are you?"

"Good," she said as she took off her coat. "Is Byron ready?"

Right then Byron walked into the living room. "Hey, Baby, you look fine." He walked over to her, hugged her and gave her a kiss.

She smiled at him. "You look pretty nice yourself, mister. So you ready to go?"

"Yep. Just need to get my coat."

"So where are you two heading off to?" asked Marcus.

"We're going to go see *A Patch of Blue*. They're showing it at the discount theatre on Prospect Street."

"I'm surprised you guys didn't see it when it came out a year and a half ago, especially given the theme."

"Better late than never," said Beanie, as Byron took her by the hand and ushered her to the door. On her way out, she pinched Marcus' arm and said, "That's for not wearing green."

"Later, Marcus," said Byron closing the door behind him.

As they walked the eight blocks to the theatre, Byron asked, "So have you decided whether or not you are going to invite Liddie to the wedding?"

"I don't know. I haven't decided yet."

"You're running out of time. June will be here before you know it."

"I'm not sure I want her to come." Beanie was quiet for a moment. "She probably wouldn't come anyway."

"Well, don't you think you should let her decide whether or not she wants to come? I mean you kind of owe it to her since she's been paying for your college."

"I don't know."

They walked in silence until Byron pulled her to a halt and said, "Have you even told her that you're engaged?"

Beanie hesitated.

"She doesn't know about me, does she?" When Beanie shook her head no, he said, "Why? Are you ashamed of me?"

"No, Byron, of course not. I'm proud to be your fiancée. And I can't wait to marry you."

"Then what's the problem?"

"Liddie doesn't like Negroes. And I just don't want to hear what she might have to say."

Byron put his arm around her and continued to walk. "Are you afraid that if she were to find out that you are marrying a Negro that she would quit paying for your college?"

Beanie was ashamed to admit that that might have been part of the reason for not telling Liddie. "I'm sorry, Byron. It's just that I've still got a year and a half before I graduate, and then there'll be law school. I won't- we won't be able to afford it if she decides to quit paying."

Byron opened the door to the theatre for her and said, "You let me worry about that. If you want to tell her about the wedding because you want her there, then tell her. But if you don't want her there, then don't tell her. Just don't base your decision on money."

When the movie was over, Byron held the door open for Beanie and said, "You want to go grab a cup of coffee, maybe get a Danish?"

"Sure."

Byron and Beanie casually walked hand in hand down Prospect Street toward the coffee shop. Beanie said, "So what did you think of the movie?"

"I thought it was good. Sidney Poitier did a great job in that movie."

"Poitier reminds me a little of you - tall, handsome."

"So you like tall and handsome, huh? That's good to know." He put his arm around her shoulder as they walked. "How about you, what did you think of it?"

Beanie sighed, "I thought it was sad. I think he really did love her, but that their racial differences kept him from allowing that love to go any further." She slipped her arm around his waist. "I felt sorry for the girl in the movie, the way her mother treated her, all the abuse, especially when her mother found out that she liked a Negro. It's sad, but I saw a little of myself in her. She had to do things that she didn't want to in order to survive."

Byron stopped and looked at her. "The difference between you and her is, I *am* going to marry you." And then he kissed her on the lips.

Two white guys walked past them on the sidewalk and saw their public display of affection. One of them said to the other, "Did you see that white chick kissing that nigger?"

"Yeah, man. What a waste of a hot skirt."

Beanie snapped around and said, "Excuse me. What did you say?"

Byron took her by the arm and said, "C'mon, Beanie. Let's just go."

"No, Byron." Beanie pulled her arm free and took a step. "What did you call him?"

The two men stopped walking and turned around. One of them said, "A pretty little white thing like you shouldn't be hanging all over no *jigaboo*. It's gross."

Before Beanie could say anything else, Byron grabbed her by the arm and in a low voice said, "Cool it, Beanie. Let's go." They turned to walk away, when the other guy said, "That's right, run along now, boy."

When they walked away, Byron said, "Don't ever do that again, Beanie. You could have gotten hurt."

"Did you hear what they called you?"

"Of course I heard what they said. But I don't need you jumping in to protect me. I can do that myself."

Tears swelled in Beanie's eyes. "It just upsets me so much when people say things like that. We've worked so hard to put an end to racial prejudice and bigotry."

He put his arm around her. "I know, but you can't confront everyone who makes an ignorant comment like that. Yes, we've helped change the laws. But it's just like I told you a long time ago, it takes time to change people's minds."

Beanie looked up at him. "So what are we supposed to do, just take it? I think about things like that movie, Liddie, those guys. People are never going to accept us. We will never be able to just *be* without having people staring at us, ridiculing us, or throwing racial slurs at us."

For the next two months Beanie and Byron kept busy with school, making wedding plans, and helping Byron pick out hospitals to apply to for his residency program. With the wedding only a month away, Beanie found herself struggling to keep her mind focused. She still hadn't decided whether or not to invite Liddie. But if she waited too much longer, the decision would be made for her.

On the last day of classes for the year, Beanie sat under a maple tree on the campus lawn waiting for Byron. They were going to go out and celebrate making it through another year of the rigorous studying it took to become a doctor. She pulled out a postcard from her knapsack.

She had never told Liddie about Byron. She always referred to him as "her friend," never by name. She never told her that he was a Negro. She certainly never mentioned that she was engaged. So to tell Liddie that she was getting married would mean a long and involved letter rather than a post card. And it would entail a lot of details about her life that she had never revealed to Liddie before. She thought maybe it would be best if she gave the information to her in small chunks. She wrote:

May 17, 1967

Dear Liddie,

How are you? I've been very busy with work, school, and a few other things.

Today my best friends are celebrating third year classes being over. They'll start their fourth year of medical school in the fall. They hope to start their own practice one day. I'm very proud of them. I only have one more year as an undergraduate and then I can start law school.

Liddie, I'm so grateful for everything you've done for me. I know I can never repay you, but I will try to become the best lawyer that I can be.

One more thing. I've met someone, and I'm in love.

Love,
Beanie

Byron plopped down next to her and said, "Did you invite her?"

Beanie handed him the card to read and said, "No, but at least it's a start."

Later that evening, Beanie, Byron and Marcus, along with a few other medical students went to O'Malley's pub to celebrate. Byron bought the first round of beers. As he set them on the table, he held up one of them and said, "Here's to the class of '68." They all clinked their mugs, and he slid into the booth next to Beanie. He gave her a kiss and said, "It'll only be another year before you start your graduate program."

Beanie laughed. "Not if I flunk Comparative Economics, then it'll be two years. I just don't ever understand what that professor is talking about."

One of Byron's friends, a young Indian man with shoulder-length, shiny black hair said, "So when are you two getting married?"

"June 17th," said Beanie.

"Will your families be there?"

Beanie looked at Byron. "No, not mine. But Byron's great aunt and uncle will be there. It's going to be a very small wedding, just a few friends here at the campus chapel."

He held up his mug of beer and said to the two of them, "There is only one happiness in life, and that is to love and to be loved. May you always find your happiness."

Byron and Beanie held up their mugs and clinked them together.

That evening when Byron walked Beanie home, he stopped on the dorm steps and said, "I know we don't need to decide now, but Marcus said he would be willing to move out and give us the apartment after we get married."

"That's really nice of him. But I thought we'd get our own little place."

Byron smiled. "Well, that'll work, too. Just thought taking that apartment might be easier than finding another one."

"Let's think about it for a while, okay?" Beanie kissed him on the cheek and said, "Good night. I'll see you tomorrow." As he walked away she said, "And congratulations. Only one more year to go. I'm really proud of you."

For the next few weeks, Beanie focused solely on her wedding. Though there wasn't much to plan, she still needed to find a dress, shoes, pick out her flowers, and, of course, buy the perfect negligee for her wedding night. *The wedding night*. She hadn't been with anyone, including Byron, since Orson. The thought of having sex both excited her and made her nervous. She knew Byron was nothing like Orson. But what if all sex was rough, just like the way Orson did it? She wasn't sure she'd be able to stand that, even with Byron.

Making plans for their honeymoon, Beanie and Byron sat at his kitchen table looking at brochures. They knew they couldn't afford much of one, but maybe a couple of days somewhere close they decided, would be doable.

Beanie handed one of the brochures to Byron and said, "What do you think of the Greenbrier? I know it's a little expensive, but it's only a few hours from here. I could take Friday off and we could go for a long weekend."

Byron perused the glossy pictures of the lush tree covered grounds, and the large, white southern antebellum looking hotel. "It's beautiful, but it's in West Virginia."

"Oh," said Beanie, the corners of her mouth drooping. For a brief moment she'd forgotten about the attitudes that people had about blacks and whites being a couple But as quick as that, it hit her in the face. She didn't want people staring at them on their honeymoon, making them feel like they were an abomination. "Well, maybe we can just get a room at the Grand Hotel, down by the White House."

"You guys, come in here, quick. You need to see this." Marcus stuck his head in the kitchen. "They got it overturned."

They rushed out into the living room and stared at the television. Pictures of a white man hugging a black woman filled the screen. "They did it. *Loving v. Virginia.* The supreme court just ruled that state bans on interracial marriages are unconstitutional."

They all cheered and hollered. Byron picked up Beanie, hugged her and spun her in a circle. "Maybe we can go to Greenbrier now that we've got the Supreme Court of the United States on our side."

Chapter Thirty-Seven

Washington, D.C.
June, 1972

Married life was good for Beanie and Byron. They made it through Byron finishing medical school, his three years of residency and he and Marcus taking over a small practice from a retiring doctor, without a hitch. And Beanie, with her good grades and the help of Liddie, got into Georgetown's law school and graduated in the top third of her class.

Still living in the little apartment they had when they first came to D.C., Beanie often reflected on how everything seemed to be falling right into place for them. The two of them had all they needed.

They couldn't have been happier.

Beanie slid into the club chair as she held the letter in shaky hands. It was from Liddie, the first letter she'd gotten from her in a long time. When she read it, she threw her hand over her mouth and whispered, "Oh, Liddie, no."

Byron came into the living room and handed her the cup of chamomile tea. "Here. This'll settle your stomach." He set a plate of sliced oranges down on the end table next to her and said, "I thought maybe these would help, too." He sat on one of the arms of the overstuffed chair, leaned over and put his arm around his wife. "What did Liddie have to say?"

Beanie handed the letter to Byron and said, "She's in the hospital. She's got cancer."

"Oh honey, I'm sorry. What do you want to do? We can send her some flowers if you'd like."

Beanie took a sip of tea, then grabbed one of the orange slices and stuck it in her mouth. A second later she spit it out onto the plate. "Yuck, these don't taste right."

He rubbed her back. "It's just your taste buds are a little off right now. They're usually that way during the first trimester."

"Thank you for telling me that, Doctor B." She gave him a playful swat on the leg.

Byron stood up and pulled Beanie out of the soft club chair. "So what do you want to do? Do you want to call her?" He scanned the letter. "Does she say what hospital she's in? I'm sure I can find the number."

"I want to go there. I want to see her."

"Seems strange. You two have never met. Now after all this time, all the years you planned on going, finally it's going to happen."

"Yeah, I know," she said. "But I would never forgive myself if I didn't go see her and then she died. The woman, whom I've never met face to face, changed my life. I owe her this, and so much more. Will you come with me?"

Byron hugged her. "Of course. I wouldn't want you to travel alone. This is a big deal, right? Meeting Liddie. So, when do you want to leave?"

"Tomorrow. I'll call the office and tell them I'm going to take a few days off."

"Can they afford to have you gone for a few days?"

"Yes. I'm sure they won't miss me too much down at the firm. New attorneys don't do much, you know that. I'm basically just their research assistant. Sometimes I think they treat me like that because I'm a woman. They'll probably fire me when they find out I'm pregnant. Maybe I'll look into doing something for women's rights next."

Byron smiled at her. "Don't go making waves."

"I won't." Beanie laughed. "How about you? Can you leave your practice for a few days?"

"Sure, Marcus can handle it. But I'm pretty sure his wife might not like him having to take on more work and spend more time at the office. But he won't mind."

Beanie took another sip of tea, kissed him on the cheek and said, "Then we're set."

Byron picked up the plate of orange slices and said, "Well, it looks like we're finally going to get to meet Mrs. Adeline Garrison. I guess she's going to find out that I'm black. No hiding that fact when I'm standing right in front of her."

Beanie smacked Byron on the butt and said, "You're not black, you're milk chocolate."

The next morning, Beanie and Byron drove seven hours to Beth Israel Hospital on Brooklyn Avenue. When they pulled into the parking lot, Byron said, "I'll drop you off at the front doors and go park the car."

Beanie glanced at him sideways. "No, I'll go with you to park it. That way we can go to Liddie's room together."

Byron flashed a mock shocked look. "You don't trust me?"

"That's about the size of it, buster."

When they parked the car, Byron walked around the car and opened Beanie's door. Taking her hand, he helped her out of the car and said, "What if it upsets her?"

"If what upsets her?" They started to walk toward the entrance.

"What if I upset her by being there? I don't want to make her uncomfortable. She could be very sick, and not only seeing you for the very first time, but seeing me as well, just might be too much for her."

Beanie hadn't thought of that. "Well, maybe it would be better if I go up there first, just to see how she's doing and to make sure she's well enough."

Byron released the tension in his shoulders. "Okay, good. So I'll just wait in the lobby until you come and get me."

Beanie nodded and then went to the information desk to find out which room Mrs. Adeline Garrison was in.

"She's in room five twenty two. Just take the elevators to your right to the fifth floor, take an immediate left and stop at the nurse's station. They will be able to tell you how to get to her room."

"Thank you."

"You're welcome."

Beanie started to walk away and then turned back around. "Can you tell me how she's doing?"

The receptionist gave her a sympathetic look and said, "I'm sorry, you'll have to ask the nurses once you get up there."

Before she got on the elevator, Beanie stopped in the gift shop and picked out a bouquet of brightly colored daisies, mums and chrysanthemums. She entered the elevator and pushed the button to the fifth floor. This was it. She was finally going to meet the woman at the other end of the line. She'd dreamed of this day and feared it. What if Liddie didn't want to see her? How was she going to break it to Liddie that her husband was black? Would Liddie hate her for it? Would she be prejudiced against him?

When the elevator doors opened, Beanie didn't move. Had it really been fourteen years since the first time she spoke to Liddie? It seemed like only moments ago, as memories rocketed through her mind, landing on the one moment when she found that piece of paper behind the refrigerator and dialed the number.

When the doors threatened to close, Beanie took a step.

Once in the hallway she walked to the nurse's station and said, "Excuse me. I'm here to see Mrs. Adeline Garrison. I believe she's in room five twenty two."

A pixie of a nurse said, "Hello. Let me check for you." She looked down at her paperwork and then said, "Yes, she's in room five twenty two. Just go down this hall, make a right and it will be the second room on your right."

Beanie walked down the hall on her tiptoes so her heels wouldn't make too much noise. She didn't want to disturb the sick. When she reached Liddie's partially opened door she pushed it open ever so slightly and poked her head in.

She wasn't what Beanie expected. She wasn't sure what she expected. The woman in the bed looked slight, but not as pale as Beanie would have thought. She couldn't see the color of her hair because she wore a pink terrycloth cap on her head. She had nicely manicured nails, and she sat up in bed reading a book.

"Excuse me, Liddie?"

Liddie lifted her head "Yes?"

Beanie took a step through the door.

"Yes, do I know you?"

Beanie took a step closer. "Liddie, it's me, Beanie."

Liddie's book fell to her lap. "Beanie? Oh, my goodness. I knew that voice sounded familiar. I can't believe my eyes." She motioned for Beanie to come closer. "Come here and give me a hug."

Beanie walked over to the bed, leaned down and hugged her. Liddie held on tight, giving her a squeeze before finally letting go.

"How are you feeling?" Beanie asked as she set the flowers on the small dresser in the corner of the room.

"I'm feeling good." Liddie wiped a tear from her eye. "They're going to release me sometime today." Liddie's eyes followed Beanie, they seemed to beam as she watched Beanie place the flowers on the table and walk back over to the bed.

And Beanie couldn't take her eyes off of Liddie.

"Thank you for the flowers." Liddie looked over at the arrangement. "They're beautiful." Liddie took Beanie's hand, rubbing it gently and said, "Why didn't you tell me you were going to come? I could have made myself more presentable."

Beanie gave her hand a squeeze and then grabbed a chair from the corner of the room and brought it to the side of the bed. She sat down and said, "When I got your letter, I just had to come."

Liddie smiled at her and patted her hand. "Well, I'm very glad you did. Our meeting each other is certainly over due." When her hand grazed over Beanie's ring, she looked down and said, "What's this?"

Beanie pulled her hand back gently, touched her wedding rings and said, "I'm married." She cupped her stomach. "And I'm pregnant."

"Beanie. That's wonderful. I'm going to be a grandmother!" They both laughed. "When did you get married?"

"Actually, it was about five years ago." Now Beanie felt embarrassed for not telling her years ago. Liddie deserved to know. "I'm really sorry I didn't tell you before. I should have."

Liddie glanced at Beanie, her brow furrowed. "Why wouldn't you tell me that you were married? I don't understand."

"I wanted to, believe me. I owe you my life. If it weren't for you, God knows where I'd be. And I hated keeping secrets from you."

"Secrets? How many do you have?" Liddie chuckled and Beanie smiled at her and lowered her head. "Well, not to worry," Liddie continued. "We'll tackle them one at time. And I'm sure they couldn't be that bad. And you know you've given me so much, too. I don't know where I'd be without you, either." Liddie wiped another tear from her cheek. "Did your husband come with you?" Liddie looked toward the door. "I'd like to meet him."

"He's down in the lobby. I can run down and get him if you'd like."

"Liddie," Glenn Randall walked into the room. "I've got a few instructions for you before I release you today."

Beanie stood up and said, "Oh, I should go."

Liddie held out her hand to stop Beanie. "Beanie, this is my friend – and doctor – Glenn Randall. He's Cassie's husband, I've written to you about her lots of times. Glenn this is Beanie."

"Yes. I remember." Beanie stuck out her hand. "Hello, Dr. Randall, it's a pleasure to meet you."

"Is this our little Beanie? Well, it's a pleasure to meet you. We've all kept up with you and your travels over the years. I'm glad to be able to put a face with all those stories."

Beanie laughed and looked over at Liddie. "I guess I'd better go. Let you talk to your doctor – unless you need a ride home?"

"No. Cassie and Arlene are coming to get me," Liddie said. "They make such a fuss over me. They and Jean, I don't know what I'd do without any of them."

Beanie walked over to Liddie, kissed her on the cheek and said, "Well, so I guess I'll go."

When she turned to leave, Liddie said, "Beanie, why don't you and your husband come to my house? You can stay there if you want. I've got a great big ole' house with nobody in it but Jean and me."

"We've already got a hotel room."

"Then come over tomorrow. Stay the one night there at the hotel so you don't lose your money, and then come to my house. I'll have Jean cook us up a feast and you can stay with me for a few days. If you can, that is."

"Are you sure you would be up for another visit?"

Liddie smiled, "You're my family, you and this elusive husband of yours. After all these years, I'd think you'd know that. And we have so much to talk about. So yes, I would love for you both to visit and to stay with me, too."

Beanie smiled and said, "I'll see you tomorrow, then. And I'll bring my husband."

"Good. Now come here and give me another hug. I still can't believe you're here."

The next morning Byron loaded the luggage into the trunk. Beanie sat in the front seat studying the map that they picked up from the hotel lobby when they stopped to check out and get directions to the nearest florist.

When Byron got into the car, he said, "Are you sure that this is good idea?"

"I don't know. I'm a little nervous about this because I want her to look past the color of your skin and see you for the wonderful man that you are."

"Maybe over the years she has softened and feels differently about blacks," Byron offered.

"But what if she doesn't? What will I do then? I love you both and I want her to be in my life."

"Let's not do the what-ifs and just see what happens. And, maybe we both should give her a little more credit." Byron reached over and squeezed Beanie's hand.

They stopped at the florist and then, without much trouble, drove to Liddie's house in Beacon Hill. Byron parked the car, and walked around to Beanie's side and opened the door. He took the bouquet of flowers from her hands and said, "Are you ready for this?"

"As ready as I'll ever be."

They walked up the sidewalk, hand in hand. Then Beanie rang the doorbell.

Chapter Thirty-Eight

Boston, Massachusetts
October, 1943

Hattie Jean glanced down at her watch. This was the third ring. Standing in a phone booth on the college campus, she only had a short break before her next class. "I know she must be home," Hattie Jean said as she tapped her hand on the side of the phone. She didn't have much time and she wanted to check on her mother and the baby.

"Hello?" Ophelia Thomas sounded out of breath.

"Hi, Momma. How y'all doing?"

"We doing good, I guess."

"What's the matter? You sound outta breath. Everything alright? Nothing's wrong with Buddy, is it?"

"Oh, I wish you wouldn't call him that. He got a name you know. But, no he's fine. We were out back getting a little air earlier and I had just put him down for a nap when I heard the phone ring."

"I know he's got a name, Momma. I gave it to him."

"I've been havin' a time with this foot, it's been givin' me the blues. That's what took so long to get to the phone. I can hardly walk on it."

"Have you been taking your medicine, Momma? The insulin you got from the doctor? You know you have to take it every day."

"Chile, I swear, sugar diabetes is just gonna have to be the death of me. I can't be sticking no needle in me all the time. I can't see. My vision is blurred and them numbers so small. I don't know how much to put in that there syringe, and them needles hurt like the dickens."

"Momma, you have to be careful. I thought someone was going to come and help you fill up a week's worth of syringes to keep in the icebox."

"Yeah, they did. But then I can't remember if'n I took it or not. I got less in there than I s'pose to have. I done probably taken more than I should."

"Momma, if you take too much you could have a seizure, go into a coma and even die. Do you hear me, Momma? You could die from taking too much."

"Yeah, I hear you, but you telling me that don't cure my memory none. I still forget. Don't matter none, though, when my time comes ain't nothing nobody can do about it. Whenever my maker calls me, I'm ready to go."

"Don't say that, Momma. You just have to hold out until I get back. If you die, who's going to take care of Buddy? I'll finish school and then I can take care of you and my son."

"I know you will. I got all the money you done sent. I done put it away, so you'll have it when you get back."

Hattie Jean laughed. "Momma, you're not supposed to put it away. You're supposed to use it. Spend it on you and Buddy. I'm working hard up here besides going to college, so you don't have to. So you can stay home, stop taking care of other people, and take care of you and Buddy."

"Well, it's in that bank where you opened up an account for me and you. I don't have nothin' I need to buy. We got everything we need. And I have stopped workin' but they still send me money every month. It's my retirement, you know. They's good people. Always have been. And that's what's making me feel outta sorts. Got me a little worried."

"What's got you worried?"

"I got a letter the other day from Boston. Right up there where you is. It was made out to Missus Stewart's dead daughter. Now that gave me a start. I'ma have to run it up to the house when they get back from they vacation. But that chile been dead for more than a whole year. How she getting a letter, and how come her letter came here to me is a mystery. I'm thinking it must be a sign of something bad to come. Maybe even death in this house."

"Don't say that, Momma. That's not what it means."

"How you know? College education giving you some kind of second sight? People get signs of death all the time. I believe in 'em."

"It's me, Momma."

"What'cha mean, it's you?"

"That letter must've come there for me. I thought that I'd changed everything I put your address on. I didn't have an address when I first got here so I used yours. After I got a place to receive mail, I put in a change with the post office."

"I ain't understandin' what you talking about. Who you sayin'?" Ophelia asked.

"Mrs. Stewart's dead daughter."

"Adeline? Yeah, a letter done come here for her."

"Yes ma'am." Hattie Jean's voice was low. "I took her name and used it to enroll in school and get a job. That letter is for me."

"What's that you say? You usin' Missus Stewart's daughter's name as your own?"

"Yes, ma'am. I'm Adeline Stewart now. I found a copy of her birth certificate when I helped you up at the Stewart's house last time I was home. I took it. Then the college sent for her school records."

"Oh my Lord Jesus. What have you done? Jesus help my chile." Ophelia's breath was short and fast coming through the phone. "Hattie Jean, you can't steal stuff from people. And Adeline was a white girl, how you usin' her name?"

"Names ain't just for one color or another. And I know she was a white girl. That's why I said I was her."

"Oh my God! Are you up there tryin' to pass for white?"

"I'm not *trying*, Momma. I am white. At least far as anyone knows."

"Oh Lord. It ain't the sugar that's gone kill me, now I see that it's gone be you."

"The real reason I came to Boston was because I'd met a man when I was in Chicago. His name is Joe Kennedy, Jr."

"Is he a white man?" Ophelia whispered in the phone as if just saying the words too loudly might cause trouble.

"Yes, ma'am. We've been dating. I know it can't last. Well, I know that now. I do love him, though. He's going off to the service soon. Fight in the war."

"He don't know you colored?" Ophelia asked, still whispering.

"No ma'am."

"And does he say he loves you?"

"He does say he loves me. He acts like he does, too." Hattie Jean giggled nervously. "But there's no way I could explain you and Buddy to him. I'll break it off before he leaves to go into the service. But that's how it got started. I wanted to be with him. But it turned out good because now I'm getting a degree in biology and maybe one day I could go to medical school. Be a doctor."

"Couldn't you find a colored man to court?"

"Didn't you hear me, Momma? I said I might be a doctor." Ophelia grunted. "Well, this is an all girls' college," Hattie Jean said, evidently not impressing her mother with her talk of an education. "Not many men around. But it's funny you should ask me about a colored suitor. There is this one colored boy, his name is Melvin Chambers. He works the grounds around the college. Just walked right up one day and introduced himself to me. I think that he knows that I'm not white. Leastways he says things that make me think that. Anyways, he's always after me. But I'm not giving in to him. I'm sticking with the white folks for now. No one else can tell the difference."

"I don't know . . ."

"And then, when I finish here at Simmons College, I'm coming home to take care of you." Hattie Jean curled the phone cord around her finger, anxious about what her mother might think of her. "I was thinking we'd move to Chicago or somewhere. I could get a medical degree at the University of Illinois. I sure couldn't be Adeline Stewart down there in Jackson and I'd have to keep her name to get a job with my degree and finish school."

"Chile."

"Really, it's alright, Momma."

"I just don't know what to say."

"Don't say anything. It's done now. And don't say anything to anyone else about this, either. This is our secret. Okay, Momma? It's so we all can have a better life. Me, you and Buddy. I came here I know, chasing after a man – a white man, when you thought I was on my way to Chicago. But being white has given me a lot of opportunities. Opportunities I could never have if anyone knew I was colored. And I'm taking advantage of those opportunities, as much as I can. I can go back to being colored once I finish school."

"I just don't see how it's gone work. You passing for white. I mean I heard it done plenty of times. Just never thought anyone in my family would do it."

"Just promise me you won't tell anyone. Let everyone still think I went back to Chicago."

"Oh, I promise," Ophelia's voice went up an octave. "I won't tell a soul. What would I say? 'My colored daughter done turned into a white woman?' Lord Jesus. People'll be done think I lost my mind."

"I gotta go, Momma. I've got to get to class. Kiss Buddy for me and tell him I love him."

"I will."

"And I love you too, Momma."

"Well now, I don't know what I'm s'posed to call you."

"You can still call me Hattie Jean." She smiled at her mother's confusion.

"Alright then. I love you too, Hattie Jean."

Hattie Jean hung up the phone and spied Melvin Chambers heading her way through the glass of the phone booth.

Why doesn't he just stick to cutting the grass and leave me alone?

She ducked out of the phone booth and ran to catch up with a group of white girls headed in the direction of her classroom. Surely he wouldn't try to follow her when she was with so many other white women. Wouldn't be proper and he knew he could get in trouble.

Turning her head to see if he was still lurking around, Hattie Jean thought, *Melvin Chambers, you are wasting your time chasing after me because there is no way I could ever like you, or even think about dating you. It just wouldn't be proper for a white girl . . . .* Hattie Jean held her books close to her chest and giggled at the thought.

"Adeline! Adeline!" Hattie Jean heard the name being called and looked over and saw Cassie Jenkins waving at her, beckoning her over.

"Hi, Cassie," Hattie Jean said after she had trotted over to her good friend who was standing with two guys.

"I want you to meet my cousin, Walter," Cassie pointed to a tall, thin man with dark brown hair. "He graduated a couple of years ago from Boston College. He's got a degree in Business Administration. Walter Garrison, this is my best friend, Adeline Stewart."

Hattie Jean held out her hand to shake his. "Nice to meet you, Walter."

"He came down for the homecoming dance. And you know Glenn." Cassie pointed to her boyfriend who was attending medical school at Yale.

"You come up for the dance too, Glenn?" Hattie Jean asked.

"Yeah, you know I couldn't let any other fellow take Cassie to that dance. They might try to steal her away. I want everyone to know that she's my girl." He wrapped his arm around Cassie's shoulder and pulled her close.

"Is Joe coming for the dance?" Cassie asked.

"He sure is. I can't wait to see him. I'm so excited."

"Walter," Cassie said looking at her cousin. "Adeline's dating Joe Kennedy, Jr. She met him at the 1940 Democratic Convention in Chicago."

"Is that so?" Walter said, raising an eyebrow. "I'd sure like to meet him."

"Well, I could introduce you to him at the dance if you'd like," Hattie Jean said.

"Sure." Walter's face lit up. "That'd be swell."

"Just stick with Adeline if you want to get somewhere." Cassie stepped close to Hattie Jean and linked her arm through hers. "She might be a girl, but she knows some pretty important people. Adeline might even become the First Lady one day." Cassie poked Hattie Jean with her elbow and they both started to giggle.

Walter eyed her and said, "Guess I'll just have to get to know Miss Adeline Stewart a little better myself."

Chapter Thirty-Nine

Boston, Massachusetts
June, 1972

Adeline watched Beanie walk in the front door, hesitantly it seemed to her. Jean had answered it while she waited, sitting on the sofa. It was sad somewhat to think that Beanie might not want to be at her house. But then, in behind Beanie came a tall, handsome black man.

The man held on tightly to a big bouquet of white roses and stood quietly at the entryway to the living room. Adeline smiled as she took him in, her thoughts going to one of her own secrets – Melvin. Gazing on them standing there worried, she surmised, about her reaction, Adeline's happiness at that moment swelled from down deep in her soul and showed on her face. She whispered, "Beanie did what I was never able to do."

Beanie had fought a battle – a battle that Liddie had told her would never benefit her – and because of it she could now openly be with the man she loved.

"Come in you two. Is this your husband, Beanie?" Beanie nodded. "Oh my goodness he is so handsome. Come on in." Liddie stretched out her arms and wiggled her fingers, beckoning them to come in. "Why are you acting so shy?"

"Hi Liddie. How are you feeling today?" Beanie asked. She and Byron stood on the opposite side of the coffee table and smiled down at Adeline.

"I'm fine." Adeline smiled back.

"I want you to meet my husband, Byron Thomas."

Adeline's breath caught in the back of her throat. "Byron Thomas?" She looked up at him, her gaze changing from puzzlement to hope. "Your name is Byron Thomas?"

"Yes ma'am. Pleasure to meet you. I've heard so much about you. Feels like I know you."

Byron pushed the bouquet into his left hand and stuck out his right to shake Adeline's. The scar on his right arm coming visible to Adeline for the first time.

"Oh my Lord, Jesus." Adeline swallowed hard, she felt her heart leap into her chest, and her body became weak.

"Excuse me?" Byron looked over at Beanie and back at Adeline, who was staring at his scar.

"That's something my mother used to say. 'Oh my, Lord Jesus.' Just seemed appropriate," Adeline said quietly, her voice shaky, and her bottom lip trembling. She looked up at Jean, still standing at the door as a tear welled up in her eye. "You see this, Jean?" Jean nodded and smiled. "Come here,

Byron, sit next to me." Adeline held onto his hand tightly, not letting go as he tried to make his way around the coffee table that stood between them.

As he sat down, Adeline took both of his hands into one of hers and rubbed the burn scar with the fingers of the other. "It doesn't look half bad."

"Ma'am?"

"Your scar," Adeline said looking up at him.

"Oh, yes ma'am, I got that when I was little."

"I know." Adeline stared at Byron, tears rolling down her cheeks. She reached over and got a tissue from the box on the end table. "Does it still hurt?"

"Uhm, no. But sometimes it itches."

"Never could keep your hands off of it." Adeline took her hand and ran it down the side of Byron's face. "You are so handsome. If Momma could see you now. What do you do for a living?"

"I'm a doctor."

"Oh my God." Liddie clasped both sides of her face with her hands. "A doctor?" Her voice was barely audible.

"Are you okay, Liddie?" Beanie asked. She had been sitting in a chair across from them. "Is something wrong? I know I didn't tell you my husband was black - "

Adeline not taking her eyes off of Byron whispered, "They told me you were dead." Adeline's words could barely make it out, tears were pouring from her eyes, and she was having a hard time catching her breath. "What happened to you?"

Beanie looked over at Jean and asked, "Is there something wrong? Is it the medication? Do you think we should call Dr. Randall?"

"Beanie," Adeline said looking over at her. "You've brought me my Buddy." Adeline's eyes were red and filled with tears. "Jean," she said looking at her. "We finally get to see our Beatrice and she has brought us my little Buddy." Liddie leaned her head on Byron's shoulder. "I just can't believe it's you."

"What is going on? What is it, Liddie?" Beanie was visibly shaken.

"It's alright, Beatrice. Adeline's okay," Jean said.

"Tell me, Byron, what did they say happened to your mother?" Adeline asked.

"My mother?"

"Hattie Jean."

"How . . . how do you know my mother's name?" Byron looked over at Beanie.

"Was that your mother's name?" Beanie asked.

"Yeah, it was."

"Liddie," Beanie said. "Byron's mother died when he was little. How did you know her name?"

"Oh no." Liddie looked over at Jean, then back at Byron. "I thought you were dead and you thought I was dead."

"Please, Liddie – someone, anyone, tell me what is going on here," Beanie pleaded. "I thought you might be upset, but I just don't understand your reaction."

"I'm Hattie Jean," Adeline admitted. She looked back at Byron. "They told me that you died in the fire. The fire that killed Momma. I kept calling her and calling her and the line stayed busy. I knew something was wrong. So, I called down to Old Man Dooley's store and he told me about the fire. He said the two bodies found in the house were burned beyond recognition. And I knew it couldn't be anyone but you and Momma. She told me that that letter was going to bring death to that house, the one addressed to the dead Adeline Stewart, and it did." Adeline lowered her head.

"It was my grandmother and another boy she was keeping while his parents were away," Byron explained. "No one knew until the parents got back the next week. At least that's what I was told. I was really young. But when the fire started, I got scared, maybe remembered somehow how bad it hurt to get burned." Byron looked down and rubbed the scar on his arm. "So, I ran out and hid. Took them a couple of days to find me.

"But my mother - Hattie Jean - died on her way to Chicago. Well, that's what everyone believed. She went missing. Never turned up again."

"Did Momma – your grandmother tell you that?"

"Well, no. She never told me that. I can remember talking to my mother on the phone while my grandmother was alive. But once I went to live with relatives in Decatur, after my grandmother died, they told me that's what must've happened to you. I mean to her."

"It was another one of my secrets. I told Momma not to tell anyone where I was. Not to tell them I had come to Boston and was passing for white."

Beanie and Byron looked at Adeline. Beanie's mouth opened in disbelief. Byron looked as if he was about to cry.

"You're black?" Beanie finally got the words out.

"As black as the day is long," Adeline said, looking over at Jean. They both laughed. "How else could I have given birth to this beautiful black man sitting right here?" Adeline patted Byron's knee.

Beanie scooted up to the edge of her seat and stared at Adeline. "I always thought you were white. I always thought you didn't like black people."

"What in the world ever gave you that idea?" Adeline looked over at Beanie. "I like – love black people. I just told you to get out from down south so you wouldn't get hurt. But, please, don't feel bad, Beanie. Everyone thought I was white, including my husband. Everyone except for Melvin. He knew all of my secrets all along. Always told me to stop living the lie about being white. He even knew about you, Buddy."

"Who is Melvin?" Beanie asked.

"Adeline had a black man, too," Jean said. "From what she told me she loved him more than life itself."

"I sure did, Jean. More than life itself." Adeline chuckled.

"This was while you were married to Mr. Garrison?" Beanie asked.

"Shhh. We don't mention that man in this house. Not even his name. But, mmm hmm. After the boy I came to Boston to be with died in the war, and my mother and Byron were killed in the fire, or so I thought", Adeline glanced at Byron, "I married him because I knew he could give me a good life. And he married me probably because I knew the Kennedys. I wasn't ever in love with him.

"Melvin was, in *my* heart, my husband. And he was so handsome, just like my son is." She smiled at Byron. "I wish that I had been as brave as you, Beanie, and married him." Adeline looked at Byron and took hold of his hands. "You don't remember me, sweetie? You don't remember that you were my little buddy?"

"I do vaguely remember my mother calling me that." Byron's voice was low. His eyes seem to desperately search Adeline's. "Or, I think I remember someone calling me that."

"Well it certainly wasn't your grandmother that called you that. She hated nicknames." Adeline wiped the tears from her eyes with the tissue. "Baby," Adeline cupped Byron's face and looked into his eyes. "I'm your mother. I'm Hattie Jean Thomas and I am overjoyed to see you – for you to be here with me Byron Charles Thomas – well, I . . ."

Byron sucked in a breath when she said his name. Tears started to roll down his face. Adeline wiped them with her tissue.

"You, my sweet child, just seeing you, made all the trials and tribulations I endured in my life, the heartaches that it took for me to make it to this day, worthwhile. To live to see the day I got my Buddy back. Well, I just don't have the words to say how I feel." Adeline laughed and dabbed at her tear streaked face.

"How do you know my middle name?" Byron bit his bottom lip, his chin started to tremble. "Are you really my mother?" He looked at her, and squeezed her hand.

"Yes. I am really your mother. And if I'd known you were Beatrice's friend all this time, I would have gotten cancer a long time ago. Just so I could see you."

"Adeline." Jean chuckled. "The things you say. We gotta get you well. Don't go wishing you'd gotten that sickness years ago."

"And you, Mrs. Beatrice Thomas," Adeline said. "Come over here and sit next to me." Adeline patted the couch and scooted over closer to Byron. "You have been a part of me - a part of my heart ever since that day you dialed the wrong number. You are truly my daughter." Adeline held Beanie's hand with one of hers and kissed her on her cheek. Then she grabbed Byron's hand with her other hand. "And now you've brought me my son *and* a grandchild. Lord, if you took me today," Adeline said looking upwards, "I'd die a happy woman."

Everyone's attention turned to the noise at the rear of the house when they heard the back door shut and someone call from the kitchen. "Hello? Where's everyone?" Cassie appeared through the dining room. When she saw Adeline's face, red and puffy from crying she gasped. "Oh no, what's wrong. Jean, did something happen?"

"Everything is fine, Cassie," Adeline spoke. "Close your mouth before something flies in it. I was just celebrating my family visiting with me." Adeline still holding on to their hands, held up hers and said, "Cassie, meet my children, Beatrice and Byron Thomas. Aren't they beautiful?"

"Oh thank, God," Cassie said. "I thought someone had died, or was about to."

Chapter Thirty-Nine

Boston, Massachusetts
1972

It was a cold, but clear December day. The black hearse pulled up in front of the house on Beacon Hill. The door that held a wreath made with roses, carnations, cushion and Monte Casino blooms and tied with a simple black bow, swung open.

Beanie and Byron had come. Due any day, Byron carefully escorted the oversized Beanie down the slippery drive. Cassie and Glenn Randall drove to the house to follow the family over to the church. Arlene rode with them. The last person out, holding a large spray of lilies, gently pulled the door shut, turned and looked out at the small group making their way down to the hearse and blew out a warm breath that turned into smoke as it hit the cold air and slowly vaporized.

The church service was short. Not a lot of mourners, but certainly a lot of tears. Those that ventured to the graveside were even fewer. The pastor, in his white and gold robe underneath a black wool overcoat, stood over the grave and proclaimed, "Ashes to ashes . . ." before his low baritone voice began singing the Negro spiritual *Swing Low, Sweet Chariot*.

Cassie threw a rose down into the grave, and walked over to the small group gathered. "Glenn and I will meet you back at the house for the repast, unless you want us to wait for you?"

"No. I'll be alright."

"Well, that was a beautiful going away service you gave Jean, Liddie," Cassie said. "I'm sure she's smiling down from heaven at us."

Adeline's oversized dark sunglasses covered her red, tear filled eyes and half her face. Her large black hat with a veil covered the other half. "She told me just how she wanted her funeral a long time ago," Adeline said, wiping underneath her sunglasses with a tissue. "Down to the letter. Who would have thought she'd go so suddenly and before me?"

"We never know when our time will come, Liddie. And you know she had diabetes. She did pretty well, that can be such a debilitating disease. But, I'm sure she was glad to have you there with her at the end," Cassie said and rubbed Adeline's arm. She looked over to Adeline's right. "Byron and Beanie, we'll see you back at the house."

Adeline walked up close to the grave and peered down in it. "You were the keeper of my secrets for these past eight years. But today I'm burying those secrets and lies with you. And I want to apologize for the lie I told on you. I'd forgotten I told Cassie you were diabetic. I just needed her to dispose of those insulin bottles I'd taken from Melvin without too many questions. I didn't think you would mind." Adeline took a long sigh. "Thank you, Jean for being with me, for being my friend, for being a part of my family. And don't worry about running into Mr. Garrison up there in heaven because I'm sure he's rotting in hell somewhere. But you can tell Melvin for me that I love him and that I'll see him soon." Adeline dabbed a tear off her cheek. "I love you, Jean. And I'll miss you terribly."

Adeline turned from the grave and looked at Byron and Beanie. "I've got one more stop to make."

A short drive down one of the lanes in the cemetery took them to a gravesite that had a marble bench placed close by and was under a small dogwood tree. The marker on the grave read, "Melvin Chambers. Beloved Husband of Hattie Jean Thomas."

"Hi, darling," Adeline said, laying the bouquet of lilies near the headstone. "I brought Beanie and Buddy by to meet you. Beanie finally came to visit and she brought him with her. Can you believe it?" Adeline ran her fingers over the engraving on the stone. "I sent you a message by Jean. Look out for her."

Adeline sat on the bench and reached out her hand to Beanie. "This is where I want you to bury me. I bought a plot next to him when he died. We weren't together in life, but we'll spend eternity together, I promised myself that. And I want my real name on the headstone. I can't keep a lie going when I get to heaven."

Adeline and Beanie walked back to the hearse hand in hand. Byron opened the door and had to give them both a little help getting in.

The ride back to the house was quiet. More than a few people came to eat and enjoy memories of Jean. Arlene didn't make it to the repast. She was dropped off at home to see about her sick husband. Cassie and Glenn stayed for a couple of hours, helping Adeline to get settled in.

After all the guests left, and sitting in the dining room around the table, Beanie asked, "What are you going to do now that Jean's gone? You got this big ole' house and you're here all by yourself."

"I'm going to sell it," Adeline said. "Sell it and move to Mississippi. Move back home. I still have that land down there. The house is gone, but the land is still mine. It'll be a place my grandchildren can come and visit me."

"Mississippi?" Byron asked.

"Yep, I don't want to stay here anymore. I don't have to live the lie anymore. The lie that I'm white. It's what kept me and Melvin from being together, and it's the reason I wasn't home when that fire started that killed Momma. If I had been there, instead of Boston pretending to be someone I'm not, things might have been different." Adeline shook her head. "My dirty little secrets."

"Well, I have to go to the bathroom – again," Beanie said and got up and headed down the hallway.

"Mom," Byron said after Beanie left. "You've been out of my life for so long. Why would you move so far away now that we've found each other?"

"I hadn't thought of it like that." Adeline looked at Byron. "Mississippi is just home."

"Home should be with us. We've decided we're going to get a bigger place and we want you to live with us. We want our children to know you. And Beanie and I want to be with you – around you - as much as we can. We've spent far too many years apart."

"I don't want to be a bother."

"You wouldn't be a bother." Byron laughed. He got up from his chair and hugged Adeline. "You're my mother. I love you," he said sitting back down and taking her hands in his. "I want to be with you. We want to be with you. You living with us would give us all a second chance on being together as a family."

Beanie came walking back into the dining room after leaving the bathroom. Her legs spread apart, she had a surprised look on her face. Adeline and Byron looked at her questioningly. "My water just broke," she said.

Byron jumped up out of his chair and grabbed her, leading her over to a chair for her to sit down. "Oh my. What do I do?" He looked from Adeline to Beanie.

"Calm down," Adeline said and laughed. "It's not going to pop out right now. Are you sure you're a doctor? Just get her coat and get her to the car, we'll take her to the hospital."

Beanie grabbed her stomach and bent over in pain. "Arrggh. I'm not going to make it to the hospital."

"Beatrice. Don't be dramatic," Adeline said. "It might be painful now, but you've still got a lot more to endure. Believe me." Adeline nodded at Byron. "That little bugger took twelve hours to make his appearance and he gave me a fit through each and every moment of it.

"Now come on the two of you." Adeline pushed herself up out of her chair, and grabbed her purse and coat. "Let's get to the hospital so we can get started on bringing my grandchild into the world."

The End

Acknowledgements

At the End of the Line was a dream come true.

We would like to give a special "Thank you," to our editor/ proofreader, Gaele Hince for her exceptional skills and the hours she spent on behalf of our book. Thank you to our beta readers, Belle Blackburn, Lisa Hall and Faith Flores for their time and the invaluable and constructive feedback they gave that helped shape the manuscript's direction. We would also like to give a heartfelt thank you to all of the people who provided advanced reviews. We appreciate their time and efforts. And to our publisher, Media Web Publishing, Inc., we are grateful to you for believing in our vision, and for helping to make it a reality.

~ Kathryn Longino

Other Books by Kathryn Dionne

The Eleventh Hour: The Enlightened Ones Book I
The Eleventh Hour: Day of Atonement Book II
The Eleventh Hour: Resurrection Book III
Derek the Fireless Dragon

Coming Soon by Ms.Dionne

The Chasing Time Series
Savannah Swift Mysteries Series

Other Books by Abby L. Vandiver

In the Beginning: The Mars Origin "I" Series
Irrefutable Proof: The Mars Origin "I" Series
Incarnate: The Mars Origin "I" Series

Coming Soon by Ms. Vandiver
The Life Keeper
Two Weeks After Forever
Honey

Media Web Publishing
11470 Euclid Ave., Suite 309
Cleveland, Ohio 44106
www.mediawebpublishing.com

1. What attracts Beanie to Byron? What attracts Byron to Beanie? Why do you think it took so long for Beanie and Byron's relationship to evolve beyond friendship?

2. What do you think is Adeline's motivation in starting a relationship with Melvin? Do you, as the reader, think that Adeline should have carried on an affair with Melvin? In what ways do you think they complemented each other?

3. Why do you think Beanie showed such eagerness and determination to be involved in the civil rights movement? Was there ever a time when you, as a reader, thought Beanie should not have gotten involved? Why?

4. What characteristic did you like the most and the least about Beanie and why? What characteristic did you like most and least about Adeline and why?

5. What was the most important lesson Adeline taught Beanie? What was the most important lesson that Beanie taught Adeline?

6. How do you feel about the way Adeline dealt with Beanie's involvement in the Civil Rights Movement? Did you, as a reader, ever feel that Adeline was a racist? Explain why you felt that way. How do you feel about the way Beanie dealt with Adeline's opinions of her involvement?

7. What stood out the most about Beanie and Adeline's friendship? What made their relationship unique? What were their biggest strengths and their biggest weaknesses?

Reading Group Questions

8. It's been more than sixty years since the Civil rights Movement began. Do you think there are lingering racial injustice and resentments? If so, what are they and why do you think they still exist?

9. Did the novel cause you to examine your own prejudices, perceived or unknown? Has this novel inspired you to think or act differently? If so, how?

10. Do you have any sympathy for Orson, Walter, or Beanie's parents? If so, why?

11. How did you feel when you discovered the truth about Adeline? What was your reaction to her secrets? When did you figure them out?

12. Have you ever experienced a forbidden relationship, or has someone in your life been involved in what someone else deemed an "inappropriate" relationship? If so, explain. If not, how did reading this book alter your feelings about such relationships? Did it change any of your thoughts or beliefs? If so, how?

13. Did you figure outwho Byron was? If so, how far into the book were you, and what gave it away?

14. Who was your favorite character, your least favorite character, and why? Who would you like to have gotten to know better? What characteristic of your least favorite character did you like the most?

15. Did you know about the Freedom Riders and the Freedom Fighters before reading this book? If not, what was your reaction to learning about them?

ABOUT THE AUTHORS

Kathryn Longino is a pen name used by the writing duo of Kathryn Dionne and Shondra C. Longino

Born and raised in Ohio, Shondra C. Longino, who writes under the pen name Abby L. Vandiver, discovered her love of writing while working in other occupations. She's published five novels and is currently working on a romance novel and a cozy mystery series. Her debut novel, In the Beginning, an Amazon #1 best seller in its category, was written on a whim, and put in a box for more than a decade before it was published. Shondra holds a bachelor's in Economics, a master's in Public Administration and a Juris Doctor.. She resides in Cleveland and enjoys spending time with her grandchildren when she's not writing.

Kathryn Dionne lives in Southern California with her husband, Jeff, and their two Shar Peis, Bogey and Gracie.

From an early age, Kathryn's love of treasure hunting sparked an interest in archaeology. As an amateur archaeologist, she's been fortunate enough to uncover some very unique artifacts in different parts of the globe. However, she's still searching for that very special scroll.

In addition to writing, she manages their five-acre property and their grove of Italian olive trees. Her husband has lovingly named their business; Saint Kathryn's Olive Oil.

In her spare time, she makes cookie jars and throws pottery in her studio. She also creates mosaics from discarded objects and sells them under the category of Found Art.

She is currently writing a new series called Chasing Time, which she hopes to have Book I published some time in 2014.